# FALLEN WATCHER

## VOLUME 1 IN THE RILEY SERIES

### KELLY HOLLINGSHEAD

North Carolina

*Fallen Watcher: Volume 1 in the Riley Series*
© 2021 Kelly Hollingshead. All rights reserved.

Published in the United States by BQB Publishing
(an imprint of Boutique of Quality Books Publishing Inc.)
www.bqbpublishing.com

Printed in the United States of America

978-1-952782-00-8 (p)
978-1-952782-01-5 (e)

Library of Congress Control Number: 2021933361

Book design by Robin Krauss, www.bookformatters.com
Cover design by Rebecca Lown, www.rebeccalowndesign.com

First editor: Caleb Guard
Second editor: Andrea Vande Vorde

*To my wife Melissa and our daughter Brynn:
Thank you for not giving up on me and encouraging
me to take this leap of faith.*

*Darkness cannot drive out darkness;*
*only light can do that.*
*Hate cannot drive out hate;*
*only love can do that.*

— Martin Luther King, Jr.

# CHAPTER 1

R ain was falling hard, and the wipers were working furiously to keep the street visible. "This weather just won't let up," Riley commented to Allison. She sat next to him, her wedding dress rumpled up in her lap. Of all days, today was the day they were blessed with a downpour, and she'd handled it with grace.

"Well, the good news is that rain on a wedding day supposedly means good luck," she said with a smirk. It had been raining off and on for the past several weeks; odd to have this kind of weather in Texas, where most of the time the humidity was so thick that you could almost shower in it.

Allison and Riley had been dating for over eight years before he finally got the nerve to ask her the big question. He could remember that in his youth he'd said that there was no way in any shape, form, or fashion he would ever be married. His friends had actually branded him "BFL" (bachelor for life), and now, as they were leaving the reception, he started to smile. He couldn't believe this day had finally come. The wedding was small, just the way the two of them had wanted it: family, a few close friends, and nothing more. They had not wanted a huge wedding but just enough so the people closest to them could share and celebrate this moment.

Allison's career had really started to pick up once she had finally broken her way into film. She had always been drawn to theatre, and she went from performing in small town plays to doing local television commercials to signing her first movie deal. Riley was much simpler. He started a lawn mowing business in high school, which helped him pay for college. The part-time lawn mowing led to a full-time business—now he had a crew that worked for him.

Riley and Allison were complete opposites, but somehow it made their relationship work. They met in high school: She was the cheerleader, but Riley wasn't the jock. On Friday nights when Allison was cheering on the football team, Riley was either in the stands watching Allison or, when the team was away, catching up on homework—or working on acquiring another client for his steadily growing business.

Allison glanced at him sideways. "What are you grinning about?" she asked. "Oh, wait, I kind of have an idea," she said, gently slapping him on the arm.

Jonathan, Allison's guardian angel sat in the back seat. Neither of them knew he was there, or that he even existed. His job was simple and complex at the same time. He was to provide comfort when she needed it, to protect her without hesitation, and to love her with the hope that one day he would be able to welcome her into Heaven. To complicate things, he now had to offer the same thing to Riley. However, Jonathan couldn't have asked for anyone better than Riley to walk by Allison's side.

"Come on," Riley started back at her. "Just think, you're the one that tamed the wild beast."

"Excuse me," she retorted mockingly, "but I believe I'm the celebrity here."

"Sweetheart, you start filming a week from today, so it's not as if the paparazzi are beating down our door just yet."

Before she could follow up with a comeback, out of nowhere, the front of a truck smashed into the passenger side of their car, too quick for either one of them to react. Allison's head jerked hard to the left and then back to the right, crashing with a dull thud against the passenger-side window. Riley's neck made a cracking sound, and then darkness seeped in with silence.

Riley started coming back to the steady beeping noise he knew all too well. At first that sound offered hope, but now it seemed to mock Riley with each steady beep. His body was in a cold sweat, and he realized bedsheets were tangled up in his legs, making him feel trapped. The strong smell of antiseptic brought him fully to his senses as he realized that, again, he'd been dreaming the same dream that haunted him every time he closed his eyes.

He was lying on a couch in Allison's hospital room. It had been over three weeks now, and each time the dream came back clearer and with more detail than the time before. Initially, his mental image of the tragic scene that stole his happiness was simply the headlights of the truck. Now everything was clearer, to the point where Riley was now starting to make out faces in the crowded, broken scene—but not of the driver of the vehicle that hit them.

The beeping machine pumping life into his wife and the soft glow of light beyond the closed door were the aftermath of a dream that had become reality.

An older nurse by the nickname "Granny," which seemed to have been given to her by everyone at the hospital, had been

Riley's constant. She always offered him a soft smile, and from Riley's perspective her work with Allison was flawless with never a wasted movement. It seemed she never left the hospital. Riley couldn't think of a time he had to call for a nurse or ask for an update.

All he wanted was for his wife to wake up so that they could go home and start their new life together. He wanted her to prove all the doctors wrong and walk out of here like he knew she could—as if this horrible thing had never happened. However, the doctors told him that she would not, and that the one thing he could do for her was to tell her goodbye and let her go.

*How am I supposed to do that? What do doctors really know? They think they can play God, but they can't. And where was God that night, anyway?* This whole thing had him questioning everything he had once believed in. His whole life, Riley was the kid that could be found in church on Sunday mornings and Wednesday nights. Anytime the doors were open, he was there with the rest of his family. Not that it bothered him growing up in such a strong Christian home; it was all he knew. This new world that seemed to be growing so fast around him that it scared and worried him. No one was satisfied as they waited impatiently for a better future, hoping that it came in a box that they could all afford.

To make matters worse, the person that had put his wife in this state was never found. Not so much as a trace. The police couldn't explain it, although they had tracked the license plate back to an owner that had been dead for the past ten years. So, obviously the truck had been stolen, but there were no fingerprints, no DNA sample, nothing. It was just too frustrating to think about. Furthermore, witnesses never saw anyone in the truck abandon the scene. It was as if they had been hit by a ghost, who then vanished into the wind. It was just one more reason he was glad he and Allison had bought a house outside the city. He didn't like crowded places and found it hard to relax in the busy streets of Taupe City.

Riley laid there quietly on the couch in the darkened room. The door opened and Allison's nurse, Granny, came in. She was an older woman in her sixties with a kind disposition. She reminded Riley of a woman full of knowledge and understanding who was never too busy to lend a hand. Her eyes were a piercing, steady blue and always seemed to hold empathy behind them. Just looking at the woman spread peace through Riley. He had grown close with the nurse over the past three weeks. While friends and family, and even Allison's jerk of an agent, had come and gone, this woman had remained, not just because it was her job. She seemed to take to Riley and was his one constant in such dark times.

Granny stood at the end of the hospital bed, picked up Allison's chart, and made a few notes. "You may want to step out for this part, sweetie. I need to move her so that she doesn't get bed sores. I'll work her muscles so that they stay strong."

This was one of the odd things about Granny: she had just walked into the room and somehow knew he was awake, watching her. She seemed to be so perfect and so caring in everything she did. It was no wonder she was head of the nursing intensive care unit.

"Granny," Riley said. "Just do what you need to. Please, don't patronize me. I'm aware of the rules and what's going on. And in case you haven't noticed, 'visiting hours' don't apply to me."

The nurse looked at him for a moment, her mouth starting to open as if to say something, but she stopped and continued with her work. Riley chastised himself for speaking to her that way. He pushed the covers off and sat up on the couch, running his hand through his sweat-dampened hair. "Look, I'm sorry, I'm just dealing with a lot right now, and it's just that I feel absolutely helpless."

The hospital bills were starting to add up, and even though Riley had a stable job and people working for him, he hadn't been able to secure more jobs to make sure that his small business kept growing and producing. Constant thoughts of money, as well as the new house, wore on his mind. Although he had plenty in savings, Riley always thought of it as rainy-day money and never touched it.

Granny walked over and put a hand on his shoulder. "No need for an apology. You're dealing with more than one should have to."

Riley looked up at her, caught a glimmer in her eyes, and found a sense of peace starting to set in.

"I can't say I understand what you are going through, but I can tell you that in the time I've worked here, I've learned that a little prayer goes a long way."

Trying not to be rude to Granny again, Riley gave her a fake smile and changed the direction of the conversation. "Any changes?" he asked, hoping for a miracle.

Granny sat down next to Riley, took both his hands in hers, and placed her calm but serious eyes on him. "This will be hard for you to hear, but you need to understand exactly what is going on and what to expect." Riley felt his face starting to warm. Granny held her gaze on him and didn't waver. All he could do was look down. "You know that when we received Allison, she was basically already gone. It was a miracle that you survived without a scratch. What this machine is doing is giving life to your wife for as long as you need it to—until you can accept things and let her go," Granny said, ever so calmly.

He continued staring at the floor, unable to meet her gaze.

The tears came too easily these days, tears of anger that blurred his vision.

"I know you're hurting," Granny continued. "I can see it and feel it all over you, but you need to understand this wasn't your fault. None of this was your fault. Things happen in life that can't be explained. It's all part of God's perfect plan. We don't always understand it, but that's what makes Him God, and in the end it all works itself out."

Riley wanted to tell her to get out, because right now the last person he needed to speak with was God.

"And blaming Him will only take you so far, and then you'll be right back where you started," said Granny. "Why not try a different approach: Turn toward Him, instead of away, and see where that leads you?"

"Granny, I do want to see the silver lining, but right now it's just too much—with my wife lying there fighting for her life."

Eyeing him, she gave his hands a squeeze. "In these last few weeks I've always told you to do what you think is best, and not to rush anything. Well, now I'm telling you that it's time for you to say goodbye, because time seems to be running out. Allison would not want you to spend the rest of your life arguing with doctors and shutting everyone out of your life until you're holding onto nothing other than thoughts of what could have been."

Realization brought tears to his eyes that, indeed, he had made quite the spectacle of himself thus far. Cursing the doctors and ordering people out, even going so far as telling Allison's parents that if they were so eager to move on then they knew where the door was and not to let it hit them on the way out. Yes, he'd made quite the spectacle thus far.

His voice was barely a whisper. "H—how do I do that without feeling so guilty that I just gave up on her?"

Granny thought for a moment. "You just realize that Allison was fighting to get back to you too, but she just couldn't, and that you two will be united again someday."

Hearing that, Riley broke down into Granny's arms. Holding him, she stroked his hair and let him cry himself out. After sitting there like that for a while, Riley realized he'd literally squeezed Granny harder than he probably should. He loosened his grip and started to get up. "Granny, I don't know if I can do this alone. Will you help me with this next part?" He trailed off again, not seeming to be able to catch his breath or finish his sentence.

She pulled him close and whispered, "We'll do it together."

After a long pause, Riley sat there, just wanting to take this all in. These were going to be his last moments with his wife. Riley looked at Granny, right into her beautiful blue eyes. Without saying anything more, she simply squeezed his hand once more.

The physicians had told him from the beginning that his wife would never wake up—she was brain dead—and that he would need to let Allison go. Every time they repeated this to him, Riley told them to get out of the room, or deflected by asking them if there was a chance that she could wake up. If so, Riley wanted to give her that chance. But this time was different. There would be no further arguing or asking about the what-ifs. Now, looking at the situation for the first time with an open heart, he realized that having a machine keep his wife alive was beyond selfish.

Walking over and standing next to Allison's bed, Riley looked down at his wife. "Sweetie," he began softly with Granny at his side. "I need you to understand that what I'm doing is out of love. I believe you gave it everything you could. I just wanted to be selfish—to keep you in this world with me. I can't explain how much I love you." With his voice starting to crack, Riley trailed off for a moment until he regained some of his composure. "I know there is a better place waiting for you. I'm just sorry that I couldn't do more for you. Know that I will always treasure what time we had together, and . . ."

Riley bent down and kissed her forehead. He noticed a small tear rolling down Allison's cheek. Granny slowly reached over and turned off the machine.

Granny whispered into the transmitter on her shoulder. "Doctor and respiratory therapist to room 317, please." She then looked over at Riley, taking his hand. "This was out of love, Riley. Don't ever think otherwise. You will meet Allison once again." She gave his hand another squeeze.

As he looked down at his wife for the last time in his life, holding onto Granny's hand for strength, Riley found he could no longer speak. Granny pulled him into her embrace as the room became busy around them with people in scrubs.

They listened to the beeps become slower and slower and then stop. A flat line moved across the monitor. Allison was gone.

# CHAPTER 2

Jonathan had failed at the one thing he was assigned to do: protect her. But now she was gone. Allison was gone. He had been her guardian angel and he had failed. The world and life as he knew it seemed to cave in around him, and he didn't know where to go or what to do next. *Help me, Father, to understand this. I know you have a perfect plan, just help me understand it.* Communicating with God offered him assurance. But in his angelic heart, he struggled with the fact that this was all part of a perfect design. He never used to have a problem believing this until now. He found himself questioning God.

However, now there was another human who, this very moment, was going through incredible pain. Jonathan was only able to save one of them from the carnage on what was supposed to be the couple's happiest day of their lives: their wedding day. Now, as he stared down at the one he had saved, feeling overwhelmed by loss and helplessness, he hated knowing that even with all his abilities, he wasn't adequate enough to do the one task asked of him.

Standing there, unseen by those passing by, Jonathan stared at the broken human and realized that not only had Riley's life changed completely, but that attempts on his life would come again and again until he was dead. The demons, those of damned souls, would continue to hunt this human because, after all, that's what they did. Suddenly, he was aware that he was clenching his fists. He didn't blame the human—he blamed himself. With all the power that he possessed, why couldn't he have been a little quicker? The power from God alone surely should've been enough—to be able to move with the speed of thought, with the power of a thousand men, in one swoop of a wing—yet it hadn't been enough.

Jonathan immediately enjoyed Riley from the first day he entered Allison's life. He loved the way Riley treated his beloved Allison—always being sweet and kind to her no matter what life had thrown at them. Watching the two of them fall in love and stand by each other through it all was a blessing. If opposites really did attract, then they were the prime example. She was outgoing, where he was not. Where she excelled in sports, academics, and seemed to be able to juggle everything with ease, he was business-savvy and able to repair anything mechanical. Together they made the perfect combination of how life and love were supposed to be mixed together. Jonathan would stay for as long as he could. Nothing was more important than staying here for his other human, the one Allison had loved so deeply.

Moving closer to Riley, Jonathan saw how fragile he had become. He studied him—his brown hair, light-colored skin and the blood-stained tux he wore. Riley was doing his best to hold it together, not screaming and demanding for someone to give him an update. Jonathan placed his hand on Riley's shoulder, willing a sense of peace to flow into Riley like a running stream. However, the peace was rejected, and where love and patience once abided, now hate and pent-up anger bit his hand, causing him to release his hold.

Jonathan heard a woman's voice behind him. "He's hurting, Jonathan." He turned to see who she was talking to and was shocked when he realized she was directing her words toward him. How could she see him? Babies could see him, and small children if he wanted them to, but not adults.

"I know what you're thinking," she said, interrupting his thoughts. "You're wondering how I know you're there. Well, that's a story for another day. I know how much you loved Allison, but she's gone now. Have you decided what you're going to do next?"

Still amazed that this woman could see him, Jonathan looked down at the elderly black woman. Although she was small in size, she had an aura about her that commanded attention. As if everyone in a room would turn to her for guidance hanging on every word that she spoke.

"You could let things transpire as they will and move on to your next assignment," she continued. "There's nothing wrong with that. There will be another to take your place and help this human through these trying times. Or, you could choose to fall, as others have done, and be the one to protect Riley the rest of his days, staying by his side instead of being assigned as someone else's guardian angel. However, you know that means you can't go back until God comes to get His children. You will never be able to serve as another's guardian, even long after this human passes on."

He had heard of angels falling before, to stay with their human, but the human lifespan was so short that it seemed a waste. He had been doing this for only a short time, just since he was assigned as Allison's guardian angel. Was he ready to become a fallen, to serve as Riley's protector on Earth? There would be so much he would have to give up.

Every time a baby is born, an angel is created. As soon as they are spoken into life by God the Father, they know exactly what they are to do and whom they are to protect and help guide for the rest of that human's life. Once the human passes on, they help welcome them into Heaven. If the human was a nonbeliever then the guardian has to say goodbye. No matter how much they wanted to give their life so that their human never had to touch the fires of hell, Lucifer had made this rule, since he had invested himself throughout the nonbeliever's life, poisoning their thoughts and sculpting the way he wanted them to be.

Nonbelievers and believers had their own guardian angel, until their life moved on from this existence into the next. Then the angel was given a choice to either spend their time worshipping in Heaven or moving on to their next assignment as a guardian to someone new.

"It's not a waste, Jonathan, but it is your choice," the woman said. "After Riley is gone, years from now, you will find other ways to help people. I do it by working in this hospital. I like to be on this level with people so I can help them through their trying times. Still, this is your choice, friend, and I will pray for you. But know that Riley is going to be put through trials. Someone, whose name I will not speak, is coming for him."

"How do you know this? What trials will Riley be forced to endure?"

"I know because I was once someone's guardian angel. I had the same decision to make that is now presented to you. The trials are always different so I have no way to tell you exactly what to be prepared for. Just know that they will bring great pain. Not only to Riley, but to you as well, if you fail in protecting him."

Even though Jonathan was new to being a guardian angel, since watching over Allison was his first assignment, he felt that he could trust this woman. Just as she was just about to walk away, Jonathan asked one more question.

"What is your name, guardian?"

She now smiled at him, as if she hadn't been called by that in such a long time.

"I don't feel as if my real name holds any value anymore." A pained expression passed over her for a second, and then just as quickly as it came, it was gone. "Just call me Granny. It's a nickname that others have given me in my role at the hospital. One that I have learned to love."

Giving him one last smile, she turned and went to Riley, Jonathan let his thoughts take him to Allison's room. Standing next to her bed, he reached out and took both her hands in his. "I'm sorry, beautiful. I will forever be so sorry for not being able to do more for you, but because of how much I love you, I will look after Riley for you, and although I won't be there to welcome you into Heaven, there will be plenty of others there. They will take you in with open arms. God the Father is there, waiting for you. I would gladly do it all over again with you, even if the result was the same. I'm so proud of the woman you have become and to have been your guardian. I want you to know that it gave me great joy for you to have been my first, and last, to protect."

He leaned down and kissed Allison, then he let his thoughts take him outside the hospital.

---

Standing there, looking at the hospital, knowing that inside this building there was both hope and pain, Jonathan shook his head and walked away. He wasn't sure what to do next, so he walked at a slow pace that matched his heavy mood. *I have to go through with this. I made a promise to my sweet Allison and must go through with this.*

Suddenly a feeling of urgency came over him as if time was of the essence. His thoughts took him to the clouds above the city. Standing atop them, he looked out across the beautiful scene of the city, lit up at night. If he were to become a fallen, he would have to give up many of his abilities, including his beautiful, but

battered, wings. He would never be asked by God the Father to
watch over another of His children as a guardian. What scared
him most, though, despite what the future held, was that he would
lose his powers—not all, at least, but most. The trials that were
coming for Riley would cause Jonathan to taste death, bleed, and
breathe air for the first time.

Stretching his wings out, adjacent to his body, he looked at
them and thought of all that they meant to him. Over six feet in
length, the feathers that at once could be as soft as a silky, smooth
cloth could also be resistant to anything that might be hurled his
way by any of the demons who, in the past, had tried to tempt
and lure his precious Allison.

Enveloping his wings around him so that he could feel the
warmth of the feathers, Jonathan breathed in deep the smell
carried upon them—the wind of the open road mixed with the
smell of meadows after the last drop of rain. This would be the
last time this scent would fill his nostrils. Stretching them out
once more, he took in their beauty. Others might look upon
them and see the flaws of countless battles, the tattered wings,
the ruffled edges that would never run smooth again, but he also
saw the complexity of what they meant to him—would always
mean to him. It was like gazing upon the most beautiful sunrise
and realizing that it was the last one you would ever see.

Kneeling down and closing his eyes, he spoke to God. "Thank
you for it all, this short time I have been a guardian. I will always
serve you. I did not come to this decision lightly, and with your
permission I would like to embark on serving the human, Riley
Smith, in these troubling hours, and walk with him for as long as
he will allow me. I love you, Father. Please grant me this."

Ending his prayer with an Amen, Jonathan found himself
starting to slip from the clouds. A hard crack of thunder echoed
off the ground, the ground his feet would soon touch for the first

time. As the ground came closer and closer, he did not fear the fall or the impact. Fear was never a factor the entire time he was a guardian watching over his Allison, but now the fear of the unknown began to drip into his thoughts. He didn't know what he was to do next.

Jonathan had always known what he was supposed to do from the beginning to the end of each and every day in Allison's life. But the unknown—not knowing if Riley would accept him and how he would comprehend all this—was absolutely terrifying. With that last thought consuming him, the ground that seemed to be so far away was now right beneath his feet. He closed his eyes and waited for the impact. Ten seconds seemed to go by, then twenty, until finally a minute seemed to have come and gone.

Opening his eyes, Jonathan found himself kneeling on the ground, his fingertips touching the cold surface and the rain pelting off his back. He felt his back muscles tense to spread his wings, but there was nothing there. The space that once bore them was now empty. The weight and meaning that they carried were no longer of any importance. It was the payment he must make for being allowed to help his new friend, Riley—that is, if Riley would have him. But the loss of Allison was deeper than words could describe.

Jonathan was now in an alley. He took in his surroundings, making sure no one had seen him, when something caught his attention. As he would soon learn, he had retained his keen sense of hearing as well as his ability to read the thoughts of someone near him. He walked toward the street and saw a woman pass by, walking alone. Perhaps she had just left work and was hurrying to get home in this weather. Her thoughts, though, were what caught his attention—all jumbled and on top of each other. Jonathan could see a nervousness all about her, something he couldn't shake. Then he saw two men walking behind her, their pace a bit quicker than hers, like predators stalking their prey.

Jonathan crossed to the other side of the street, behind the two men. The young woman turned the corner and the two men followed. In an instant they were out of his sight. Quickening his own pace, Jonathan turned the corner only to find they had disappeared. Scanning the empty street as it was being blanketed by rain, he couldn't see anything. Suddenly, a scream pierced the night. He followed it to an alley and rushed over to find the two men had cornered the woman. She was doing her best to fight them off. One was behind her, holding her, while the other man was in front of her, tearing her purse from her hands.

"Please, stop, I don't have anything valuable!"

"Oh, sure, like we've never heard that before," one of them sneered at her as he held her by her arms. "You have something that's better than cash."

The other man began rummaging through the contents of the purse. He pulled the wallet out and tossed the purse aside. "Bingo," he said, opening it. Finding no cash, just cards, he cursed under his breath and closed in on the woman, "No cash, so it looks like we're going hungry. You'll have to pay for that." He bared his ugly, stained teeth. "Hold her still, Joe, I'm first." The woman screamed, but the man behind her put one of his hands over her mouth. "Let her yell, Joe. I like it when they yell."

"Stop it now, before you do something you'll regret."

The man turned abruptly to see Jonathan behind him. He was significantly bigger and taller than either man. "Whoa, what kind of a freak are you?"

"You two can still walk away from this, but let her go, or I'll make you do it myself," Jonathan said coolly.

"Get a load of this huge freak, thinking he's gonna get a taste of our catch," Joe said. "We aren't playing, you big freak. You know the saying, 'the bigger they are, the harder they fall.' Get him, Mike, mess him up good."

The other man pushed the woman aside and pulled out a knife. "Let's go, big man. You wanna play?"

"Yes, I do want to play," Jonathan said as he walked toward him. "You see, it's been a bad day. It might cheer me up to teach you two some manners." He showed no sign of fear at the knife being waved back and forth in front of him.

Mike lunged at Jonathan with the knife, but Jonathan caught the man's wrist and snapped it with one quick movement, causing his fingers to go limp as the knife fell to the ground. Still gripping the man's wrist, Jonathan gave him a direct punch to the throat. The man dropped to his knees, grasping his neck.

Jonathan then turned his attention to Joe.

"Enough of this," the second robber said as he reached behind him and pulled out a handgun. Before he could squeeze the trigger, Jonathan was upon him, taking his weapon and pitching it to the side. He held Joe's head in the palm of his hand and slammed it against the wall. As Jonathan released his hold, the man fell limp at his feet.

Jonathan then turned around to see if he could help the woman, but she had grabbed something from her purse and sprayed him in the face with it. Sticking his hand up to block the spray from his mouth he looked at her dumbly. "Miss, are you okay?"

Still aiming the can at Jonathan, she had a look of pure terror on her face. She stared at the spray can and then dropped it. "Please, please don't hurt me," she said, her voice trembling. "Take whatever you want, but please don't hurt me. I won't tell anyone, I swear."

"I won't hurt you," Jonathan replied. "I'm simply here to help. My name is Jonathan, and I promise I won't hurt you." He wiped at his eyes to get whatever solution she sprayed into them out of his vision. A bitter aftertaste followed, causing him to perform an act that he'd never done before. Spitting several times to be rid of the solution that had gotten into his mouth, satisfied that most of the bitterness had dissipated, Jonathan spoke.

"There's a hospital not far from here. If you like, I'll take you there so that you can be checked out."

The woman, still shaking and trembling, put her hands over her face and began to sob. Not knowing if he should approach her, Jonathan turned his attention to the woman's belongings. He gathered them up and put them back in her purse. Jonathan then stood, walked over to the gun and knife, and picked them up. Lastly, he walked over to one of the assailants still lying on the ground and shook his head at him in pity.

"I can tell you that you and your friend are traveling down a path that only leads to hurt, torment, and pain. All the wrongs you have done in your life will be nothing compared to the fires of Hell that will one day nip at you. There will only be more torment for you unless you take up a new path."

"Please—I don't want to die; please don't kill me!" the man begged. Jonathan crouched down until he was face-to-face with the man and gave him an icy stare. He showed him the gun in his hand, and the man began to beg for his life. "Oh no, please, don't do this! I'm sorry!"

"The things that I have seen would cause you to soil yourself," Jonathan replied. "You cannot imagine what I could do to you. Turn yourself into the cops, own up for your bad deeds, and I won't come back for you."

Jonathan closed his hand around the gun and squeezed. He opened his palm and revealed nothing more than a twisted, misshapen piece of metal and dropped it on the ground. He then bent the blade of the knife back on itself, rendering it useless.

"I'm not joking. Turn yourself in and choose a new path. Seek refuge in the Lord our Savior. And know that if I wanted you dead, I would have done it by now." And with that, Jonathan stood and turned to walk away.

"Who are you?" the man called out.

"My name is Jonathan. Remember what I have told you."

Walking over to the woman, still not knowing how to comfort her, he simply offered her the purse. Not looking at him, she took the purse. "Thank you," she offered in a small, nervous voice.

"May I accompany you to the hospital?"

Looking up at him, new tears began to well in her eyes. "Okay, yes, thank you."

"You are very welcome." Jonathan offered her his arm. She shied away.

"Not to be rude, but, um . . . you smell like pepper spray."

"Pepper spray," Jonathan said, running his tongue along his mouth and then looking down at his coat and pants, and then back at the woman, with a puzzled expression. She shrugged her shoulders, and her mouth relaxed into a small smile, revealing an attractive young woman, whom Jonathan guessed to be in her early thirties. She wore a business suit under her now dripping wet overcoat.

"Most people," she said, "are not immune to pepper spray as you seem to be."

"Oh," he said. "I see. Well, I'm not immune to it—it must be the rain—it's washing it away."

"I'm so sorry."

Jonathan led her out of the alley. "Don't give it another thought, Miss. I'm just glad we both came out of this alive."

"My name is Allison," she said. "Well, my actual name is Mary, but everyone calls me Allison. But my parents and a few friends sometimes call me Mags since it's my initials."

Jonathan suddenly stopped. He felt the sting of that name, his beloved he had failed. The person he had watched night and day her entire life. What he wouldn't give to hear her laugh again.

"Is something wrong?" she asked.

Hoping the shock he felt wasn't registering on his face, Jonathan quickly composed himself. "No, nothing is wrong; just this weather sure will take it out of you, and it seems to be doing that to me. I must be getting old. Let's get you inside where it's warm."

She chuckled. "You, old? Please, you can't be more than thirty."

The light conversation continued all the way to the hospital. Once there, Jonathan asked Allison if there was anything else that he could do to help.

"You're not coming in?" she gave him a queer look. "I figured you'd need to be checked out as well."

Jonathan tried to think of an excuse as to why he didn't want to walk back into the building where his sweet girl lay dead. "No, there are other young women I must rescue," he said, giving her a small smile. He started to extend his hand, but then remembered the pepper spray and pulled it back. She grabbed his hand and squeezed it hard. While looking up at him, her eyes started to tear up.

"Words will never be able to express how grateful I am for you. Thank you, so much." Releasing his hand, she dug inside her purse and took out a card. "This is my business card. If you ever need anything from me, please call." He hesitated, not sure what to say, so she took the initiative and put the card inside his top right jacket pocket.

With that, she turned and walked away, and then called over her shoulder. "Seriously, if you ever need anything . . . job, help, money, or just a friend, please call me." With that, she walked into the hospital and disappeared.

Reaching inside his jacket pocket and pulling the card out, he looked down to find her name, *Mary Allison Gregory.* Underneath the name read, *CEO of Gregory Portal Provider* with two phone numbers. He placed it back inside his pocket.

# CHAPTER 3

Karen sat in her small, empty one-bedroom apartment, hearing the distant noises from outside that promised the excitement of good times and bad decisions: the alcohol and substance abuse that would eventually lead her to waking up next to a stranger, confused about the aftermath of the night before, knowing that her actions would take her further down a road of frustration and confusion.

She wondered how her life choices had led her to this moment. She had tried to follow a dream that somehow always seemed just out of reach, no matter how hard she tried to grasp it. That dream had brought her here, reveling in the one fact that life had just given up on her as she listened to her conscience confirm what she already knew.

*Do you honestly believe you will be missed? Well, let's look at the facts, shall we? Number one, your husband couldn't pack his shit quick enough to get away from a crazy bitch like you. Number two, do you really believe your parents are going to help you after disgracing their good name with a second divorce in less than a year? Unless, of course, you want to return to being daddy's little girl, and we both know what that means. And as for your son, that little punk is damaged beyond repair. And by the way, did you ever figure out who the father really is?*

These ugly thoughts seemed to be coming at her from everywhere at once, dripping into her weariness as a water spout not completely turned off. Karen closed her eyes, giving in to the thought of how she'd been wronged her whole life. Now here she was, a payment behind on rent, another man in the world who couldn't stand her, and losing another job. And, come to think of it, his exact words were: "Damn, woman, how many jobs can you go through in a year, and exactly how hard is it to pour a cup of coffee? Seriously, I'm tired of being the only one working around here."

She had grown up in a small suburb where the women either got married and started a family right after high school or tried to make it on their own. Most who had failed in their pursuit of wanting something more came back and joined society's simple way of life, raising a family and knowing this was as good as life would ever become. Karen, however, had wanted what every teenager wanted—fame—and she thought she could get it if she worked hard enough. So, she left her small town and came to Hollywood in pursuit of an acting career. But her plans turned into working as a waitress at any restaurant that would hire her. She had been bouncing from job to job, and party to party, for as long as she could remember, and it was all due to the pipe dream that she kept chasing.

Unfortunately, those dreams quickly fell apart when she found out she was pregnant, and God only knew who the father was. Crazy part was, she was not that kind of girl. Small city, sure, but when she had first moved out to the West Coast with stars in her eyes, some supposed manager with a slick-talking way about him had gotten her into adult film, promising this is where everyone started till they made a name for themselves. She wasn't naïve but wanted fame to knock on her door quickly and saw this as a means to an end. Before she knew it, she was working at sleazy gentlemen's clubs, being used up by anyone who could help keep her afloat. Once her looks faded, the only dreams she held onto now was how to make enough money to put food on the table and a roof over her head. Now her life was all about taking extra shifts, hopefully getting good tips, and hoping to catch a glimpse of her eleven-year-old son, who seemed to have hit puberty with the way he was already talking and acting. She looked down at the worn carpet on the old apartment floor and wondered, *Where did this go so wrong, so fast?*

There was not so much as a spark of hope left for Karen or her son. Now all she wanted to do was simply make it all end, to close herself off from the world and just go into a soft, peaceful sleep. Her son was honestly better off without her, no matter how she looked at the situation. She was pregnant at an early age, and all she wanted was to get out from under her mother and stepfather. Her mother was constantly doped up to the point that she never noticed her husband was straying a little bit—into Karen's room, most nights.

A shiver ran down Karen's back, and the small hairs on her neck stood up. She looked at the bottle of pills on the coffee table. *Why not? Let's quit playing around and just get it all over with once and for all.*

Legionaries sat there watching his master, knowing very well not to interrupt what was taking place. Master truly was miraculous at what he did, coaxing humans into believing that it could all end with just one simple act. Master started in again. *Karen, it won't hurt nearly as much as what you have endured. This can all come to an end. Just let go of your troubles and relax.* He knew he almost had her, but then he was interrupted by the phone.

It rang a second and a third time, and Legionaries wondered if she would pick it up.

Legionaries watched with wonder and said quietly, not wanting to disrupt what was transpiring right before his very eyes, "Master's work is so excellent, nothing seems to be enough of a distraction. But then, Master has had thousands of years to perfect the art of whispering his thoughts."

There was another presence in the room as well. Legionaries picked up on it as soon as it appeared. An angel sat right next to Karen, touching her hand, praying for her, and sending out an aura of peace that made Legionaries feel sick to his stomach. It was none other than Karen's so-called guardian. But Legionaries knew the angel hadn't been able to prevent Master's influence on her, swaying her with such ease. The guardian paid no attention to Master or Legionaries, even though he knew they were there. He just kept on praying to the point where he had tears of sympathy running down his face.

Then, to Legionaries's delight, Karen grabbed the bottle of pills, jerked the top off, sending pills flying everywhere, and emptied what was left of the bottle into her mouth, followed by a long pull from a bottle of cheap vodka. She came up for a long breath, filling her lungs to capacity, and let the tears start to roll down her face.

The guardian at once threw itself at her feet and cried out so hard that Legionaries felt the room almost expand with the power that the guardian emptied from its being. Knowing he could do nothing for her now except sit and wait, the guardian took his place next to Karen and wrapped his massive arms around her. "I'm sorry I failed you. From the moment you drew your first breath, I felt compassion for you. I will stay with you for as long as I'm allowed. I love you so much, Karen, and I'm sorry that it came to this."

Feeling defeated, Karen leaned back into the couch and took another long drink. With her vision starting to blur, she fought to keep her eyes open only to be overtaken by a thick darkness as she slipped into a feeling of peace. Or so it seemed. Karen awakened and looked around. Seated to her right was a man with a face of pure beauty, but with eyes darker than the black of night. Another being stood behind him, with a sorrowful look on his face, and years of frustration etched into his forehead. He had a freakishly large build, yet there was something so vulnerable about him, he seemed weary. Karen's attention returned to the man sitting next to her. He took her face in one of his hands.

"Karen, Karen, Karen, it is my pleasure to welcome you to your own personal Hell. I will take extreme delight in your screams as you experience terror unlike anything you could ever imagine. And just when you think you can endure the pain no longer, I will personally see to giving you more upon more. There truly will never be an end to what I'm about to do to you, and all I can say is that I hope it was all worth it." With that, he released her face and grinned at her. "By the way, you can call me Master—or Lucifer—whichever you see fit."

Karen began screaming as something grabbed her by the hair and pulled her to the floor. She felt unimaginable pain as if she were being eaten alive. Amidst the pain and misery, she realized she had just been pulled into Hell. She began to scream, but no one would hear.

Master chuckled to himself as his new lady in waiting was dragged out of sight. He turned to face Legionaries, whose size alone would frighten off any man. However, he was more of a bookkeeper than a fighter. Master kept him around simply for the fact that he grew tiresome of the battle to claim more souls and enjoyed being able to lay some of the burden on this lackey. He also kept him close, for he knew he couldn't trust him. After all, Legionaries knew too many of his secrets and could possibly use them to lead an uprising against him. But keeping him close, abused, and under his thumb, there was no reason for worry.

Karen's guardian, still in the room, sat on the floor of the old apartment and watched the soul of his beloved Karen being dragged away from him. There was nothing more he could do for her. Karen, unfortunately, had made the decision to end her life without ever becoming a believer in God. Guardians weren't allowed to save their humans once that choice was made. It wasn't suicide that caused a soul to taste the fires of hell. Only the fact of whether a person was a believer or a nonbeliever determined what would happen to their soul. Finally, the guardian rose to his feet and looked directly at Legionaries, and then at Lucifer, with disgust. Behind his own blue eyes lay the pure belief that one day this would all be repaid.

"My name is Simon," he said to Lucifer. "I will be there at the end of days when Michael casts you into the fires of Hell for all eternity, and all the souls that you so cowardly took from this world will tear you apart limb from limb. On that day, Heaven will rejoice, and you will come to terms with what you are . . . a wretched fallen that God will no longer hear."

"Hold your tongue!" Lucifer all but screamed. "That will never happen, and it is I who will be triumphant in the end."

The guardian began to laugh, mocking Lucifer as he placed his hand against a wall as if in need of support. As if the moment was too rich to not find the humor in Lucifer playing the eternal part of a fool.

"Silence, you imbecile!!" Lucifer yelled again.

The guardian held a small smile on his face. Then he stood before Lucifer and gritted his teeth to control the rage seething in him. "It is written in scripture, and guess what? You lose." And with that, the guardian was gone.

Legionaries watched as Master stood completely still as if

contemplating what he was just told, letting the words echo around inside his head. He then looked at Legionaries standing beside him.

"What is it, Legionaries? You seem to have a lot on your mind. You must have a good reason for disturbing me with your presence. Must I sic the hounds upon you once more to gnaw at your bones?"

"Master, I thought you should know that there has been another botched job. And an angel has fallen!"

This was only known to happen once every hundred years or so. Lucifer's dull black eyes began to sparkle with excitement. An angel falling meant that the angel had decided to come to Earth to help out instead of being, as one would say, behind the scenes. Lucifer was once an angel himself and knew the rules. Sure, a fallen angel would be able to return to the false God one day. But until then, the fallen would be stuck on Earth with only limited powers, waiting and doing God's work in near-human form.

Still brimming with excitement, Lucifer held it back as he spoke. "Legionaries, so help me but if you are not a hundred percent certain, then I will personally be the one to pull your insides out and chew on them while you beg for me to stop. The delight in knowing that each time you cry out as I feed on you like a rat on a carcass sends a unique pleasure to my core, making me hope that you aren't sure of what you heard!

"Now, with that said, take a moment and consider how angry you want to make me if you are wrong. Are you sure that an angel has fallen?"

Legionaries stood there, standing as straight as he could despite the constant pain being driven through him. Then he summoned all his confidence. "One of the twins told me this morning. I'm simply the messenger . . ."

Lucifer pounced upon Legionaries, throwing him to the

ground and hissing, "You may be the messenger, but you know very well what I do to messengers. However, since it's one of the twins reporting it, I'll take some time to look into it. Which one? Do you at least know that much?"

"Master, I have no clue; there are far too many for me to even imagine and—"

Lucifer stood up, leaving Legionaries lying on the ground, and started to massage his temples. "So help me, Legionaries, so help me. I keep you around like some stupid pet just so I can kick you every now and then for pure amusement. Not which angel has fallen, you dumb, simple-minded fool, but which of the twins . . . which, for Hell's sake, of my twin sons informed you?"

"Oh." Legionaries stood up slowly. "Bryce, sir. He was in the southern section when it happened—almost three weeks ago now. One of the elders reported that something strange seemed to be happening in that section, and Bryce confirmed it."

"Well, Legionaries, tell the twins I would like to see them tonight. We have quite a bit to talk about, and we really should catch up. Now leave me. I have no further use for you."

"Master, where would you like me to have them meet you?"

"Have them meet me in Heaven, Legionaries," Lucifer hissed with sarcasm. "We will see if Saint Paul can secure us a reservation and, who knows, maybe even the false God himself would like to sit down with us."

Legionaries looked down, expecting the hounds at any moment would begin their treacherous gnawing on him.

"My own personal chamber, Legionaries, just like the last thousand times I've gotten to see my boys."

Legionaries stood still for a moment longer, listening for the sound of hounds at his back. He then quickly left Karen's apartment and began his long descent into the fiery pit to make his way to the southern section. The fires rushed up all around him with the force he'd long ago learned he was powerless against. He'd taken this trip every day for a millennium. He heard the unending cries of unseen faces begging for help, begging for mercy. He proceeded to his own little passageway that always remained unlocked, just for him. It was his personal pipeline to the twins' section. He would inform them of Master's demand. Suddenly, he felt a touch on his shoulder. He turned around to see Karen standing before him.

What was she doing here? She wasn't supposed to be here. He was Master's right-hand man. He and the other region leaders were to be left alone from the other residents of Hell. This was their privilege. However, sometimes one of the damned was still able to get their hand on him, just for a short moment, and tried to claw their way out. Legionaries looked at her, annoyed. Her eyes were wild, and the face that was once beautiful had been nearly chewed off, only to appear confused as to where she was a moment later. She began thrashing and slapping uncontrollably at her face, and pulling her own hair out in strands, begging for Legionaries to help her.

He kicked at her, but missed, as she was pulled down by arms that seemed to come up all around her from nowhere. He heard the screams and then—nothing. He'd been down here for as long as he could remember. He, too, once went through the constant ritual of being tormented, until Master gave him a seat at the table. His job was to ensure all was kept running smoothly. Legionaries was grateful for the new role. A rush of fear overtook him, and he knew he had to get back to the surface as soon as possible. He closed his eyes as he said, "southern section" and was whisked away.

# CHAPTER 4

R iley sat on the edge of the bed, talking on the phone with his realtor. He wanted to sell the house, the house he'd bought for Allison. It was just him now, and the house seemed to be more of a tomb than a home. Everything around him, from the newly furnished rooms all the way to the hardwood floors, irked him about being here, and he had come to the conclusion that there was just no way that he could stay here any longer.

The house was a two story with four bedrooms, three baths, a kitchen, dining room, living room, and an amazing patio that overlooked the four-acre lot behind the house. Riley had gone all out because he believed that this would be the place where he and Allison would grow old together. It was the absolute perfect place to raise a family—out of the city, but not too far. They could be in downtown Taupe City in thirty minutes. It was a cozy neighborhood with nice people that Allison and Riley had gotten to know over the past several months as the house was finished. But now, the quietness that surrounded him and what used to be the comfort of knowing everyone was too much, and it all seemed to be closing in.

"Are you listening to me?" Alex said on the other end of the line. "You can't sell the place. You haven't been in it long enough. Besides, this isn't a seller's market right now. As your friend, I'm telling you that you're going to be upside down on this thing for a long time. I understand you want to sell, but trust me, this is the last thing you should do." Alex was not just a real estate agent who had his own company, Ayala Dream Realty. He was a close friend to Riley, someone he trusted when it came to big decisions and financial advice.

Staring at the open closet door, Riley was taken back to when the house was being constructed. Allison had stood there looking at it. "Perfect! Just big enough to fit my shoes," she'd said with a wry grin.

The whole picture played out in front of Riley. He closed his eyes hard and pressed the receiver of the phone to his ear with his shoulder as he put on his other boot.

"I hear you, but I'm going crazy, and this just isn't going to work," he said. "I need out of here. What about leasing it out and I'll just hire someone to manage the property?" There was a long pause on the line followed by a hard sigh.

"Look, Riley, when I was showing you the location, I told you that it was an up-and-coming area that was going to explode in a couple of years to where you could sell for almost double what you bought it for, but as for selling now, you will literally get less than what you already sunk into the place. I'm telling you this as a friend; you don't want this over your head. On top of that, leasing it out is not an option because no one is really looking in that area—not right now. You're the first person I've actually sold a house to in quite some time. That's how bad the market is."

Just as Riley was about to fire back with an insult about feeling cheated into buying this lot and building, the doorbell rang. "Hey, uh, Alex, I really don't care about the financial aspect. I just want out. So, pull some strings, kick down some doors, put up some flyers, I don't care. But get me out of here and soon. Gotta go, someone's at the door." Riley disconnected the call before Alex could respond. The doorbell rang once again.

"Coming!" Riley yelled as he jumped off the edge of the bed and tossed the phone toward the chair in the corner. He crossed through the living room. It was a spacious room with an open concept, hardwood floors, and oversized windows with an amazing view of a field right behind the house. No one else could build there, since a waterline system hadn't been put in. He stopped in the foyer, did a double take at his reflection in the mirror, and opened the door to find a man the size of a giant standing there, sporting a huge smile.

Well-dressed in khakis and a jacket, the giant extended his hand. "Hi. My name is Jonathan. It means 'Gift from God'."

Overtaken by the man's size, Riley accepted his large gift-from-God hand. "Whatever you're selling, I'm really not interested. If you have a business card, I'll look it over when I get a minute, but right now I'm pretty busy."

"Oh, I'm sorry, but I'm not a salesman."

"Well, if you're a Jehovah's Witness, then I should probably just tell you I have no interest in religion right now, or any other kind of belief system for that matter."

"Hmm . . ." the giant said, releasing Riley's hand. "I'm not one of those either, but I'm sorry to hear that you're not a Christian. Would you mind if I ask why not?"

"That's a strange question for someone who's not a religious fanatic."

"Well, that's where you're wrong. I never said that I wasn't religious, I just informed you of what I'm not. Actually, the reason I'm here is to comfort you in your time of loss. I was a close friend of Allison's, and it saddened me deeply to learn of her passing."

Riley was just about to close the door but stopped himself when he heard the man speak of Allison. "Oh, I'm so sorry, it's just that lately I've been a little more than on edge. Pardon my rudeness, but I don't believe in the eight years I knew Allison that she ever even mentioned you."

The man smiled back at Riley. "What I'm about to tell you may take a little while and may be hard to wrap your head around, but everything I tell you will be nothing but the truth. You see, Riley, where I come from, we are forbidden to lie, and this conversation is better shared somewhere where you can be seated."

Taking a long moment to look the big man over, Riley was struck, once again, when he looked at the man's face and saw that he had the same gentle blue eyes as the kind nurse, Granny, who helped him through the weeks he was at the hospital. "Tell you what," Riley said. "I don't know you from Adam, and although I am leery," he said, looking up into Jonathan's blue eyes, which seemed to offer peace and the promise of being truthful. "I think getting out of this house for a little bit could do me some good. How about I grab my jacket and we go for a walk instead. Maybe over to the park?"

Jonathan smiled and nodded. "Sounds good to me. I have always loved the cooler weather."

Riley returned the smile, excused himself for a moment, and grabbed his jacket out of the front closet. When he turned around, he saw that the giant had already let himself in and was now standing in the entryway looking at the vaulted ceilings in the living room. Finding the man's size a little more uncomfortable now that he was inside closed walls, Riley quickly put on his jacket as if nothing was wrong and proceeded toward the door, about to usher the giant out. Without having to be asked, Jonathan turned around and walked out onto the front stoop as if he were just a big kid waiting for someone to tell him it was time to go.

They started off toward the park, which was just a couple of blocks away. Their pace was slow, as if they were two old friends just catching up. At first Riley wondered how this conversation was about to play out. Who was this man? What was he really here for? How come Allison had never mentioned him? All these questions rolled around in his head. The whole time Jonathan just kept the same easy pace as if he didn't have a care in the world. Neither of them spoke a word.

# CHAPTER 5

**A**rriving unannounced, Legionaries watched in silence as the twins Bryce and Abel focused on their job that would happen shortly. Wanting to deliver Master's message then leave at once, he broke the silence. "Your father has demanded that both of you come to dinner tonight."

Bryce turned abruptly, shocked at how Legionaries had just snuck up on them. Abel didn't seem to care as he remained focused on the region below. Trying to show that this lackey hadn't surprised him, Bryce glared then spoke sarcastically. "Did you hear that, Abel? It seems as if we're being summoned, and Master's right-hand man is the dutiful messenger."

Abel, the taller of the two, didn't seem to pay even a moment's notice to Legionaries. The "twins" didn't look a thing like one another—nearly everything was different about them. For starters, they weren't actually sons of Lucifer's, just simply two whom he had taken in. No one asked questions. One was short and muscular, and the other tall and lean. Bryce was loud and quick-witted. Abel was quiet and spoke only when he found it necessary. The only reason Lucifer called them twins, according to what Legionaries could determine, was that when it came to completing tasks that others could not, these two were more than adequately equipped to do what was asked of them.

They put Legionaries on edge. Being around the two at the same time, he never knew what would happen. However, these two were definitely connected at the hip and had been inseparable in all the time that Legionaries had known them.

"Fine," Abel quickly said, to satisfy Legionaries. "We'll be there. Now, if you could return to wherever you came from, we have things to do."

"Thank you. I will inform Master that you will both be at dinner."

"And so on and so forth into eternity. Now get the hell out of here," Abel said with a laugh.

"Some of us have more to do than follow the Master around, awaiting his every order," Bryce joined in. "You're nothing but a worthless piece of shit whose purpose would be better served feeding the maggots down below," he finished, with enough sarcasm to make Abel look up from where he was perched. Then Bryce leaned back and laughed a sick little laugh that made Legionaries's skin crawl.

With that, Legionaries turned and left, making his way once again through the halls of cries and screams of countless souls begging someone to end their torture.

"A little abrupt even for you, brother," Abel said as he continued to watch the activity taking place in their sector. There was a busy intersection he was keeping a close eye on.

"Do you think it was a bit too much?" Bryce asked, feigning concern.

They both laughed mercilessly. Now they awaited what was to be another huge catastrophe, scheduled to take place soon, according to the data Legionaries had reported earlier. There was going to be a pileup and it was their job to do the collecting.

"Can't have spirits just wandering around like chickens with their heads cut off now, can we?" Bryce said with a grin. Their job was simple: Collect the dead souls that belonged to Hell and deliver them to their Master. It was what they were created to do and their way of winning Master's approval. "Shouldn't be too much longer, right?" Bryce continued. "I feel like we've been sitting here for a millennium. And I, for one, am ready to go and see what's so important that Father sends the fool to fetch us."

Abel just sat there staring, waiting, and didn't say a word.

"In all seriousness, what do you think he's summoning us for? Our records have been perfection through and through. Do you think it's about the fallen angel that slipped through our fingers and that I didn't immediately report it?"

Still silence, just the long stare and the wait.

"Nonsense. It was one minor mishap. And it's not as if we see an angel fall every day. He can't be that angry with me. Hell, it wasn't even our failure. We were just there and saw it happen. Why should it fall on us to report it? We have enough on our plates as it is."

With that, Abel picked up his tote bag and tossed it over his shoulder. "It's time," he said dryly and then jumped off his perch.

In the middle of the intersection below them, a drunk driver had crossed the center line and hit another vehicle with a family inside head-on. The collision would forever alter several lives and end others, all because of one person's recklessness. This pleased Abel and Bryce. The man, wife, and child were all killed on impact. The drunk driver would walk away with little more than a broken arm, knowing the rest of his life that he was the cause of killing a child.

"Three deaths and only one of them is ours?" Bryce scowled. "That is unacceptable! He believes that only hounds and Father can cause pain. Give me five minutes in one of Hell's rooms with him and I'll change his mind."

Abel grabbed the dark spirit of the woman in the car and tucked it in his bag. The tote bags that all region leaders carried were only a couple of feet long, slender, and made of a mesh material. The bag didn't fasten close. Once a soul was forced inside, the mesh held it in place, making it impossible for escape as the occupant pulled and stretched, trying to be free. Souls of the damned were the actual form of the human body that it inhabited.

When souls were released upon death, they acted just as a child did after birth. Squirming back and forth, innocently taking in the new world they now occupied. To carry out the process of actually capturing it, leaders simply snatched it up, since it weighed nothing and offered no resistance.

However, if it wasn't collected immediately, after a few minutes the soul would begin to comprehend what had happened and would go from childlike to adult in the space of a few minutes.

Realizing what they hadn't wanted to believe when their mortal body was alive. Understanding now that the choices they made decided what afterlife would be their new destination. The soul would flee, making it far more difficult to catch over time as it learned about its new existence and the new way of survival.

The leaders had all heard tales of how some still occupied Earth, eluding capture time and again, hoping for a second chance at life. Growing in frustration as the false God of Heaven ignored their cries for help. The more frustrated the unclaimed soul became, it could eventually cause havoc on its surroundings, which could lead to an uprising of which other leaders would feed off.

A soul that belonged to Master, that was left unclaimed, could only lead to doubt and frustration. Doubt that would breed among the ranks of region leaders, leaving them to wonder if they had been forced to follow rules that were outdated.

Or frustration, believing that they had been forced into a belief that was outdated. Causing leaders to wonder why they followed a fool who couldn't control lost souls. Especially those who were fed to fires of hell.

Why should they suffer the rules that Lucifer commanded when they could now choose what they would and wouldn't do?

"Damned misfortune!" Bryce continued. "We were up on top of that building for four straight hours, and we only claim one? Maybe we should cross over and grab the little one; maybe then Father wouldn't be too hard on us."

Abel raised an eyebrow. "You know the rules just as well as I do, and I'm not going to go back to the pits to be fed for your sake. Now come, let's go push this soul into Hell where it belongs and head to Father's."

---

Lucifer's house was covered in black marble with a straight-line connection to Earth. The front door led into Hell and the back door faced Earth but was unseen by the human eye. It was a thing of perfection and magnificence. No one, including Bryce and Abel, had ever seen all of the house, not even Legionaries.

"Bryce, Abel, it is good to see you both," Lucifer said to the twins. "Seems like a century since I last laid eyes on you," he said, pleased with himself. "Please, come in and tell me how things are going in the southern section. Don't be shy, boys, what's mine is yours, and there are no secrets between us. I would hope that by now you would feel comfortable in my presence . . . that it would come to you just as naturally as collecting souls."

Lucifer was dressed in black slacks, a white button-down shirt that he always buttoned all the way to the top, and his black slippers. He was breathtakingly beautiful to look at. He could take on several appearances, but when he saw Abel and Bryce, he always appeared to be a man in his later years, with a full set of white, pearly teeth, salt-and-pepper hair, and fair skin.

The room that they were in was divided by a table that stretched the entire length of the room. A vast chandelier hung overhead. The art on the wall depicted souls in one form of agony or another, some frozen in the state of begging for forgiveness. They were the damned and tormented.

"Ah, yes, Bryce, I see that you have an eye for talent."

Bryce was staring at one of the depictions on the wall—two people clutching one another in desperation as they tried to shield themselves from the constant wind of flames that threatened to engulf them.

"They look so elegant, don't they?" Lucifer said pleasantly. "They were among my first catch, which helped me build the empire that we have now.

Abel broke the silence. "Father, I know that we should be honored that we're with you this fine night, but there seems to be an issue of importance we must discuss."

At the head of the table, Lucifer stared impatiently at Abel and then gestured for the twins to take their places to the right and left of him. "Don't worry, we will discuss the fallen in a moment. I don't want to keep the chef waiting, as she's been preparing all day."

As soon as they were seated, the door behind them opened and a line of bare-breasted servants carrying various dishes walked in, placing the food upon the table and then lifting the lid off each dish, exposing what the chef had been working so feverishly over.

"Simply extravagant," Lucifer said and clapped his hands in respectful appreciation. "Bravo, I do say, bravo. Chef has really outdone herself this time." He gestured to the server closest to him. "Please inform the chef that I would like to personally thank her. Thank you, that will be all for now." The servers left the room. "Well, boys, dig in. I'm simply famished."

Lucifer began filling his plate with large helpings from the various dishes of greasy fattened meat. Once his plate was full, he leaned down over it, the steam rising up, and breathed deeply. "I tell you what, boys. If I close my eyes and focus long enough, this could almost seem real, couldn't it?"

A moment later, the chef walked in and fell to the floor beside Lucifer's chair, kissing Lucifer's feet and praising him for allowing her to prepare the meal.

"Rise, my child, rise please," Lucifer said. "You are simply too much." When the woman stood up, there were tears running down her face. "Please tell me what you prepared. It looks simply scrumptious."

"Well, my king, I used a couple of old recipes that I remembered you enjoyed. Liar's tongue, cancerous intestines, and wandering eyes. The tongue is from a woman who cheated her way through life and left so many ruined along the way. The intestines are from an oncologist who was sued more than once for malpractice, treating patients like guinea pigs while he experimented on them. And last is the wandering eyes of a priest who did more than take confessions from his congregation."

"Astounding, absolutely astounding," Lucifer exclaimed. "You outdo yourself every time. Such a talent in the kitchen, just as you were in your past life. Except this time, I hope you don't intend to poison me as you did your late husband and child." The chef, unsure of what to say, simply nodded and left the room.

"Let's not spoil the mood," Lucifer said, returning his attention to the table. "Please, let's just eat and converse about what Bryce witnessed not too long ago, shall we?" His tone changed as he gave Bryce an icy stare.

With that, the fork that was on its way to Bryce's mouth stopped. He couldn't look at Lucifer, knowing if he met his eyes, his soul would be set aflame. Finally, Lucifer stopped staring at Bryce in disgust and began to eat. Silence filled the room as the scrapes of silverware finding plates replaced it.

"I hope you know that the reason I put you both in charge of the southern section was due to my belief that you were up to the challenge," Lucifer said. "But I've been wrong before, now, haven't I?"

"No, sir," Bryce answered.

Abel, quick on the recovery, added, "It's just that we haven't found our bearings yet, but we seem to be getting the hang of it, Father."

Silently, Bryce breathed a sigh of relief, knowing that calling Lucifer anything but Father was a sure way to be cast into the eternal depths and to never be thought of again.

"Hmm, yes, this is true," Lucifer replied. "And it is a large area, but I would surely think that with two of my finest on the job that this would be so easy to overcome. However, let's just forget all about it. What do you say, boys?"

Abel knew something was up, and that this matter wouldn't be put to bed this easily. "Father, I know we can get the job done. We've done it up to this point, but I do understand why you are angry with us. The fallen angel—it was our mistake for not telling you. It won't happen again, I promise you."

Lucifer reached out like a bolt of lightning and struck Bryce, throwing him from his chair. Suddenly standing over him, Lucifer put his foot on his neck. "Usually, son, you're so talkative, as if you're hemorrhaging words, and now you just sit here at my table while your brother tries to cover for your mistake. What do you have to say for yourself? Tell me, what do you believe makes you so different from the others who are just begging for me to give them a chance to be free of the flames even just for a short while?"

Struggling to get out from under Lucifer's foot, Bryce knew he must placate him. "B-because—I . . . I worship you, Father."

Lucifer stood back and reached down, pulling Bryce to his feet, and embraced him. "You see, that's all I was looking for. Now, please, let's just sit and enjoy the rest of this dinner, and you can tell me about everything that happened and how you're going to make it all better for me."

They all sat down again. Bryce was unable to look Abel or Father in the eye. Abel once again took the lead. "Approximately three weeks ago, we split up to cover more territory, since the day was to be a busy one, according to the morning report. When we met back up, Bryce said that while he was out patrolling, the sky seemed to open up, and it looked as if there was a ray of sunshine that broke the clouds, just long enough for something to fall out of the Heavens. We weren't sure what it was. Then we remembered the stories about the last fallen. We put two and two together and, well, there you have it."

"That was all?" Lucifer asked, staring first at Abel and then holding the stare a bit longer at Bryce.

Bryce composed himself. "No, there is more. When it happened—the falling—the rain completely stopped, and there seemed to be a loud shot, as if a cannon was going off. But at the same time, it was as if the whole world stood still. And an unfamiliar pain seemed to come over me. Then the rain continued and the light that had once broken the Heavens disappeared."

"Good to know all the facts," Lucifer said coolly. "Would you like to know what this means—what you just told me?"

Abel and Bryce sat motionless, at complete attention, waiting with anticipation.

"It means that an angel failed," Lucifer continued, "and then decided it was best that he or she fall. Since it couldn't save the mortal life it was sent to protect, the fallen had the option, and took it, to fall and reside on Earth in order to stay with the mortal's partner. It thought it owed the human."

He threw his half-eaten portion of food off the table, his plate shattering to pieces as it found the wall. One of the women servants from earlier appeared and began picking up the mess. Lucifer then hissed at her.

"Do not ever come to a room unless I ask for you."

He snapped his fingers, causing the woman to burst into flames. She began screaming for mercy, as Master ignored her, till at last he snapped his fingers once more, causing her to disappear to a place where neither Bryce nor Abel could see any longer.

"It repugnant to think of something or someone giving up their life to help someone they supposedly loved. Even the word 'love' is pathetic. Used to describe an emotion of weakness and short-sightedness. Do you boys honestly believe that I would give my kingdom up for you or, for that matter, offer myself to the fires of hell and be fed upon the multitudes of the damned? Just so that you both could continue to live out your pitiful existence in my place? As a prince, a king, or a new God!"

"No, Father," both replied in unison.

"Not only would I never do such a thing for either of you, but I would do anything I felt as needed to assure that I remain as the god I am."

Bryce and Abel broke eye contact with Father to look at each other, shocked. Not at what Father had told them of ever being important, but that a fallen had actually happened on their watch and, even more, it happened in their region. Bryce now understood why he had received such punishment for not reporting what he had seen at once.

The fact that it hadn't taken place in such a long time was

no excuse. Every leader knew that to capture a fallen was more important to Father than gathering the damned ever would be. For if a leader was able to complete such a task, then they would immediately become godlike in the eyes of other leaders. Father would not only look upon the individual with favor. But he may very well learn the definition of the word "love."

## CHAPTER 6

Jonathan and Riley arrived at the crowded park. Children were playing games like hide-and-go-seek without a care in the world.

"Magnificent to watch them at this age," Jonathan said. "So free and unharmed by the world's values and judgments. If I could just freeze this moment and stay here like this, I really think this would be perfect." He turned and looked at Riley. "I'm glad you suggested the park, Riley. This is always a nice place to come and just relax and be with people."

Riley, not really paying much attention to his surroundings, was focusing on this giant of a man. How did he know his wife? Why had Allison never told him about this guy?

"Yeah, they're real cute," Riley said numbly. "Hey, why don't we grab a seat and you can tell me what brought you to me? Not to rush you, or anything; it's just that I have some other matters to tend to today."

Jonathan just looked at the kids and smiled. "Splendid, I tell you, absolutely one of the most precious things you may ever see. People are always wanting to hustle to this place or that, not even aware that some of the best things that you may ever see are literally right in front of you."

Having no interest in talking about the kids at the park, Riley chose a picnic table out of the way of the others. He was still taken aback by Jonathan's size. He was easily close to three hundred pounds, and by the look of him, Riley figured he must spend most of his time at the gym toning each muscle to perfection. Riley enjoyed working out, but not to that degree. Jonathan reminded him of a huge defensive lineman for a pro team, yet he didn't seem as if he would hurt so much as a fly. He was simply a gentle giant.

Jonathan sat down at the picnic table opposite him. Riley could swear he actually heard the metal frame beg for mercy under the man's weight. Finally, Jonathan took his attention from the kids and looked directly at Riley with those stellar blue eyes. The friendly smile disappeared from his face.

"I've made it a point to seek you out," Jonathan said, his tone solemn. "I cared deeply for Allison. I can't begin to express how saddened I am by her passing."

"Hold on a second," Riley interrupted. "I knew Allison for eleven years before we married. Not once did she ever speak of you. For you two to have been so close—how is it that I've never heard of you? We didn't even send you an invitation to our wedding. And I would know, since I helped fill out every one of those invitations. So, cut the crap and tell me what you want." Riley was trying hard to control the pain and anger that now consumed him.

Jonathan paused for a moment as he saw pain flash across Riley's eyes, as if someone had just hit him. "If you will be patient with me, I can explain this. You may or may not understand, but what I tell you is the absolute truth. I cannot tell a lie."

Riley sat, staring at the big man. "Sorry, but I'm under quite a bit of stress, and then you show up out of the blue, claiming to know my wife!"

"I understand, and no need to apologize, but I didn't just know your wife," Jonathan explained. "I know you too. But please, allow me the time to explain everything. And please listen carefully. From this day forward, your life will be in danger.

Nothing will ever be the same as you once knew it. Plans have been set in motion and things will start to change for you, almost immediately. I have only a short time to catch you up to speed, and then to beg for your forgiveness. I only hope that you will allow me to help you through these trials, but you must trust me."

Riley said nothing, not quite sure about what he had just heard.

Jonathan paused a moment before continuing. "Do you know the Bible verse, Matthew 19:5-6?"

Riley, once again was taken aback, not sure if this guy was preaching at him or was about to tell him a story. He could say no and tell him to leave, but he had promised to hear what Jonathan had to say so remained silent.

Jonathan leaned toward Riley. "The verse says, 'For this reason a man will leave his father and mother and be united to his wife and the two will become one flesh so they are no longer two, but one. Therefore, what God has joined together, let no man separate.' I know you don't understand what all this means and why I'm throwing scripture at you when all you want to do is get as far away from it as you can. So, I'll tell you what this means: When a man and woman are united, they become one. However, what you probably don't understand, nor can you begin to fathom, is that guardian angels cover all of God's people—the believers and nonbelievers alike—and we help them on a daily basis, although we're behind the scenes, unseen by mortal eyes."

All Riley could do was stare at him, not sure what he was hearing.

"I was Allison's guardian," Jonathan continued. "And her death is my fault. I was distracted by a demon and was fighting it while another one set into motion something terrible—the car accident—that would change your life forever. I failed at my duty to protect Allison. I failed her and I failed you."

"What the hell are you saying?" Riley spat, unable to stay quiet any longer.

Jonathan reached out and touched Riley's arm with a powerful tenderness no mortal possessed. All at once, a sense of pure peace flowed over Riley. He looked deep into Jonathan's blue eyes. He felt, more than heard, the words: *I have no intention of harming you; I simply am here to beg for your forgiveness and to offer my help, if you will allow me.* Riley, without hesitation, simply nodded. He felt the truth of Jonathan's words.

Jonathan released his grasp of Riley's arm. "Your memory of the accident is not clear to you. Part of it has been erased, as it would be too painful, too difficult for you to comprehend, or to even live with. I'm sorry. I failed Allison. I failed at my duty of protecting her. Although we are not able to prevent everything that happens, I should have fought harder to overcome that demon who caused me to look away from Allison. For that, my friend, I am truly sorry." Jonathan paused for a moment, to steady himself. "Following the accident, I was given a choice: I could accompany Allison to the most beautiful and perfect place—one you have heard stories of, so that we could finally meet after all these years. Or, I could fall to Earth and stay with you.

Riley once again became aware of the sounds around him—other people in the park, children laughing, the stiff breeze in the trees promising colder weather was on its way. He noticed the blueness of the sky. He turned and looked back at Jonathan. "This is so hard to understand, or even wrap my head around. I really don't know what to say, or where to go from here. I just feel lost. I want to curse you for not protecting her. Just the fact that you're really an angel; not just any angel, but mine. I'm at a loss right now. I need to go home."

"Wait, my friend. Please don't go just yet. There's more I need to tell you."

Feeling as if he didn't have a choice, Riley stayed, but was sure that he felt the pulse of a migraine coming. He didn't know if he could handle hearing more from Jonathan.

"These events I speak of—the danger you are in—you are going to face endless trials. Riley, you were supposed to die in that crash with Allison. That was the demons' plan, but they also failed at their mission. Lucifer doesn't like botched jobs, and he will send his demons after you, to take your life, to finish his work. As a believer, your soul has been claimed, which makes you a thorn in his side. However, so was Job in the Bible, and Lucifer was able to put him through trials similar to what you will go through. But in this case, he will overstep the rules to take your life."

Riley couldn't believe what he was hearing. "I don't understand. I'm no one, nothing really. I'm not a preacher or evangelist, I don't speak to multitudes. I'm a very simple man with no great attributes to speak of."

"You're wrong there, my friend," Jonathan said with a sense of knowing. "You're a son of God, a believer, and a survivor, and that alone makes Lucifer furious. Where this road will take us, I do not know, but I will be with you every step of the way, if you will allow me."

Riley, still hesitant about everything Jonathan was telling him, couldn't shake the sense that what he was telling him was the absolute truth. He had just one question.

"So . . . where do we go from here?"

# CHAPTER 7

"This emergency meeting has been called so that we can discuss the best way to deal with the fallen that was witnessed three weeks ago," Legionaries said, standing at the front of the room. "We must take swift action, for we know that in times past we have not been able to capitalize on the opportunity. And today, friends, I say that those days have come to an end. With that said, this meeting will now come to order."

All the heads of every region around the world had been gathered, totaling 666. Although each had their own followers, they all answered to one: Some called him Master or Lucifer— the true prince and king of all kings, known on Earth as the Devil. All the demons were now in one auditorium-like room with a podium at the front, where Legionaries stood, and to his left, the Devil himself.

The walls were made of gray rock, the floor was white marble with gray streaks running throughout. The podium was a black, shiny rock shaped like an upside-down cross. The chairs each leader occupied were leather with high backs. A table was placed in front of each chair, making the space look like a large courtroom. Legionaries wore a red robe with a brown rope tied around his waist, as did all the other leaders of the regions. Lucifer was dressed in a white, large silky sheet that covered his body. Upon his head was a crown of thorns, just as Jesus wore the day He was crucified. The appearance Lucifer took on was neither male or female—it was indescribable pure beauty, yet hard to look upon.

"The only reason that—that sniveling, conniving son of a . . ." Bryce mumbled.

"Do you have anything to add before we are in session?" Legionaries asked, staring down at Bryce, wearing a slight grin on his face as he asserted his position of authority over him.

Abel blew out a breath of annoyance, and Lucifer gave Legionaries a look as if to say, *Proceed cautiously; after all, those are my sons.*

"All right," Legionaries continued. "The only reason that we are all here is to discuss how to capture the fallen and hang him on our Master's wall to show that a false God truly cannot protect His own. I will now open the floor for discussion. Oh, and I must remind you all, let's stay on topic, and no interrupting. We are, after all," he said while looking right at Bryce, "friends."

Bryce tensed up in his chair, ready to rush to the front of the room and tear Legionaries's head right off his shoulders. Abel cleared his throat and leaned over to Bryce. "Not today, brother. His time will come."

One of the leaders, Tristan, stood up. "To begin, I have one of the biggest regions and would love to take down a fallen." Tristan's area covered all of the northern hemisphere. He was the most reliable out of all the heads of the regions and earned the reputation as a conniver that would do anything to get ahead. When he first started, he was a follower of someone else who headed a region, but through schemes and lies, which Lucifer enjoyed the drama of, he took charge of the region. Over time he had been given more responsibility when other leaders failed at controlling their region due to uprisings from followers—or if they let Master down.

"It's been over a hundred years since the last one fell, and now she's living out her days working in a hospital, where she is loved by all," he sneered. "That mistake will not be made again. I will take my best hunters and make this fallen a sacrifice for our king of kings. It would truly be my honor to serve you in this way," he said, bowing toward Lucifer. "In fact, I can think of nothing better to give you, your highness." Tristan looked around as if daring others to say otherwise, and then took his seat.

A soft murmur moved around the room. Legionaries hammered the gavel down a few times to quiet the crowd. "This is not a simple situation that can be resolved with lofty speeches, but I for one believe that you can get the job done," he said, nodding toward Tristan with approval.

"Nonsense," Bryce called out from his seat. "Pure and utter nonsense. You, Tristan, simply wish to get in the good graces of my father."

"Is someone speaking?" Legionaries goaded. "If so, that someone knows the rules and needs to follow them. You will stand and properly address the group. The leaders gathered here deserve the respect they have earned since the dawn of our time."

"Simpleton," Bryce mumbled, standing to his feet, ready to pounce on Legionaries for calling him out. "You, lackey, are of no importance, and I will snap you at the knees one day and watch with delight as you are dragged away by the hounds that stalk your dreams at night."

"This is getting us nowhere," Lucifer said. As he stood, Legionaries stepped aside and took his seat. "Please, son, take your seat. Your wounded pride will not go unattended." Lucifer then turned his attention to the gathered throng. "Friends, I have called this meeting, not because I desire another trophy for my walls, but because we have never successfully captured a fallen. This is our time to rise up! Now, I know that I cannot go and take this fallen down myself, since the rules prohibit it, but it doesn't mean that I will sit idly by, either. I like your idea, Tristan. Thank you for doing whatever is necessary to bring me honor.

Your record is simply outstanding, and I have confidence that you—and your hunters—will get the job done."

Once again the crowd started murmuring. Several of the leaders began to stand, wanting to get in on the challenge that lay before them all, aware of the consequences if they failed at capturing the fallen. Someone from the back of the room began to speak. "Please, Master, I have served you for as long as I can remember. My region is small, and although I do not have hunters as great as Tristan does, I too would like to be considered for this task. I know my reputation is questionable, and that you leaders look at me as worthless. However, I have always been loyal and continue to work to prove to everyone here that I am your equal."

His name was Mikell, and Abel almost admired the demon, not because of his past, but because despite being constantly put down, he always seemed to rise to any challenge. The only reason he had never been moved into one of the larger regions was due to his one mistake, which, in truth, wasn't even his. One of his followers had overstepped and wanted Mikell's title. The only way of getting that title, from any of the leaders, was to give them a beating and force them back into the darkest pits of Hell. The follower had almost done it, but he didn't act alone. While Mikell was sleeping, several of the followers jumped him, beat him, and managed to overthrow the region. There was nonstop mayhem for a period of time, and several of the leaders had tried to take the region back, but the group of followers had formed an alliance and were successful at defending their newly proclaimed territory.

It took Lucifer himself to break the alliance apart and return things back to working order. Mikell was restored as the leader but was still considered an outcast; promotion would never happen for him. The followers were punished. Their power of speech was removed and they were cast into mindless hounds from Hell with one job—to feed on the unfortunate who constantly begged for mercy from the depths of Hell.

"You all know of my past," Mikell said. "I am ashamed, for I let down my Master. But I will take this job, not to get back in your good graces, king of all kings. I do this to prove to those in this room that I will succeed with my duty."

The room grew completely still. Everyone was aware of Mikell's past. Others continued to question his position. The silence was broken by an evil laugh, followed by a sound that only comes from the depths and cries of Hell. Lucifer rose once again and stilled the room. He glared at Mikell.

"You poor, pathetic wretch. I had to clean up your last mistake, something I will not do again. The only reason I left you in charge was to give the others a place to dump the trash they don't want. And you will accept it, all of it. You're a stupid, simple-minded fool. What do you think you could do to a fallen? They're much stronger than the ones that overthrew you. Although the fallen no longer have the powers of guardian angels, you are no match for their physical strength, speed, wit, and cunning intensity to see the job through till the end. Make no mistake, you are no match for them."

Once again, the crowd was hushed. Lucifer's eyes, completely dead and black, looked around the room, scanning for anyone who might dare to say something. If they did, they would be the next to fall victim to his unending wrath. At once Mikell sat down, making sure not to look at his fellow companions, and most importantly, never looking at the beast itself, waiting to be fed. Lucifer sneered at the crowd. "No one else should dare to patronize me. Listen closely. I want this fallen, and I want it now!"

"Father, I have a solution," Bryce spoke up, seeming to be the only one in the room who was unafraid of what Lucifer may or may not do.

Abel turned to him and whispered under his breath, "This is not the time to be messing around. Did you not just hear the sounds of the hounds aching to be let loose?"

Ignoring him, Bryce continued. "I have the solution! I saw everything take place in my region. My region! Not in Tristan's and certainly not in Mikell's." He paused and looked directly at Lucifer. "I will bring the fallen back to you, Father, to give to you as an offering for all your glory." He stopped and stared directly at Tristan. "I can do this. I will do this."

Abel stood up, positioned himself next to his brother. "*We* shall do this. After all, brother, it happened in our region."

"Splendid, absolutely splendid!" Lucifer said, his anger subsiding. "I was hoping you two would step up for this. I'm looking forward to what my sons will achieve. I know you will not disappoint me, but first, I would like to meet this mortal, the one the fallen failed. What is his name, Legionaries?"

"Riley," Legionaries replied.

"I should like to see into the mind of this mortal. I will make him an offer. If he doesn't accept it? Then, sons, it falls to you. That will be all. Everyone may go back to your regions. Sons, Legionaries will let you know if the job is yours."

At once the room started to clear as the followers murmured amongst themselves. They were relieved that things didn't escalate into a feeding. Lucifer and Legionaries stood at the front of the room, watching the crowd disperse.

Tristan positioned himself next to Bryce. "I would say good luck, but then that wouldn't allow me the opportunity of getting my hands on the fallen," Tristan said condescendingly.

"When we need an ass kissing, we will let you know," Bryce fired back. Tristan simply grinned and then disappeared.

Abel looked at his brother. "Sometimes I could strangle you."

"Yes, I know. But then who would keep eternity interesting for you?"

Once the auditorium cleared out, Lucifer remained at the front with Legionaries. A menacing look crossed his face as he glared at Legionaries. His voice lowered to a growl. "Hounds!"

At once, Legionaries screamed, for he knew what was coming. "King—Master—please! I beg of you! I—I didn't mean . . ." The hounds came all at once, and the feeding began.

"You make a mockery of one of my sons," Lucifer sneered, "in front of all the leaders, and you don't expect repercussions?" A gurgling sound was all that could be heard coming from Legionaries as the pack of hounds tore at him, consuming him. "I should banish you to the depths, where worms would consume you daily!" Lucifer screamed. "The hounds will be the last thing that stalks your dreams."

Where skin once covered Legionaries's body, now was just torn meat and broken bone. Blood dripped from the mouths of the pack. "Enough!" Lucifer said. And the hounds vanished. Legionaries's body slowly started to repair itself. Lucifer bent down over his broken, torn body. "I think your tongue gets you in far more trouble than Bryce's ever will. His I find amusing. Yours is a constant annoyance in my ears. Like a puny fly that I swat and swat, and it pesters me still."

Lucifer pried what was left of Legionaries's mouth open and seized the tongue that was starting to rebuild itself. "I will cut this thing out and hang it in my viewing room." With one swift move, the Devil vanished, taking the tongue with him.

Unable to scream, Legionaries let out sobs and gurgling

noises. He clawed at his throat and the inside of his mouth as the tongue started to rebuild. It would take hours for his tongue and skin to grow back, but in Hell, an hour could last an eternity.

# CHAPTER 8

**R**iley and Jonathan sat in Riley's living room listening to the fireplace crackle, each with their own cup of coffee in hand. The sun had begun to set while they were leaving the park, and now the soft breeze that had blown earlier started to pick up the cool air from a northern front. It was official, winter was here to stay.

They were sitting across from each other, Riley in his favorite recliner and Jonathan sitting on the couch. They stared at the flames and sipped their coffee. Drinking coffee seemed to come just as naturally to Jonathan as fighting off demons and flying from cloud to cloud just to enjoy the view. It was hard for Riley to even begin to imagine what Jonathan had told him in the park. There were so many questions he wanted to ask, but he knew that if he started asking them, he may not stop, much less begin to understand it all. However, he was definitely not going to sit here watching the big man drink his coffee like everything was normal.

"Where would you like to start?" Jonathan asked, interrupting all the thoughts rolling around in Riley's head. "You're over there just winding yourself up, so let's talk, and I'll do my best to answer everything."

"Thing is, I don't even know if I want to start firing questions. I mean, I'm not sure about what I want to know."

Jonathan finished his cup and put it on the end table. "As a fallen angel, I will live forever. Although my abilities are limited,

I am still stronger than any human. I have the ability to read others' thoughts, which you may come to dislike."

Great, Riley thought. Now I have to not only watch what I say but what I think as well.

Jonathan smiled at Riley, choosing not to address the thought. "To sum it all up, you could consider me virtually indestructible. However, there's a flip side to all that. I now breathe air just like you, and I bleed. Demons can hurt me, but I can sustain more than any human can."

Riley shook his head. "Why did you save me and not Allison? That's the only question that I'm really wrestling with."

Jonathan looked down at the floor. He seemed to be searching for the right way to put the answer into words that would help Riley understand. Jonathan finally looked up and said, "I didn't choose you, my friend. It wasn't my decision. I loved Allison very much. I was with her throughout her entire life, ever since she was first brought into this world. I was there through every fall, triumph, pain, joy—everything that she went through, I went through with her. She was my world, and I would have done anything to protect her. There are crazed demons that can cross over to inflict damage on anyone they choose. Sometimes it's random. For whatever reason, you and Allison were their victims that day."

Jonathan paused a moment before continuing.

"They have rules in the underworld, just as there are rules here. Man was the first human that God put on this Earth, then he made a woman for companionship and to bring love. Any guardian who watches over a male must leave when the man marries because the bride's guardian will now look over both of them while the man's guardian will be assigned to someone new. So, your guardian handed you off to me. It was my job to watch over you both.

"Don't get me wrong, I loved you from the moment Allison met you. You were shy, but you had a good heart. And I knew you loved her and would do anything for her. That was good enough for me. In fact, it was more than good enough for me; I couldn't have asked for more. So, when the accident happened, I could have gone and helped welcome Allison to Heaven, but your good nature and your gentle heart started to become dark with anger, and I felt compelled to stay and help you. You see, you don't remember it because it's been wiped from your memory, but you saw the demon who caused the accident. You weren't supposed to, but I feel that I should tell you everything so that you understand. Call it an act of rebellion, but I want you to know why your life has changed and will continue to change drastically. It rarely happens that a guardian chooses to fall, so that it can be part of their human's life. The demon wasn't supposed to reveal himself to you. He made a mistake, and now Lucifer will try and correct that problem by sending other demons after you. Without me, you are like a sheep among wolves, but I will do anything to keep you safe, since I failed you and Allison once already."

Riley stood and walked over to the fireplace, then began to stoke the flames. He said nothing as he focused on the fireplace, lost in the thoughts of an actual guardian angel sitting in his living room, opening up to him about the afterlife. Why had this happened to not just him, but to his beloved Allison? Furthermore, why would God allow such a thing to ever happen to begin with? Jonathan could hear the steady stream of thoughts and questions taking shape in Riley's head.

"I will never be able to take back Allison's death, but I can help you find solitude, and I will answer anything that you ask of me," Jonathan finally said.

Riley turned to look at him. "Thank you, Jonathan. I don't want to continue right now, but I have one last question."

"What are we waiting for, and how do we stop them?" Jonathan answered.

Riley didn't say anything; he just turned back to the fireplace.

"It will begin tonight, that I am certain. I imagine the demons have had their meeting and set a plan in place to take you out of this world by any means necessary. I suspect there will be many who will be competing for you. I believe they are already on their way."

"Great," Riley blurted out. "So, the rest of my life I will be chased by demons until they succeed, and let's face facts here— it won't take too long, will it? And I have to depend on you to protect me?"

"They can be hurt. They are nowhere near as powerful as I am. They are just like you when they are on Earth. They bleed and suffer injury as you do, but they will come in groups, I'm certain of that. The last angel who went through this—you've actually met her—the kindly nurse at the hospital who helped you with Allison. You know her as Granny. She is a fallen angel, like me. We've all learned from her experience."

"Wait a minute. Granny was an angel? She seemed so . . . normal."

"Not *was* an angel, she still is an angel. She spends her days at the hospital helping people. She believes she is better able to serve in that capacity. Her human passed on quite some time ago."

Riley was numb by everything he was hearing. It was too much to comprehend. He swallowed hard. "Was she successful in helping her human—or do I not want to know the answer to that?"

"The odds are not in our favor, Riley. I told you I will never lie to you. She did everything that she could, but even we can't see the future. Only God knows what will happen next."

Riley took his seat again, and then stood and started to head for the kitchen. "You want some more coffee?" He grabbed Jonathan's cup before he could respond.

After filling the two cups, Riley leaned back against the kitchen counter. *I'm going to die; it's just a matter of time, and my hourglass has just about run out, it seems.* He grabbed both cups off the counter and headed back into the living room, handing Jonathan his as he sat on the couch. Riley turned to take a seat across from him. Suddenly, Jonathan was standing, looking down at Riley with an air of seriousness.

"Tonight, Lucifer—the Devil—is coming. I can feel it. He's coming to talk to you, but he will not harm you, not tonight. However, I won't be able to be in the room with you."

"Wait. He's coming here?" Riley was astonished to know that he would be entertaining the Devil himself. "How do you know all this? And why aren't you going to be with me?"

"He is simply coming with an offer. He will not hurt you in any way."

"Well, maybe your other angel friend got it all wrong. After all, her human died, so just maybe the one who's coming is coming to end it all right now."

Jonathan placed a calming hand on Riley's shoulder. "Trust me, my friend, that's all that I can ask."

Riley's worry seemed to slip away under Jonathan's hand. He looked squarely into Jonathan's blue eyes. "Okay, I trust you. But I still worry."

"Don't. You have God with you. No harm will come to you tonight. It's just an offering. And it's up to you whether to accept it or not. Whatever you decide, know that the decision will carry heavy consequences."

# CHAPTER 9

Sitting in the guest room of the two-story house, just down the hall from the master bedroom that would have been his and Allison's, Riley wondered about all the things that were going to play out tonight. What had his life become in these short weeks following his wife's death? Everything seemed to be a bad dream that he so desperately wanted to wake up from, and to top it off, an angel was just down the hall, vowing to do everything he could to protect him.

Riley leaned back on the guest bed. Jonathan had a look of sadness when Riley had met his eyes to tell him goodnight. They'd held something inside them: worry. "I will never lie to you," was all he'd said. And with that, he had closed the bedroom door.

Sleep usually came easy, with all the things that Riley did during the day. He was a successful landscaper and ran his own business. That's how he had first met Allison. He was her parents' lawn boy all those years ago, when his business was just getting off the ground, while they were both still in high school. Nowadays, he stayed at home, fielding calls and scheduling appointments for his three crews. Winter was his slow time, but his business still flourished. His crews were hardworking, and he treated them all like family. He liked it best when he could work with them side by side, carrying his share of the workload; but at times it was too much to take appointments, manage scheduling conflicts, and manicure all the grounds. But he still made a point to work with them as much as he could.

His thoughts drifted back to Allison and her smiling face and good-natured personality. She had been absolutely perfect and everything he could want in a woman. His eyelids started to close and his mind went back to that day in the car—rain was coming down hard, and the wipers were working furiously to keep the street visible. He immediately saw Allison, so lovely in her wedding dress, like a glowing light that he shouldn't be allowed to look at. The conversation started to play out as it always did in his dream. He could rehearse the lines and describe every detail; it was that clear to him. The light turned green, and he was well aware of what was about to happen. He felt himself start to jerk and yell, but no sound came out. Allison just continued to smile at him while the headlights of another vehicle came barreling down upon them.

This time, though, no darkness.

Riley pulled his head away from the airbag that deployed and tasted the salty blood in his mouth. All he could hear was a loud hum, as he looked over at his wife. The passenger-side window had been knocked out, and his wife's pretty blonde head was starting to take on the color of red, way too fast. As he struggled to reach for her, the seatbelt held firm, and the locking mechanism would not release. Just as he peered up at her again, panic started to set in; he was trapped and he couldn't reach his wife, who was lying motionless just inches away.

The driver of the vehicle that crashed into them stepped out of his truck and rushed over. Riley couldn't make out the face yet, because the rain was now coming down in sheets. Finally, the driver made it to the passenger side, leaned in over Allison, and breathed deep, like a dog smelling the air. The face was still unrecognizable to Riley. Finally, a voice, an unnerving, eerie voice said, "Wake up, Riley. We have a lot to discuss."

Riley jerked awake, drenched in sweat, just as he had every

night since then. The room was blanketed in darkness with a soft glow coming from the bathroom light down the hall. A figure appeared to be standing—no, sitting, at the end of his bed, but the mattress didn't yield under the weight of the figure. Riley rubbed his eyes with both hands and strained to see in the poorly lit room.

"You aren't dreaming," the voice said. "If you would like, I can turn on a light. However, if you scream, the fallen will not hear you. I know very well that he can hear your thoughts, but this, Riley, this decision I'm about to offer is for you and you alone."

"What are you?" Riley asked into the dark. "What do you want?"

"Precisely what you hope I'm not. You've known about me your entire life and know of me as the opposite of good. I have many names—adversary, enemy, serpent, great dragon, Satan, Lucifer; but the one I'm most fond of is Carrier of the Light. To keep things simple for our little meeting, you can simply think of me as the Devil."

Riley felt the goose bumps rise all over his body. The room itself suddenly took on a strange feeling, as if he were falling and had yet to land—just like those dreams where you wake up right before you hit the ground. Riley struggled against what was taking place, right here in his own home. "What do you want with me?"

"Right to the point. I like that. I wish my sons acted that way. But boys will be boys now, won't they? Ah, my apologies. I just remembered your wife passed not long ago, so you don't know about children just yet. Yes, that's too bad," the Devil mused.

Riley jumped up as if to lunge at the Devil.

"I wouldn't do that if I were you. I'm not here to harm you, but if you push me, I will snap you at the neck like a twig—lines crossed be damned. It's been years since I've shown myself, and I mean truly shown myself, to anyone, and if you believe you have what it takes to try me, then this will end abruptly."

Riley stopped cold in his tracks. "Go back to Hell where you belong."

"Are you familiar with the Bible, Riley? The reason I ask is because if you were, you would know that I don't abide in Hell. I walk this planet just as freely as you do. The difference is, one day you will rot in the ground, as your wife is doing now, and I will, supposedly, be cast for eternity back to where I have taken so many. But that's not what I came here to discuss, you ignorant, pathetic little cockroach. You see, just as you've been told, I come with an offering, and it's really simple. I'm here to give you your life back, the way it was not too long ago. I have the power to make all of this feel like nothing more than a long, bad dream, and when you awake you will be in your vehicle, leaving the wedding with your beautiful bride, Allison, right by your side."

"Don't you dare say her name, you lying ass."

"I do lie. Hell, Riley, I'm the king of kings when it comes to manipulation, but for this I'm telling you the truth. I only want one thing in return, and then you can have everything back, and you and your bride can live happily ever after."

Riley was stilled by what just hit his ears. He could have his wife back, hold her, and never let go. Grow old with each other, raise a family—it was everything he wanted and it could be right at his fingertips. Just to hear her quick-witted remarks again, and the laughter that followed them, made tears sting his eyes. It was too good to be true. "What do you want?" he asked.

The Devil smiled to himself in the dark room. "Not what do I want, but whom. You see, you have a strange guest staying in the room down the hall, and as of now he belongs to no one. He fell from Heaven, as I did long ago. So, this is how it works: you say yes, you get your wife back, and I take that oversized buffoon down the hall back with me, and you go on happy as can be, but . . ." he paused so Riley could take it all in. "You say no, and I will send my demons after you, group by group, and they will hunt the two of you down and bring you to me. Either way, it's a win-win for me, but I'm feeling generous and giving you a choice here. In the end, all I want is the fallen. Don't be a fool, Riley. He failed your wife, so face it: he can't protect you forever."

Riley sunk back into the bed. All he wanted was his life back, and he could have it back, right now. But to hand over an angel, one of God's angels, could he live with himself? Are there some sins you just can't be forgiven for? Would he be sent to Hell for sacrificing an angel?

Lucifer stood there, hearing the thoughts playing out in Riley's head, smiling a little wider with each passing second as Riley tortured himself. He whispered into Riley's thoughts, *This fallen ended your wife's life. He failed Allison and you. Did he really choose to fall from Heaven, or was he cast out and simply seeking your forgiveness?*

Riley's head started to ache from all the thoughts rushing around. Why had Jonathan put him in this kind of predicament? Why didn't he just do his job? It was Jonathan's fault he was going through all this. Pressure seemed to come from everywhere, and these thoughts . . . where were they coming from? Why was he even considering such blasphemy against God, to trade one life for another?

*To not consider this is an outrage! Your wife—all she ever did was love you and want the best for you, and it was all snuffed out because your so-called God let this happen. Where was He if the angel couldn't get the job done? Isn't He the one that can see everything before it happens? Ask yourself where, Riley, where was He? You're a good man, you do well by anyone you've ever come across, and your wife, she wanted only good for others. Why would God let this happen if He's all powerful?*

Tears that once stung Riley's eyes now flowed in a steady stream down his face. The thought of never being able to hold Allison again cut at his heart as strongly as the day he watched her casket being lowered into the ground. All the what-ifs could have been gone in the blink of an eye. Then, as clear as if she were standing there next to him, almost as if an apparition, she walked over to him, took both his hands in hers, and said, "I love you still, but this decision is not yours to make. I will see you again, but not right now, my love."

Riley's eyes opened, and in the dark room he heard the movement of the Devil behind him. Moonlight poured in from the window, and as he turned, he could see for the first time, the Devil's face—the black and horrific eyes peered into Riley's now, the face so evil, something that only Hell itself could produce.

"I know your answer, Riley. Nothing more needs to be said. Just remember when you're gasping for your last breath, and you're thinking about what could have been, that there is no turning back. I will make it a point to end you, and it will not be quick."

Riley, tears still streaming down his face, looked right back into the horror which was no more than a foot from him, and with no fear at all, he spoke. "I am washed in the blood of the lamb, and in the name of Christ I demand you to leave this place."

An ear-piercing scream escaped from the Devil's face, as if everything inside him was consumed by fire. And in an instant, Riley was left standing in an empty room, staring at the place where the beast once stood, with only the sound of his own heavy breathing to break the silence.

# CHAPTER 10

E xiting his room, Riley couldn't believe that he had actually just met the devil and, furthermore, that he had just turned down an opportunity to have his wife back. He was of the understanding that the devil wanted him, according to what Jonathan had told him.

But now he knew that it wasn't he whom the Devil wanted—it was his guardian, Jonathan. Riley felt like he had been lied to on both sides. The Devil he expected it from, but he wanted to believe everything Jonathan was telling him was mostly true. Only to learn now that he had more questions for the new addition to his life.

The door to Jonathan's room was wide open. As Riley looked inside, he discovered that the room was empty. It was late now, but sleep was not going to come tonight, so Riley headed downstairs to the kitchen. Once on the landing, he saw Jonathan sitting in the living room, sipping a fresh cup of coffee. Some sort of steam appeared to rise from him, as if he'd just walked out of a sauna.

"Jonathan, what's going on? Are you okay?"

The giant figure just sat there in the recliner, seemingly unaware that Riley was in the room. The steam continued to rise off him.

"Listen, I think we should talk," Riley said, his voice growing louder with anger. "I want to know about these rules and why you came to me offering protection when you're the one the Devil is after. My life has turned upside down, and I feel completely and utterly lost, so either start talking or get the hell out!"

Jonathan turned and looked at Riley. The last of the steam seemed to finally lift off of him. He sat quietly, looking up at Riley. He sipped his coffee, not looking at anything else in the room except for Riley. Finally, Jonathan spoke.

"Remember what I told you before you went to your room?"

"Yes, you said you would never lie to me."

"That's right, I never will. It's not in my power to tell you a lie. Tell me what took place tonight, up there in your room."

"What? Why? I thought you could read my thoughts."

Jonathan looked at Riley, and his eyes requested to oblige him.

"He told me that if I hand you over, I can have my life back, that I can have Allison back, that everything would go back to normal. All I had to say was yes, but that you would be handed over to him."

Jonathan stood and walked over to Riley, placing a large hand on his shoulder.

"For that, I will forever be grateful to you. The Devil's gift is lies. He can bend anything to make it look good, but he wasn't lying. I would have to go with him without a fight. The whole reason the devil wants me is to one, prove to the demons who serve him that we are not as powerful as we are made up to be—it's basically a win for what I guess you would call his side—And two, he believes that if he has me, he can possess my abilities and make himself stronger. However, that isn't possible, but he is a fool and believes what he wants to believe."

"Well then, why does he want me?" Riley asked.

"You should have died with Allison. I prevented that, and in doing so, you became a target for him. With you out of the picture, I think he believes I will just give in and go with him. I can also tell you that he doesn't have the power to bring people back from the dead. You know of the only one who can do that. Your life would have been snuffed out as soon as you handed me over. Lucifer himself would have stolen your soul.

"You see, there are so many rules—I wouldn't even know where to start, but I am yours, more or less. I will do whatever is asked of me, to the letter, but we don't have the time for me to explain everything to you right now. There are things you simply aren't meant to know. Things that, as a human, you cannot comprehend. However, we must leave here. It isn't safe for you here."

"What do you mean we have to leave here?"

Jonathan placed both hands on Riley's shoulders, gripping them tightly. "You must trust me. This place is not safe for you. I cannot protect you here. We are too vulnerable in this house."

Unsure what to think, Riley reluctantly went back up to his room to pack a bag, although he didn't know what he was packing for. Where were they going? How long would they be gone? Riley struggled to let this all sink in. Sure, he had told Alex, his realtor, that he wanted to sell this place, but to think he had to leave like this was too hard. This was going to be his and Allison's, the house where they would raise a family, and now he had to leave in the dark of night and would quite possibly never see it again. It made his heart ache.

No, he had to shake those feelings away. He needed to keep moving. This was not the time to be thinking about the past, when time was of the essence.

Jonathan stood next to the window that looked down on the street in front of the house. He whispered softly to himself, "Holy, Holy, Holy is the Lord God, the Almighty, who was, who is, and is to come." He repeated the chant over and over as he waited for Riley.

Riley finished stuffing his bag and took one more look around the room. Jonathan left the window, picked up Riley's bag, and quoted Matthew 18:20, "Where two or three are gathered in my name, there am I with them."

They made their way downstairs and headed for the garage. Jonathan tossed Riley's bag in the back of the truck as Riley got behind the wheel. "Where are we going?" Riley asked.

"We need to go to your lake house. It's remote; we'll be safer there," Jonathan replied. "I know you and Allison used to love spending time there. You see, demons can take on a human form when they crawl out of Hell—that's how they disguise themselves—but the human has to be a nonbeliever with a weak will. The less populated the place, the fewer people who can fall prey to being overtaken by demons. Plus, it will take the demons longer to reach us. Once they've overtaken a human body, they have only the powers of that body."

"That's as good a place as any, I suppose," Riley said as he put the key in the ignition. He looked across at Jonathan. "If we're heading to the lake house, we'll need to get some groceries and supplies. I haven't been up there in a year."

Riley had built the lake house because he loved being away from everything. He and Allison looked forward to the serenity that could always be found there. But for now it would serve not as a peaceful place but as a hideout that could mark his fate if his new friend could not protect him. Just thinking about how crazy everything had become sent chills down his spine.

"Not a problem," said Jonathan. "We won't run into too much trouble until we actually get settled, then things will change. But we need to get to the lake house and secure it as best, and as quickly, as we can. We'll need to set traps all around the perimeter, make it difficult for them to get in." He paused for a moment. "Also, do you have any firearms?"

Riley looked at Jonathan. They were going to need guns? Jonathan couldn't just use his powers? He decided not to ask, not right now.

"Be right back."

Riley got out of the truck and hurried back into the house. He emerged a few minutes later, carrying a large duffel bag containing three rifles, two handguns, and several boxes of shells. Riley didn't like guns but had inherited them from his father and decided to hold onto them. He never imagined he'd ever need them. He got back in the truck, throwing the duffle in the backseat. The truck started right up, and they pulled out of the garage and onto the road that led past the park where they'd talked earlier in the day. It all seemed so long ago.

Completely uncertain of what awaited him, all Riley could do was hope this wasn't the end for him. Maybe he was losing his mind. As the heater blew the last of the cold air out and the warmth started to come, Riley wondered what powers angels really possessed, or in Jonathan's case, fallen angels. He glanced into the rearview mirror, thinking this might be the last time he saw the place that he'd come to feel was only a burden. His normal life seemed a thousand miles away.

# CHAPTER 11

"*Legionaries!*" Lucifer yelled, even though his lackey was standing nearby. "The time has come for my boys to take the honor that I have ordained upon them to prove their worth to me and all the leaders of the regions. It is imperative that they show themselves as more than just my sons, but as the leaders that I have raised them to be. I want that freak, and his human, suffering at my fingertips. The nerve to decline my offer! I could have very easily crushed him like a beetle. What ties this human and his loyalty to this fallen, and so quickly?"

Lucifer, dressed in a full dark suit, with his signature style of buttons that ran all the way up to his chin, was pacing back and forth down his long hall. The walls were covered with the same kind of paintings that hung in the dining room. Multitudes hung on every wall in the place, portraying humans and their greatest sins. They were captured here, forever, to amuse Lucifer. Hundreds of halls like this connected the house directly to Hell. There were only two ways in—and out: The back door opened up to Earth, where only Lucifer could walk among the mortals as if he were one. The front door led to Hell, where the eternal screams of terror were just on the other side. This house was Lucifer's alone. Others were invited but never stayed, not even the twins.

"Did you not hear me, Legionaries? Pay attention, or you too shall become nothing more than a painting upon my wall."

"Yes, Master. I—I . . ."

"Never mind," Lucifer said sharply. "We've had fallen before—humans are so quick to give them up just so they can have a little taste of what life used to be like. And then I snatch it back," he said, smirking. "All of them simply give in to their emotions, and I receive what is rightfully mine, even if it is just for a little time. I have perfected the art of whispering into their thoughts. After all, I invented it. They all follow the path when it comes to what could have been. So, why does this one not allow me to play on his emotions?"

Lucifer stopped and turned to look right at Legionaries, who had a confused look on his face as if asking for someone to help him try and make sense of this puzzle. Knowing when to offer his opinion—and when not to—Legionaries cleared his throat. "Master, it seems to me—and this is just me guessing, or offering what I have gathered on the matter, and not really myself understanding all that is taking place—"

"Oh, for the sake of Hell, speak!"

"The human is being guided by more than just impulse. Not just what the angel—I mean fallen—has told him, but I sense that, in some way or another, his wife is still guiding him. Perhaps she comes and visits his thoughts and brings peace to his mind."

Lucifer stood there, glaring at Legionaries. His first thought was to beat him, but on second thought, he remembered that this is exactly why he kept Legionaries around. Lucifer knew that Legionaries had been around since biblical times. He could read humans and sense things about them. He was an asset in that way to Lucifer.

Legionaries had been Lucifer's lackey for thousands of years. He'd never been given a territory to look after. He had no one that served underneath him. He was basically the custodian of Hell, running about and keeping things in order. Lucifer regularly tortured him, sometimes simply for his own amusement, other times to keep him in his place. Lucifer knew Legionaries well and had to be kept down so as to never be a challenge to him.

Turning his back to Legionaries, Lucifer considered that this very well could be what was happening. Did the human really have the all-trusting faith in God like that of a child?

"Call the boys. I want this over with, and soon," Lucifer hissed. "That damn human! I'm ready to set the world ablaze if that's what it takes to get that fallen."

Legionaries quietly dismissed himself.

Lucifer walked down the long hallway, not stopping to admire the art that hung on the walls as he usually did. He had been cheated by a fallen, outwitted by a fool, and a human who denied him his claim. "Damn!" he yelled. The walls rattled as he turned a corner and entered the chamber where his oversized throne overlooked the large entry into Hell. "I must be losing my touch," he snarled.

The room was strictly for observing his hounds as they dismantled new souls. He loved the smell of fear in the air, longed for it, so thick that it rested heavy in his lungs, burning like pure desire. The only furniture in the room was his throne. He could push a button to open up a wall to reveal a view of Hell itself. There was nothing better—with the exception of seeing his hounds tear something apart, then leaning back in his chair, letting his worries drift away, watching the flames dance, with people begging for mercy. His was like a large fireplace with flames that would not end.

Sitting back, grinning to himself, and thinking of his magical kingdom, his hounds, and how their presence alone satisfied him, he snapped his fingers. Immediately, one of the hounds came to him. Lucifer stretched out his hand, and the hound came to his side and let him pet it. The red, glowing eyes locked on Lucifer's face.

Suddenly, Lucifer heard voices coming from the hallway, distant but coming closer. The hound showed no emotion. It just sat there staring, never breaking eye contact. Lucifer snapped his fingers again, and this time several hounds came to his side. Legionaries and the twins came into the room. Legionaries trembled when he took notice of the hounds.

"Calm yourselves," Lucifer said to the four other hounds who began to growl at Legionaries. Each hound was close to two hundred pounds of pure muscle, capped off with pure hatred.

Bryce smirked, knowing how fearful Legionaries was of the hounds. After all, they had feasted on him quite often. He squatted down. "Come here, boys." Not one of them so much as made a move toward Bryce. He continued to coax them, but, of course, nothing. They knew who their master was.

"Father," Abel said. "When would you like us to go?"

Bryce was still cooing to the hounds, not paying any attention to the matter at hand, while Lucifer, himself occupied, simply stared at the hound he held with both hands. "Immediately. I want this all taken care of—the sooner the better. This task will define how you will be viewed by the other leaders of the regions and what kind of support they will show to you from here on out." Lucifer made a sound to one of the hounds, directing it to go to Bryce, but never broke eye contact with the one he was still holding. The hound that he directed went and sat before Bryce.

Imitating Father, Bryce pulled the hound's face directly into his, letting it know that he was not afraid of it and that it should be the one to fear him for the position that he was in. The hound, however, only returned the stare, its red, predatorial eyes seeming to look directly through Bryce. "Father," Bryce said, his face still only inches away from the hound. "How many did you let tear into him this time?"

"Do not take this assignment lightly," Lucifer replied. "You have never taken on a fallen. Their strength, speed, and agility will be more than one of you can handle. With two of you, there is a chance that you'll have a shot in bringing him down, but remember, they can read thoughts. It will be one hell of a ride for you two, but I'm counting on you getting the job done. The one thing you and Abel have that the fallen does not, is your tyranny whips. Bryce, don't be a fool and think you can take him on by yourself."

Bryce paid little attention and seemed more interested in trying to sic the hound on Legionaries.

"For if you do"—There was a snapping noise which made Bryce turn around to see Lucifer holding the detached head of the hound in his hands, while the body lay at his feet, twitching— "the fallen will snap you like a twig. You take this lightly and come back to me without the fallen, you will spend eternity with the hounds chewing on your insides like sticks of gum." He dropped the head of the hound. "Eat!" he directed the other hounds, and they at once pounced on the body of the dead hound and began feeding.

Bryce replied nervously, "Father, we shall not fail you."

"See that you don't. I will not be made a fool before the leaders. I expect you two not to fail me, for I will show no mercy when disciplining." Lucifer sank back into his chair and crossed one leg over the other, his eyes turning a faint red as the shadow of the chair enveloped his figure. "Like sheep among wolves, my sons, go and do your job."

The hounds now stood motionless around Lucifer's chair, fresh blood dripping from their snouts, as they stared at Bryce and Abel. The twins nodded in unison and backed away swiftly, never turning their backs to Lucifer, or the hounds, as they left the room.

"Legionaries," came the voice from the chair. "Please, by all means, stay awhile."

As they reached the door, Abel took one last look and saw Father slither out of the chair toward Legionaries, and with that, the door closed and a chill ran down his spine.

# CHAPTER 12

The lake house was outside Potogi, a little town about four hours away from Taupe City. The town had about 3,300 residents, most of them retirees, some of whom had grown up in the area. It was a friendly little town where people still waved at strangers passing by on the highway and most kept their doors unlocked at night. Riley only hoped that whatever evil was coming for him wouldn't spill out onto the small town.

As he maneuvered down the one-lane gravel road leading up to the clearing where the lake house stood, he couldn't help but notice how strange Jonathan seemed to be acting. He was like a kid taking in the view for the first time. He couldn't sit still, constantly looking this way and that, like he could see something Riley couldn't.

"You okay over there?" Riley asked.

Jonathan gave no reply; he just kept his eyes peeled, looking at everything. The long drive had been filled with silence despite all the questions Riley had.

Riley knew that if he began asking questions, his head would soon swim with every answer that came, half of which wouldn't even make sense to him. It was the same as his life had now become. He did wonder how long his life would remain this way. Jonathan had told him that it would change drastically from here on. But did that mean forever, or would there ever be a time of normalcy again where he didn't live in fear that it could be the day he was killed?

The view of the lake house was breathtaking. It was off the main road with just a small road leading up to the driveway. The place was surrounded by thick, lush evergreens that left a heavy smell of pine in the air. The lake house held great memories for Riley, especially in the summer when the lake was busy and filled with excitement. In the winter time it was peaceful, with most home owners leaving for the season, except for some of the locals that maintained the grocery store and the retirees that stayed year-round.

The house itself was a one-story with a basement and a wraparound porch. There was a trail which led down to the dock and the boat house, all of which was maintained by Luis, the groundskeeper. Riley had called ahead to let him know that he would be staying a while and that his services would not be needed. Riley would call him when he was leaving. Riley lived on the lake right across from Luis, and over the years they had become good friends.

Luis was a boxer in his spare time. He was short and stocky and was somewhat of a legend in the area for his "will fight anyone at any time" attitude. His greatest bout was when he fought in a tournament in Taupe City and took second place. At the time, he was an average boxer and hadn't taken the sport too seriously, but since then he had been training a lot more, actually had his own gym, and was quickly coming up in the ranks.

As they pulled up to the house, Luis was out front finishing up mowing the yard. Jonathan gave a quick side-glance at Riley. Then they both got out of the truck. Riley felt his muscles finally release from the long drive. It had been a tense twenty-four hours with meeting an angel and encountering the Devil.

"How the heck have you been?" Luis asked Riley, as he walked up and gave him a hug. It was one of the things Riley liked most about Luis; he was soft-spoken around most people, but once you got to know him you had made a friend for life.

"The grounds and house look great," Riley said as he took it all in.

"Well, I'm so glad that you approve," Luis said jokingly. "Figured I would show up to give the yard a once-over. Who's the giant?" he asked, looking Jonathan up and down.

"Oh, I'm sorry, where are my manners? Luis, I would like you to meet Jonathan. He's a, uh, friend . . . well, really an employee of mine. He needed to get out of the city for a bit. Traffic and the quick pace of life in the city was starting to make him a bit stir-crazy." Riley hoped the lie wasn't too transparent. He was relieved that Luis didn't seem to question it.

"Oh, I completely understand that," Luis said and offered Jonathan his hand.

"Nice to meet you, Luis," Jonathan replied as his hand enclosed Luis's and the pleasantries were exchanged.

"That's quite a grip you have there. You ever do any boxing?" Luis asked.

Jonathan gave a quick look toward Riley. "No, I was just blessed with big bones, I guess."

"Well, I'm just glad that I don't ever have to worry about exchanging blows with you; I might be biting off more than I can chew," Luis said with a smile. Jonathan smiled in return, looked at the place once more, and then went back to the truck to start unloading the bags.

"Well, the lake looks peaceful," Riley said. "I sure do wish I could come up here a lot more."

"Yeah, brother; y'all were missed this summer . . ." And then

Luis stopped, looking as if he had put a foot in his mouth. "I mean . . . I'm so sorry about Allison, Riley; it pains me that I couldn't be there for you."

"Completely understandable, thank you. It's . . . well, it's getting a little easier," Riley replied, lying.

When the accident happened, Luis had been in Vegas for his first big opportunity in boxing. He was on the undercard of the event but had gained some notice for demolishing the other boxer in the first round.

"I've got to head to my last job and then head over to the gym," Luis said, "but how about we get together soon and cook out on the grill?"

"Sounds like a perfect way to welcome me back," Riley said.

"I'm going to be heading out of town for a month. Heading to train with a legendary coach in Las Vegas. He wants to add me to his list of fighters. Convinced me that in a year I could be headlining main cards." He chuckled. "Honestly, I really think he's bringing me in as a punching bag for one of his upcoming talents that everyone is talking about. What he doesn't know is that I've sparred with this kid already, and he didn't last two rounds!"

Riley couldn't help but smile at Luis. He never gave himself credit for how good he really was. As for any fame that may come his way, he had no doubt that he would shrug it off with a laugh.

"Oh, before I forget, here's the spare key." Luis dug the key out of his pocket and handed it over to Riley.

"Nonsense, I told you to keep that. Besides, I have my own."

They shook hands with the promise to see each other in the next day or two, and with that, Luis loaded his lawn mower and weed eater into his truck and drove off, honking as he exited the circular driveway.

Riley stood there and looked at the place, taken aback by all the memories that this place held for him. Seeing the wraparound porch brought back a memory that choked him up and brought tears to his eyes. The porch was where he had asked Allison to marry him. All of the memories that now came back to him felt like being doused in cold water. He remembered how the sun had begun to set that day and how the light sparkled off the water. Then, thousands of stars with their faint light illuminated the sky. The soft breeze blew through the trees and the easiness that nighttime brings was about to be upon them. They had sat there in the swinging chair with their lemonades, the glasses sweating from the heat of the day.

There was a nervousness in the air between them. The conversation had been uneasy, and Allison suspected that something was up until, finally, Riley got down on one knee and looked into the eyes of the one he loved and would always love. He somehow got the words out, and her response followed with kiss after kiss, assuring him she would always be his.

Riley squeezed his eyes shut, trying to restore the thought. He just wanted to stay in it. It was by far his happiest day, but it seemed so long ago now. When he finally opened his eyes, he saw Jonathan watching him.

"Sorry. This place . . . well, it holds a lot of memories for me."

"I know it does; that was an amazing day," Jonathan said. "I was so happy for you both."

Riley looked at Jonathan. "Okay, I hate to ask, but how do you do that? I mean, how do you know what I'm thinking?"

Jonathan simply smiled and started to head to the house. Riley followed. When they reached the door, Riley paused before putting the key in the lock and turned to Jonathan.

"Don't you think it's time you tell me about all your capabilities, so that when everything finally does hit the fan I kind of more or less know what you can and can't do?"

"Yes, I agree that you should have as much knowledge about me as possible," Jonathan replied, "but first we need to put some security measures in place and develop some plans. Then you and I will talk." With that, not waiting for Riley to insert the key, Jonathan opened the front door. Riley gave him a quizzical look. Jonathan smiled. "The door was already unlocked."

"Oh," Riley said as they walked into the house. All the furniture was covered in sheets. "Looks like we may have to do a little spring cleaning, but it shouldn't take long. It's been awhile since I've been back here. Let me flip the breaker in the garage so we have some electricity, then I'll get started on cleaning this place up." Riley went back out the front door and headed for the garage. Jonathan followed.

"I'll be right back," Jonathan said. "I'm going to check everything out. Won't be long, then we can check on supplies and get everything we need before nightfall. We don't want to be outside at night."

Riley turned around. "What's wrong with the night?" he asked sheepishly, not sure if he really wanted the answer. His whole life he had never really been afraid of anything, but the night always made his mind play tricks on him, making him wonder what might really be out there.

"Your visibility isn't as keen as mine," Jonathan said. "Other than that, no reason to fear the dark, Riley." With that, Jonathan was off the porch and walking across the lawn before Riley responded.

"I'm not afraid of the dark!" he said as he turned and went to the garage. Once inside he flipped the breaker and looked around. He chastised himself for letting the big angel get inside his head; or was he getting inside his own head? It had been a long night, and day, thus far. Being scared of the dark was for kids and shouldn't bother him, but it did. However, maybe fear was justified since he seemed to be on the run for his life.

He headed back inside and started pulling the sheets off the furniture. He then tucked them away in a large tote and put it out in the garage. Coming back inside, he looked around but didn't see Jonathan. He started wiping everything down and then broke out the vacuum. After finishing all the chores, he proceeded to the kitchen and started checking the cabinets, pantry, and fridge for any food he and Allison may have left behind the last time they were there. Taking out a pen and paper, he started writing a grocery list and discarded other items that they had left behind.

Jonathan walked into the kitchen. "Where do you keep the rest of your hunting supplies?"

Riley, without looking up from his list replied, "I don't have anything other than a couple of fishing poles and a tackle box. If whatever is coming after me is afraid of stink bait and plastic lures, then we're set. Anyway, never saw the use for guns since I don't hunt. Only ones I have are the ones we brought along, and I inherited those."

Jonathan contemplated for a minute. "Okay, so add plenty of ammo to your list. We're going to need it."

Riley looked up as Jonathan sat down opposite him at the kitchen table. "What good are guns going to do against demons anyways? I thought that's what I had you for."

"They're demons, yes, but they have to take human form to walk on this side. There are very few who are allowed to actually walk this side with their powers still intact. The others have the same vulnerabilities as you. Whatever human they overtake, they must then assume that host's abilities. Let's say your friend, Luis, is overtaken by one of them—they're going to pack one heck of a punch and know how to take a hit and keep moving forward. They'll have more speed than you, but nothing else."

Riley put the pen down and looked at Jonathan. "So, if they

can't come to this side without taking human form, then how do they ever get to this side of Hell in the first place?"

"They are given a small window of time. In your time, it would be as little as a minute tops, and if they're not successful at their attempt, then they're pulled back into Hell. Demons have to kill the person they're taking over by inhabiting their body, but they can only take nonbelievers. Guardian angels can only do so much for the nonbeliever since, as angels, they have to work behind the scenes. Believers are washed in the blood of the Lamb, and demons have no influence over them—they can't harm them or inhabit their body. They can be manipulated as all mankind can, which is why there is sin in the world, but they can never be overtaken by a released demon. Not even the Devil himself has that kind of power."

"Okay, I understand," Riley said. "But I need you to understand that if a demon takes over a human life, I don't know if I can kill it."

"That's what you need to understand—what you're going up against has no feelings for you and will do anything to succeed. If they fail, then they go back to the pits of Hell where they came from. There can be no hesitation. You need to be strong and certain when you do take aim and fire. You can't hesitate. This isn't a game, Riley, and there are no second chances."

"I know you're right, but this is just surreal."

Jonathan leaned back and crossed his massive arms across his barrel of a chest. "I'm sorry, Riley, I just need you to be ready when this all goes down." He knew Riley wanted to change the subject but there was more that needed to be addressed. "It's been a while since you fired a gun. We should probably shoot a few rounds, just as soon as we get all the supplies. We're going to need more guns—and ammo," Jonathan said. "We need to have enough to hide around the property." He paused again, looking around the house. "Don't worry, I have a plan all laid out for how to best protect you."

Needing a break, Riley got up from the table. "How about some stale coffee, and you can tell me how the hell you're going to save me from what's about to take place."

Jonathan let out a quick breath. Riley turned to see the big man holding his side as if someone had punched him. He rushed over to Jonathan. "Are you okay?"

Jonathan caught his breath and looked at Riley. His bright blue eyes were dimming, changing to a shadowy gray. A moment later they returned to their brilliant blue. "You remember those rules I was starting to tell you about?" Jonathan asked. "Rule number one is no swearing. I feel the sting from your sin and it weakens me."

"I thought only God felt pain when humans sinned. You're telling me that you feel it as well?"

Jonathan looked at Riley and gave him a simple nod as if not needing to say more on the subject.

Riley, not satisfied, was about to continue with this line of questioning till Jonathan elaborated.

"I don't know if I feel the pain from your sin as God does. I just know that it does weaken me. Remember, after all, I am your guardian angel."

## CHAPTER 13

After regurgitating the remains of Legionaries, Lucifer looked down at the mess as it began slowly piecing itself back together. Lucifer returned to his human form and smoothed his black jacket. He then walked back to his throne where he started to coo over the hounds once more. He waited for Legionaries to return to his old self.

"I want you to go into the depths and pick me a handful of the damned," Lucifer ordered. "Inform them about the subjects they are to go after. I don't intend for any of them to succeed; I just want to see if this big, stupid, wretched fallen is up to the task that is before him. Regardless if those chosen fools are capable, my sons will finish the job that is asked of them. Soon the fallen and that weak, defiant human Riley will suffer for the trouble they have caused me. However, if the others are able to wound either of them, then my sons' job will be that much easier. Do you hear me, you pile of worm filth?"

Legionaries was finally able to make it to one knee with half his face still covered in a slimy mucus. He doubled over in pain and started to vomit violently on the floor.

Lucifer kicked Legionaries and sent him across the room, crashing into a wall. "I feel prideful tonight. I think I may go see what I can shake up and work on my next painting. There's a place that I believe would be best suited. Inform me when you have released the damned. And don't be overzealous and send out a whole army; they'll be Hell to keep control of, so be sure to keep track of how many you release. Do you hear me!"

On his feet, but still trying to recover, Legionaries nodded. "Yes, my king."

Lucifer started to fade into a mist.

After containing himself, Legionaries proceeded out the front door and down the staircase into the depths of Hell, listening to the blood-curdling screams of the damned begging for mercy, asking for water, and even some crying for their mother. He followed the staircase farther and farther down. The flames of the inferno nipped at him. As long as he kept Master happy, then he would be spared the pains of Hell.

The madness all around him began to settle in his head. He had to stop. Legionaries could no longer stand the screams nor block them out. To continue on, even just one more step, would drive him beyond madness. He could always gauge how far he'd descended when a steady stream of red began to trickle from his ears and down his cheeks—that's when he knew that he had reached the point where he could go no farther. The rest of the way was only traveled by Lucifer himself.

On either side of the narrow staircase stood two walls of which one could never see the end. On the other side of the clear walls were the faces of men and women, all pressing against it, trying to break free. They begged and pleaded for help. The walls never bulged, no matter how many faces were pressed against them. Sometimes one of the faces would smile maniacally at him. It made his skin crawl.

"I only need six," Legionaries said in a calm, smooth voice, trying to exert his authority. With the promise of release, the faces seemed to multiply, begging to be selected. They began tearing and gnashing at one another. Legionaries could stomach no more and started to point randomly at the faces. He didn't care which ones. After counting six, he stopped and proceeded back up the stairs. The chosen six exploded from the wall, and it sealed up before any others could escape. The screams intensified as the six fell in line behind Legionaries, leaving the flames and the worms behind. Four of the six were male and two were female. Completely nude, they were clothed in a state of ecstasy at being released. They followed Legionaries to the top of the stairs.

"Your task is to take down a fallen and a human," Legionaries said. "When you get to the surface, breathe deeply and follow the stink to the fallen. When you find him, you will find the human. Kill them both, but I warn you now, the fallen is a giant. He will not be easy to take down. However, if you succeed, Master will have a room prepared for you. You will work as a unit, and each of you will be rewarded the same. If you fail, you will be sent back to where you came from."

With that, Legionaries turned and went back through the front door, closing it behind him. As soon as the door closed, the six turned into a mist and were dumped in the middle of a street. People passing by were completely unaware of their presence. The six, still only a faint mist, raced toward them, searching for a nonbeliever's body to take.

Being back in the world they had once lived in was crueler than any kind of punishment that hell could inflict upon them. The promise of hope if they succeeded, and yet the promise of a quick return to hell if they failed.

Now each begged for the chance to be a part of a world that would never accept them. To once more experience life and know that each day was a blessing. Where other damned souls weren't trying to hurt them with the intent to just make their own pain cease. The race was on, with time being just as evil as it always would be.

# CHAPTER 14

Heavy rain fell upon the ground as people scurried about. The six souls raced frantically to see if they could take over the human body of a nonbeliever. The idea was to find a human walking alone so they wouldn't be noticed. One by one, the six loomed over the unaware pedestrians, scattering this way and that, for they knew the rules. Sixty seconds, just sixty seconds is all they had. If they failed at overtaking a nonbeliever, then Hell would drag them back. It was the only way Lucifer could keep the damned from walking around freely. Some had more privileges and could harvest a person when the right opportunity came along, but for these poor souls, time—just sixty seconds of it—was of the essence.

The fight between a demon and a nonbeliever's soul wouldn't be a fight at all. Since a nonbeliever's soul had never tasted the pain that a demon has gone through, it still hung on to the notion that life would always remain this way, clueless to the fact that everything eventually would come to an end.

The demons pounced on the first nonbeliever they came across just so they wouldn't have to return to the pits. All they cared for was one more chance to be able to taste actual water and look out at the world they once knew and belonged to.

The first demon quickly overtook a body, a man in his late fifties, which would surely be a challenge when it came to his stamina for a fight, but at least it wouldn't have to worry about being pulled back. Then another, and another, until five of the six were safe, at least momentarily. The last one, knowing that the timetable was almost up, started to panic, searching wildly at this point, floating in a crazed panic over the pedestrians on the street. When his time was up and he had failed to overtake a human, he was sucked back to the pits of Hell, unable to let out so much as a scream.

The five looked at each other and began dancing around, celebrating their freedom. Then stopped and looked up at the sky, tilted their heads back, and opened their mouths to let the rain trickle in to quench their thirst. Water was precious to them, having been trapped in the pits of Hell for so long, still able to remember the coldness with each swallow. They could remember the taste of things from their past life, and every now and then a memory of a loved one would surface, inflicting more pain than Hell ever could. Knowing that those days would never return. The damned could only hope they didn't find a loved one in Hell because instead of embracing, they would feed on each other as if they were foes. Just as they were enjoying their drink, and starting to make a further spectacle of themselves, the demons heard a voice that sent shivers down their spines.

"I asked for a few of the damned to help my sons in their quest, but instead I have been given a coterie of imbeciles who enjoy announcing to the passing public that they have indeed escaped from the asylum. One was too foolish to survive for more than sixty seconds, and five others that I believe would be better off as feed for my hounds."

The demons looked upon the face of Lucifer, who had taken on the appearance of an overweight secretary on her way home from work. Even the eyes, a sparkling green, masked the blackness that lived behind them.

One of the five immediately fell to its knees, begging for mercy, but was quickly dispensed back to Hell before it could become yet another spectacle on the street. The host that the demon had overtaken fell lifeless on the sidewalk, immediately grabbing the attention of passing pedestrians. The crowd began to multiply as they looked on in concern. A woman tried to help revive the teenager, as others took out their phones and called 911. A few in the crowd began taking pictures and video of the scene.

Lucifer then looked at the remaining four, his eyes black as coal once more. However, everyone that was crowded around the body didn't seem to notice, since all eyes and phones were on the lifeless teenager.

"Well, that one went just as quickly as the other fool," Lucifer said with a chuckle. "I have no need for begging or grandeur. Just get the job done," he sneered under his breath. And with that, the plump secretary turned, then gave a surprising nodding smile to the other pedestrians and walked away, never once looking back or offering any advice to aid the last four. She simply made her way along the street, blending in with the passing crowd. If those around the kindly old woman knew who, or what was really in their midst, there would have been mayhem.

None of them were affected by the sudden death of someone, but the crowd seemed to have doubled, everyone wanting to help or catch a glimpse of what had happened.

"Let's get out of the way so we can have a little privacy," the woman of the group of demons said.

After placing a good amount of distance between them and the onlookers, one of the remaining four, the man in his late fifties said, "Let's get started." He reached in his back pocket and pulled an ID out of his wallet. "Hmm. My name is Bill. Everyone, quickly, find out who you are—we all need to know who it is we've overtaken." The other three began to reach into their pockets and bags.

Thomas was in his early forties and looked like a skinny librarian showing the signs of too much fast food as the punch of his stomach pushed out. His reading glasses hung onto the bridge of his nose. Jason was in his early twenties, extremely skinny, and wearing baggy pants that were cinched tightly in place with a gray belt. Cassandra was a young black athletic woman also in her twenties.

Bill, the oldest of the group, positioned himself as the leader and started laying out a plan. "We will have better odds of getting the fallen and his human if we work together."

"Wait just a minute," Jason interrupted. "We aren't doing a damn thing together. There is no 'us'! I say we do it alone and let the pieces fall as they may. First, I intend to get a warm meal, quench my thirst, and find some female companionship to help out with some other much needed attention. So, I'll see your asses back in Hell."

"Stop!" Cassandra commanded. "We're only limited to the abilities of the bodies we've possessed. Legionaries told us if we take on the fallen individually, we'll never win. Look, we all have desires and want a second chance at life. Well, this is our best shot. We started out as six and now we are four, so Bill's right. We need to work together."

"That's right, and you're about to be three," Jason said. "We aren't here because we're the most qualified to win. We are here as appetizers for the real main course. I have no idea how long I've lived in Hell, but I do know that if we go against a fallen, then our stay will soon be permanent. You act like strength in numbers is the answer. Ha! Look at yourselves! We have between us two out-of-shape, middle-aged men and a woman who looks like she could make more money if she were turning tricks on a corner. And as for my host—this puny body has probably never even seen the inside of a strip club. How in the hell will we ever take down a fallen and his human like this?"

"That's why we're going to come up with a plan," Thomas said. "We are all aware that we don't have a chance to take on the angel. In these bodies, there's not a chance we'll match his skills alone. Stay and help us think of a way to get us out of that worm field. I don't want to go back to being fed upon and endlessly tortured. We've got to stay together."

"All very heartfelt, except for the fact that I've been down in that hole for too long. This is my break, and I'm taking it," Jason said. "They're going to have to send Lucifer himself to pull me back, because this is my lucky ticket, and I'm going to enjoy it for as long as I can." As he turned to walk away, he said over his shoulder, "The only thing that any of us are guaranteed is a one-way ticket back to Hell."

His comment drew attention from an older woman passing by.

"Forget about him," Bill said to Cassandra and Thomas. "We'll just have to make do, but first, let's get out of this weather and find a place where we can talk without drawing attention to ourselves."

"This weather is refreshing," Cassandra commented. "I would much rather stay and be rained on than eaten alive."

"Or burned to eternity," Thomas offered.

Bill agreed but knew that if they stayed out in the elements like this, the attention they didn't want would find them. They needed to rest somewhere to grow comfortable in their host bodies and try to blend in as much as they could.

Bill turned and walked into the café across the street as Thomas and Cassandra followed.

The place was small and reeked of cigarette smoke. Booths

lined one wall with large windows looking out on the street. Tables were scattered about, and there was a bar where several people sat on barstools. There was a '50s feel to the place, with a jukebox in the corner that, by the looks of it, no one had played in a decade. Old advertisements and flyers lined the wall beside it. Bill led the group to the back of the place so that no one would overhear them talking.

As they were waiting to be served, Thomas said to Bill, "You know, the kid may very well be right."

"To hell with him," Bill scoffed. "All he did was weaken our chances and leave us out to dry."

A waitress rolled up to the table on roller skates. She was a young, blonde teenager. Her nametag said Peggy. "You got that right, to hell with them all. What can I get you three to drink?"

"Water," the three replied in unison.

"Really thought this through," Peggy said. "Have you had a chance to look over the menu?"

"Just water for now," Cassandra said.

Peggy rolled away, and the three looked at each other and began to crack a smile. Who would have thought that they could simply ask for water and just like that it would be served?

"Okay," Bill said, turning the group's attention back to the issue at hand. "We know we don't have much to work with, but ..."

"Wait, do you smell that?" Cassandra interrupted.

"Yes, and it smells ... awful," Thomas said.

"I smell it, too," said Bill. "I could smell it when we first walked in."

"What is that?" Cassandra asked. "It's horrible."

"Remember Legionaries told us to follow the stink? Do you suppose this is what he meant?"

Peggy rolled back to the booth and put the three waters down in front of them. Thomas grabbed his and downed it, a small trickle running down his chin.

"Whoa, slow down there," Peggy cautioned. Thomas choked and started to cough. "See, told you to slow down. Don't worry, there's more where that came from. Have y'all had a moment to look at the menu?"

Thomas wiped his mouth and looked at the young waitress. "You never want to end up in Hell, Peggy. All you'll hear are the screams of the damned and the gnashing of teeth. There is unending and unimaginable pain," he cautioned her. "Hang on to everyone and everything that you love now, for you don't know what tomorrow could bring and— "

"Just bring us a pitcher, would you," Bill interrupted, "and we'll pour ourselves. We've been working all day and have a lot to discuss."

"Whatever," Peggy replied and rolled off again.

"Damn, Thomas, why don't you just set up shop and start preaching," Bill said.

"I know, but I just feel for the ignorance of others," Thomas replied.

"Good to hear, but that isn't our job. We— "

"I know what our job is," Thomas blurted out. "You don't need to tell me what we have to do."

Cassandra passed out the menus to distract them. "What's the plan, Bill?" she asked while looking at the menu.

After taking a long swig of water, Bill put his glass down. "We need guns and vast amounts of ammunition." He reached inside his pockets and pulled out a credit card. "We buy everything that we think we will need, find a vehicle, and follow this smell until it's so strong that we can smell nothing else. Then, we watch the fallen and this human so we can pick up on their routines. Get inside their lives. Once we start, we can't go back. Like Legionaries said, we only have one shot at this, and then we're all done for."

Peggy returned and set a pitcher of water on the table. Thomas immediately began refilling his glass.

"You ready yet?" Peggy asked impatiently.

"We'll start with three cheeseburgers and three orders of fries," Cassandra said curtly. "Just keep the water coming."

"Whatever," Peggy said and rolled away once again.

"If she's working for a tip, she can kiss that goodbye!" Bill said. Thomas started to laugh, since the old man seemed to be loosening up.

"I think we can all agree that she definitely doesn't deserve a tip," Cassandra replied. "But I think Thomas already gave her the best tip anyway—hang on to what's precious in your life."

That brought the mood down again, and the three sat there watching people pass by outside, all of them in a rush to get wherever they were going. None seemed to have a care in the world.

# CHAPTER 15

Riley concentrated on the target twenty yards away and slowly squeezed the trigger. The sound of the shot echoed off the lake and distant pines, but the target remained untouched.

"Jeez!" he yelled.

The whole morning thus far had been a waste of time and ammo. They had gone through two boxes so far, and still the target remained upright. It was as if the aluminum can was almost mocking Riley. He scowled at Jonathan.

"I told you I wasn't much of an outdoorsman. You might be reaching for the sky when it comes to me hitting aluminum cans. Seriously, I think I would be better off just throwing the gun at the target!"

Jonathan stood, looking at the missed target. "Rome wasn't built in a day. And I believe, with more practice, you can only get better," he said, a grin starting to spread across his face.

Riley started to smile. It was the first time since losing Allison that he'd been able to smile without it feeling forced or painted on. It felt good. "Well, if we're going to continue this, we're going to need to head back to the store for more ammo. Besides, I think I could use a break." He looked down at the blisters starting to form on his palms. "How about some lunch?"

"Lunch sounds good to me," Jonathan replied.

"Let me put the gun up and grab my keys. I'll be right back," Riley said.

It was around eleven o'clock, and the day was nice and cool. The sky was clear and the water was calm with a soft, cool breeze coming across it. The high of the day was only going to be in the sixties. Jonathan set about the task of gathering up all the empty shell casings. Then he removed the remaining targets and put them in the garage before heading toward the truck where Riley was sitting. Jonathan opened the passenger door and squeezed his body into the truck.

"Whoa, wait!" Riley shouted. Immediately, he saw he had caused Jonathan to go into defensive mode. In a flash, Jonathan had placed one of his giant hands upon Riley's chest, holding him in place like a parent sheltering a child from harm. His face was lined with concern, and his muscles seemed to tense one upon the other as he quickly scanned their surroundings: the house, the pines, the lake, and beyond. Riley couldn't help himself and laughed. "Wait, it's okay. It's just that the tires popped when you got in." He realized his little joke had just fallen flat.

Jonathan looked at Riley, his face serious. "No, Riley, there's something out there watching us at this very moment. They're here."

Riley felt a sudden panic kick in. He looked around, scanning as quickly as he could. He squinted hard into the sunlight pouring through the pines, trying to imagine what might be out there. What was he looking for? He turned to look at Jonathan, who was now smiling at him—he had just turned the joke around on Riley.

"Wow, you totally had me. And here I thought this whole time you were just going to be the serious, fatherly, overbearing type." Finally remembering to breathe, he blew out a breath and shook his head. "You totally had me."

"You think of me as a fatherly type?" Jonathan asked. He removed his hand from Riley's chest.

"Well, maybe not really fatherly . . . just kind of like, I don't know, an authority figure. You know, like someone you would look up to. That kind of thing."

"Hmm, kind of like a role model."

"No, not really a role model," Riley said, searching for the right word. "I don't know, just someone who is . . . more serious. You making a joke, it just took me off guard, that's all."

"I get it," Jonathan replied, "but I'd rather be your friend."

Without confirming whether they were really friends, or just stuck in this situation because they had to be, Riley put the truck in drive, and they started down the long driveway leading to the main road.

"So, since we have some time, how about you finally tell me some of these rules?" Riley said.

"I guess we could do that. However, there's not really an order to them and there's hundreds for all kinds of situations."

Riley turned onto the main road. "Just break it down for me, then, pertaining to our situation. Like, what I should be aware of and what you can and can't do."

Jonathan paused for a minute, pondering where to start. "How about I begin with demons and their nature and what they can and cannot do once they're here on Earth?"

Riley simply nodded, keeping his eyes on the road ahead of him.

"Demons are released only at the direction of the Devil. They only have one mission, and that is to come after a fallen and his or her human. When they climb out of Hell, they have just sixty seconds to find and overtake the body of a nonbeliever. Once they do that, they assume the human's physical form, age, and abilities."

"Okay, but what's in it for them, the demons?" Riley asked. "Why not use their freedom to beg for forgiveness from God, or—or do whatever they choose, like try to pick up their old life where it left off?"

"Hell itself prevents them from pouring out of it as they please. No one leaves unless the Devil says so, and then he commands them to carry out the job he assigns them."

"What about those people who the demons overtake? What happens to them?" Riley asked.

"Well, there are basically two types of demons. There are those that can walk Earth without worry of being pulled back because the Devil has allowed it. And then there are those that have sixty seconds to take a mortal body, whose attributes are limited to the body that they inhibit.

"The nonbeliever's soul is then cast into Hell. God himself feels each one that is lost. The demons do as they are commanded because, basically, there is no way for them to come back to God. They aren't able to speak his name, or even imagine being given the opportunity at a second chance."

"Sounds so harsh," Riley said. "God creates person, person screws up, gets cast to Hell and is never heard from again."

"It's a horrible thought, indeed," Jonathan said. "I wish I could answer all your questions, Riley, but I can't. I'm sorry, my friend, but these are questions you should ask God someday."

Riley shook his head. "Okay, so let's get back on topic. How about with you? Say we manage to survive all this. What happens next? Do you automatically head back to Heaven?"

Jonathan repositioned himself so he could face Riley. "If we get through this, I will stay at your side and aid you the rest of your days, if you will allow me."

Riley looked at Jonathan with growing anger in his eyes. "Not really looking for a constant reminder of why my life is the way it is now. I've already had a soul mate." It was a low blow, but Riley didn't know how to feel about Jonathan—after all, it was his failure that allowed Allison to be taken from him.

Jonathan turned back in his seat and stared at the road ahead. "I understand," he said simply. "When our business is concluded I will leave you if you command me to. As for me, my rules are simple: protect you and love God. It's not really even a rule. Loving God, for me, is like breathing air—it's natural, perfect, and it's impossible not to want to. God gives willingly and only asks that we believe in him."

"So, you've met God, huh?" Riley asked, frustration still in his voice.

Jonathan's smile returned. "Yes, many times. And every time it makes me wonder how something so good and perfect could love something that isn't. Just like me and you."

Riley slowed the truck and pulled over to the shoulder. Pushing the gearshift into park, and not once looking at Jonathan, he just breathed in and out in slow, deep breaths. His frustration with God, Heaven, and do-gooding angels had pushed him over again. He really hated God right now and felt as if God was being forced upon him.

Jonathan felt the tension in Riley. He remained quiet and waited for Riley to calm himself. Riley turned the engine off and got out of the truck. Jonathan went to open his door but Riley barked at him. "Stay in the truck, or do whatever you want, but I need some time to myself, so stay away from me."

Jonathan knew he must stay close to Riley, to protect him. He waited a moment and then climbed out of the truck as Riley headed for a stand of pines.

Riley didn't know where he was going, so he just followed his feet to wherever they were taking him as a jumble of thoughts raced through his head. *Something so perfect, huh? Praise, laughter, good feelings, on and on.* "Well, perfect my ass!" he yelled.

He kept moving until he was no longer in sight of the truck. He went farther and farther into the pines, until finally, when he felt he'd gone far enough, he sat on a fallen tree to collect his thoughts. Fallen tree branches and pine cones covered the ground.

*You may be perfect and all-knowing to some, and have your great plans, but you took my perfect little life and turned it upside down. Then you give me an angel that I have to look at every day as a constant reminder of one of your failures. It screwed up, and now my wife is dead. Great job. Really, you should be applauded more for your efforts. Oh, and you want to know what the best part is? I get to hope, and imagine, that this freakishly huge thing can protect me from an onslaught of demons.*

Riley bowed his head and started to sob. "You took everything that I wanted in this world, do you understand?" he cried out through his tears. "Can you even comprehend that? I'm empty to everything, and I don't know where to go or what to do. I want to just give up, and for all this to end, but this little adventure hasn't even started yet!"

There was no other sound but the wind coming through the pines, with a coolness in it that caused Riley to shudder. *Just as I thought. When it feels like my darkest hour, you give me nothing.* With his face still pressed into the palms of his hands, Riley released the last of his tears. Then he felt the weight of a hand gently squeezing his shoulder. Riley jumped up and turned around, expecting to see Jonathan there. But it was a chubby older woman with a kindly face smiling softly at him.

# CHAPTER 16

**H**er outfit didn't suit her surroundings at all. The plump lady was dressed in black heels and a blue skirt and blouse. She had red, short, curly hair and green eyes that were fixed on Riley.

Riley was stunned and speechless.

The old lady looked up at him. "Whom are you talking to, dear?" she said, in a tone that reminded Riley of his grandmother. Where had she come from? What was she doing out here?

The woman was staring at him, not saying anything; just staring at him with her very intense green eyes. Riley felt himself shiver. He was becoming increasingly more uncomfortable. "My—my name is Riley," he finally said and awkwardly thrust his hand out.

The woman took his hand with both of hers, but her hands were ice cold, and he immediately pulled away. The woman just stood there looking at Riley.

He started to fumble with his words. "I was, uh, out here just, uh, trying to understand some things that have been wearing on me," he paused and thought for a moment. "Um, could I offer you a ride somewhere? Back into town, maybe? My truck isn't far from here."

The lady looked at him a moment. "Well, aren't we all?"

"Excuse me?"

"We all are trying to just understand some things. For instance, when people are given an opportunity, why don't they take it? Instead, they circle around, wondering why things are the way they are, and whether they should have chosen a different path. What I really can't wrap my head around, Riley, is why someone like you would put his life into the hands of someone who botched a job and is now a daily reminder of what you lost!"

She was staring harder at Riley now. He watched in disbelief as her eyes began to blacken, even the whites of her eyes turned black as night. A coldness swept over him as he realized he was standing face to face with pure evil, the Devil himself. Riley's knees began to buckle. He wanted to turn and run but knew he wouldn't get far.

"I give you a chance to get your life back, to get your Allison back, but you refuse it," the Devil seethed at Riley. "Are you trying to make up for old sins—or a guilty conscience? So, here we are on the road that you picked, Riley. And I find you out here, alone in the woods, feeling sorry for yourself, no better than a wounded animal."

"Why are you here?" Riley demanded, fighting back against his own fear. "Have you come to do your collecting? I'm through with waiting and wondering when your demons are going to come and do your little deeds. Do it yourself, you piece of filth, or leave me alone!"

The Devil smiled and then transformed himself back into the little old woman with the shining green eyes. "Soon enough, dear. I'm going to enjoy this so much! And believe me, I'm in no hurry."

Riley turned away, wondering where Jonathan was. But then he felt an icy hand grab his shoulder and spin him around.

"Don't turn your back on me," the old woman said.

Riley made a fist and swung around, connecting with her nose and sending her to the ground with a thud. His hand throbbed.

He took in a large breath of air to prepare himself for what might come next. Rubbing his hand, he stood over the Devil.

"Don't put your hands on me ever again."

The Devil broke into a wildly hysterical laugh that began as an old woman's cackle before descending into the growl of a wild animal. "You are just full of surprises, aren't you, Riley? Not only am I going to put my hands on you, but I'm going to watch with great delight as the fires of Hell nip at you." He paused. "I did the same to your wife, you know, and all the while she just begged for the pain to stop."

Riley knew the Devil was feeding off his anger, so he closed his eyes and started to turn away once more.

"Her first night in Hell," the Devil continued, "I welcomed her by letting my hounds feast on her, and then I ravaged her on the floor all while she was calling out your name. But to be honest, I think she rather enjoyed it."

With that, Riley turned and, without a second thought, stomped on the old woman's head, driving it into the ground. The old woman evaporated into a gray mist that lifted Riley off his feet and slammed him to the ground. It disappeared into the wind.

Adrenaline was coursing through Riley's body now. He began to tremble. He hadn't expected this would all be happening so soon. He thought he had more time. Trying to gain control of himself, he turned and headed back to the truck. Although he hadn't been gone long, the sun had already begun to set. He picked up speed and finally made his way through the pines until he saw his truck with Jonathan sitting there waiting for him.

"They're here!" Riley screamed at Jonathan. "The Devil is here! I can't believe what just happened. How did they find us so quickly?"

In a panic, he jumped into the truck and, without waiting for a response from Jonathan, Riley fumbled to put the key in the ignition and start the truck. He glanced at the dashboard clock. "You've gotta be kidding me. Five thirty? That can't be right!"

To Riley's shock, Jonathan simply sat there, quietly. Then he nodded. "It is right, Riley. Your little run-in with the Devil back there just means that the time is getting closer, for one. And, secondly, he manipulated your time. You went into the trees with anger, almost inviting trouble, and it found you. Needless to say, you're a marked man. Riley, the Devil put you into a sleep and, although it felt very real to you, the old woman, the Devil, was nothing more than a dream."

"You're telling me that just because I lost my temper the Devil was able to take control of me? The demon—or whatever it was—came to me dressed as an old woman but I ended up hitting her, wanting to kill her. I mean, I hit her. My hand is throbbing! No, it couldn't have been a dream. I felt the impact. I stomped on her head, Jonathan. I saw the blood."

"You likely hit something in your sleep, nothing more. As for the details of your dream, it's just like any other dream; it feels real to you until you wake up."

"Then how do I know I'm not still dreaming?"

Jonathan reached over and pinched Riley's arm.

"Ouch."

"Yup, you must be awake now."

With that, Riley looked at his hand again. The red marks promised to turn into stiffness and bruising. Then he thought of what the Devil had told him about Allison—he had to know despite how much he feared the answer.

"I have to know something, and no matter how much it may hurt me, I want to know."

Jonathan could hear the question playing out like a loud drum in his friend's head, but knew not to pry or answer before Riley built up the nerve to ask. He just sat with patience and waited.

"Did my wife get damned to hell? We weren't church-going people after high school—I always had excuses as to why we shouldn't go, but I know she was a Christian. I worked nonstop, and my only day off was Sunday, so I chose sleep and a little peace before I had to start the week all over again. I felt I deserved one day to myself." Knowing he was trying to rationalize his laziness, he shook his head at the ignorance of his actions. His whole body started to shake with frustration. "Was I my wife's downfall? What have I done?"

Jonathan wanted to place a hand on Riley to soothe him, let him know it wasn't his fault Allison died. He knew the answer would set him free from this built-up anger. "Riley, look at me," he said. Riley sat there with his eyes closed and his head resting on top of the steering wheel. "Riley, please look at me."

He lifted his head and looked up at the roof of the truck for a moment, then blew out a long breath. He turned in his seat and looked at Jonathan. The angel spoke.

"That day, when Allison was in the eighth grade and went before a packed auditorium at youth camp and gave her life over to our God, I knelt beside her as the youth pastor led her through the prayer. She cried tears of happiness, and ever since that day, she never wavered in her beliefs. I remember sprawling out on the floor after she whispered that prayer and weeping. I knew that one day, the two of us would actually meet, and I would be able to hold her in my arms. All we guardians want is to meet our human and hold you and tell you what we enjoyed most about watching over you."

Riley couldn't help but smile at the thought of this massive angel picking up his small Allison and holding her and being by her side for what he could only imagine would be all of eternity. Riley kissed the tips of two fingers on his right hand and placed them on Jonathan's cheek. "Thank you." He then eased back into his seat and, looking ahead of him, started the truck. "Well, let's go get some shells."

Riley could see that Jonathan wanted to say more of what just happened between them. However, he hoped that he wouldn't ruin the moment with offering some form of bond that they would forever share. He was pleasantly surprised when Jonathan replied back.

"I'm interested to see if maybe you could hit at least one target before the end of the night," he mused.

Neither one spoke during the drive into town. Riley preferred it that way. It was hard to know how to take his new companion. He wasn't really a friend. He was a protector. Maybe he should simply see it as a business arrangement.

A short while later, they pulled into the parking lot of Paul's Grocery. Riley jumped out and headed to the front door, leaving Jonathan to follow. They were greeted by Paul, the store owner.

"Riley!" The balding, elderly man said. "So good to see you. What can I do for you . . ." his words trailed off when he saw the massive figure standing behind Riley.

"Paul, it's great to see you too," Riley said. "And this is Jonathan."

Jonathan extended his huge hand toward Paul, and the two shook hands.

"My, you are huge," Paul exclaimed. "I don't believe I've ever seen anyone so big . . . " He stopped himself, realizing he was being rude. "Oh, I, uh, I'm sorry to be so blunt."

"No apology needed, sir. I am large. You're just stating the obvious."

"So, a friend of yours, I presume?" Paul asked. "Where's that pretty little girl of yours?"

The innocent question stung, catching Riley off guard. Most of the locals never got out of town and only heard about people's lives through the comings and goings of others.

Taking in a breath, Riley looked at Paul. "Allison passed away recently . . . in a car accident . . . about a month ago."

"My God. I'm so sorry, Riley."

"It's okay. You didn't know."

Wanting to end the conversation and get out of the small shop, Riley said, "We're just going to grab a few things and be on our way; promise not to be long."

"Take your time, Riley. I'm just sorting through some orders. Once again, I'm so sorry for your loss."

With that, Riley headed toward the hunting section with Jonathan following. The place had a total of four aisles. Three had grocery supplies, and the last, containing fishing and hunting supplies, took up a whole wall and ran around to the register at the front of the store. It wasn't nearly as big as the outdoors shop down the road, but it had what Riley and Jonathan needed. Finding the shells for the shotgun, Riley grabbed box after box.

"You okay?" Jonathan asked.

"We need a basket. They're at the front. Can you go grab one?"

Jonathan made his way back to the front of the store. Riley overheard Paul talking to Jonathan. "You need some help?" and the rest of the dialogue faded away.

Standing there with four boxes of shells, Riley closed his eyes and went back to that rainy night. He took in Allison's face and her dress, even the way her hair was done. He could smell the rain in the air and hear the sound of the raindrops landing one by one on top of the car. This time, a sense of peace started to run through Riley instead of the anxiety over what he knew would come next. He opened his eyes to see Jonathan and felt his touch on his shoulder.

"What are you doing?" Riley asked, startled, as he dumped the boxes of shotgun shells into the empty basket. He grabbed four more boxes and dumped them on top of the others. "Don't ever do that again. You have no right to invade my thoughts, and I don't need you to make things better for me."

Leaving Jonathan standing there, Riley headed to the next aisle over and started to pick out random items he thought they might need. Jonathan caught up with him, and Riley dumped more items in the basket before Jonathan could speak. Riley hurried through the aisles, grabbing this and that, looking like an impulse buyer, just grabbing random items until, finally, he turned to put more in the basket and found that the basket was full. The weight caused the basket to bow out at the sides and the handles were strained, but Jonathan held it as if he were holding a pillow full of feathers. Riley shook his head, and then started to laugh.

"I could see if Paul has a shopping cart," Jonathan said. Riley shook his head no, continuing to laugh.

The day had almost been too much for him—the lousy target shooting, his angry talk with God, meeting up with the Devil once again—if only in his dreams—and now, another person telling him they're sorry for his loss. All he had left was to laugh.

Riley placed a hand on Jonathan's shoulder and smiled up at the big man. "Thank you."

"For what?" Jonathan asked.

"For giving me hope that I may have another day and just being here for me. I realize it wasn't your fault, and I'm going to do my best to stop blaming you."

Jonathan smiled back. "It's okay. Hey, if you're done with your impulsive shopping, I'm kind of hungry. How about we lay off practicing tonight and finally get something to eat?"

# CHAPTER 17

L uis woke up, sweating from the nightmare about his younger brother. He remembered how close they had been and how guilty he still felt that he had survived the drive-by shooting. From that day forward, Luis hadn't owned a gun and never would.

His family grew up on some poor streets, and one day, when Luis and his brother Juan were waiting at the bus stop, there was a drive-by. Apparently, the person sitting next to them, waiting to catch the bus, had been caught up in drugs and was affiliated with a rival gang. When the shot rang out, the intended target walked away without a scratch while Luis's brother paid the price with his life at the age of eight.

Luis's anger drove him through the next several years—the resentment and wanting payback. He found his release in boxing and ended up getting really good at it. He never learned the name of the guy who was supposed to be taken out that night, but he hoped he had turned his life around. Luis never wavered in his decision not to own a gun.

A loud knock came at his front door, pulling him fully awake. Checking the clock on his nightstand, he saw four-thirty in glowing red lights. "You have got to be kidding me."

He was a long-time bachelor, lived with no one, and hadn't been in a relationship in a very long time; it seemed he never had the time. He always had a heavy workload doing upkeep on other properties around the lake and spent the rest of his time at the gym.

He crawled out of bed and made his way down the hallway to the front door as the knocking continued.

"I'm coming!" he barked angrily.

He flipped on the light switch to the porch and opened the door to find a man who appeared to be in his forties. Before Luis could say anything, the man pulled a gun from his waistband. In a flash, Luis smashed the man with a right cross that sent him staggering backward off the porch as a shot rang out from the gun. Luis slammed the door shut and ran to pick up the telephone only to find that the line was dead.

"What the hell!" He dropped the phone and headed back down the hallway to grab his cell phone. He could hear voices outside.

"God! He broke my damn nose!"

"Shut the hell up and go around to the back."

There were sounds at the door again—someone was trying to kick it open.

Reaching his bedroom in a panic, Luis spun around, looking for his cell phone, checking the pockets of the pants that lay on the floor, and then the nightstand. "Of all the cursed times. Where is that phone?" Giving up, he rushed to turn off the lights so that whoever was out there wouldn't have such an easy pop at him. He started looking for anything he could use to defend himself.

The front door finally gave in. In the silent darkness, Luis could hear someone's heavy breathing. He realized where his cell phone was and shook his head. *I left it in my truck, on the charger.* He'd gotten home late that night after working all day and sparring at the gym until almost midnight. After the thirty-minute drive back from the gym, it was close to two by the time he got in bed. Running only on two hours of sleep, he and his muscles felt drained. But he was fully awake now, having had a gun pulled on him.

Thinking of a plan to get to his truck, he grabbed his keys, stuffed them in his pajama pants pocket, and didn't bother with throwing on a shirt or shoes. Looking down the hallway, he saw the door—dented and hanging open. He didn't know if someone was in the house.

Crouching down to stay clear of the windows, he worked his way toward the front door but stopped cold when he heard a creak on the porch. "He's still in there," he heard a voice say.

*Maybe three or four, tops* Luis thought and hoped. Still unarmed, he reached the guest room and grabbed a bat that was hanging over the bed. He only used the room for other boxers who would come and track him down to train with for a week. Other than that, he kept sports memorabilia in there. He had signed boxing gloves framed in shadow boxes, football helmets, and so on. But his most prized possession was this bat that he and his brother had signed when they were younger and played on the same minor league team.

Gripping the bat in his hands, he looked down at the signatures that had faded away with time. They had it signed before the season had begun, and their father had told them it would be a season to remember. It turned out to be the season his brother had been killed halfway through. After that, baseball was no longer fun, and the bat got put away since it brought back difficult memories. Right now, though, he would not go down without a fight. He willed himself forward. *I will make it to the truck, I will call the police, they will come and help me, and if anyone gets in my way, I will move them. No one will keep me from reaching safety.*

Holding the bat low and making a quick dash to the front door, he froze when a man came in low, a gun in his hand, scanning the room as quickly as he could, not even seeing Luis. Before he could pull the trigger, Luis smashed the guy right across the face and sent him back out the front door screaming and cussing. Luis quickly kicked the door shut and leaned against it.

*What the hell is this about?* He was a simple guy who had built his own little gym and provided groundskeeper services to several owners on the lake. He lived a normal life, owned his lake home, allowing him to work and train close to home. *What the hell is this?*

His closest neighbor was Riley, but he lived across the lake, and who knew if he was even there? Thoughts of despair started to circle around his head. *No one is coming, and no one heard the first shot.* He forced the thought out of his head. Leaving the front door, he started for the back door, hoping no one was on that side of the house.

"Oh my God, oh my God," he heard again from the front. "I can't see a damn thing!" And then more swearing. Then he heard a woman's voice. He stopped.

"Easy pick, huh?"

*So there's three of them, including a woman! Three of them— maybe more, but not sure. Three of them. Yeah, three, I can handle three. Two in the front now, and one somewhere in the back. God, please, let there be no more. You can do this, Luis, you can do this.*

He knew he could get outside, but he must do it quickly. Having been in some pretty tough boxing matches, he was counting on that. He knew one of them couldn't see very well. It was pitch-black out there, and they didn't know their way around. He crouched down and held the bat in one hand and put his other hand on the door handle. He pushed into pure darkness and then closed the door softly behind him. Nothing, not a sound coming from anywhere. Maybe he was just this lucky, but then he heard a noise coming from the right, maybe a few yards away.

The moon was concealed by clouds, which was in Luis's favor. Carefully, he made his way to where he heard the noise, until he came upon the outline of a person with his back to Luis. He laid the bat on the ground and then lunged at the figure, punching him hard right below the ear, where the jawbone starts to curve. He knew where to locate the sweet spot for a knockout. The guy dropped with a thud, face first. Luis grabbed the gun. Just the feel of it in his hands made him uneasy. After taking out the cartridge, he tossed it into the tall grass along with the gun, where they both disappeared. Searching the man, he came up with a wallet. He dug out the license and pitched the wallet. Knowing the guy was going to be out for a while, he slipped the ID into his pocket for the cops. He then gathered up his bat and slowly rounded the house.

He could hear the front door being kicked open once again. *Good, now's the time to make a run for the truck.* He checked his pockets to make sure the keys were still there. Rounding the front of the house, he gave a quick look and saw no one. *They're inside; here we go.* He made a rush for his truck, feeling his heart thumping. He opened the door, and there on the seat was his charging cord—but no phone.

*They have my phone!*

The truck was sitting lower than usual. Luis checked the back tire and then the front; both were flat, and from the look of the truck, they were all flat. They had him trapped, and Luis knew it. He could swim but would likely get shot trying to cross the lake, or drown before he reached the other side. He could make a run for it but would end up getting gunned down on the long, narrow roads that encircled the lake. He gripped the bat tightly. "If it's a fight they want, it's a fight they're going to get," he whispered under his breath. Crouching down, he headed back to the house. Once he reached the front door, he saw a tall young woman in the living room.

"He isn't here!" she yelled. "Let's go out front. He's probably already in the water, or on foot."

She turned and came face-to-face with Luis, who smashed into her ribs with a thunderous left. She tried desperately to cry out, but all that came out was a dry heave, as if her lungs had just collapsed. She dropped to her knees, wheezing, completely vulnerable to whatever Luis wanted to do to her, but instead of taking the bat and finishing her off, he kicked her hard in the ribs, lifting her off the ground and dropping her on her back.

Someone else in the back of the house yelled, "When I get my hands on this guy, I'm going to empty this whole damn clip in him!"

Coming down the hall from the bedrooms, the older man walked into the living room and saw the woman on the floor, convulsing.

"What the—"

Luis whipped around and smashed him into the wall with a body shot that would make any boxer proud. The man's graying and thinning hair and pudgy body made him look like some average office worker with kids close to graduating high school, not a man that would kill for sport or pleasure. Luis hit the guy again, twice to the face, fast and hard, and the man fell to the floor, unconscious. The woman behind him was still trying to catch her breath. She stayed on the floor, panting. She'd had more than enough.

Although he wanted to triumphantly throw his fists in the air, Luis simply allowed himself to grin at what he had just done. What a story this would make! *Boxer takes on three armed fugitives with nothing more than an old Louisville slugger and a few good punches.*

Standing there looking at the intruders, one with blood coming from his nose and mouth, and the other sprawled out, still gasping for air, Luis wondered once more what they could possibly want with him. And why these three? They didn't look like your average criminals except for being dressed in black.

Luis remembered there was a third assailant somewhere outside. He started to get a little uneasy. He spun around, only to see there was no one there. Not wasting any time, he went to the kitchen, opened the cabinet below the sink, and pulled out his tool chest. After fidgeting with the chest for a few seconds, he located what he needed. Pulling out zip ties, he proceeded to tie up the woman first. She sat, wide-eyed, staring at Luis, trying to figure out how he had gotten the better of them. She didn't resist but simply held her wrists out in front of her in defeat.

"No," Luis said harshly. "Put your hands behind your back."

The woman did as she was told, and Luis slapped two zip ties on her, snugly; enough that her hands started to redden from the pressure being applied. Luis then proceeded to do the same to the other assailant. He looked at them both and then said to the woman, "There are three of you, right?"

She had a blank look on her face, as if all the life had just been sucked out of her. She nodded.

"I'm going to go get the other one, and then I'm going to call the cops and they can sort this out," Luis told her. "If you so much as move, I will have no problem beating you within an inch of your life."

The woman continued to sit still, blank-faced. With that, Luis turned and headed toward the back door. He reached down, picked up the pistols, ejected the rounds, stuffed them in his pajama pant pockets, and then placed the guns in one of the kitchen cabinets so that they were out of sight. The memory of his younger brother came back to him once again. He shook his head to clear his thoughts; this wasn't the place or the time to think of him. Picking up his bat, he walked to the back door, opened it, and was gone, once again, into the night.

Moving quickly, but low to the ground, he headed to the end of the house where he left the last assailant. When he reached the spot, his mind started to race.

There was no body.

Starting to get a little frantic, he began to scan the area as fast as he could, but without any light he couldn't make out anything. This time his mind became his worst enemy, playing tricks on him about where the guy could have gone. Maybe he had gotten the jump on him and was back inside the house, freeing the other two. Or maybe he was playing games with Luis, waiting for the opportune time to take a shot at him.

As Luis turned and headed toward the back door, he stumbled and fell on top of the third intruder, who let out a startled breath. Luis rolled off of him and, without a second thought, raised his fist and started to pound on the guy. Adrenaline rushed through his body with each blow that he landed. Finally, he grabbed him by the hair and dragged him to the back door. Suddenly, Luis felt a cold chill. He opened the door to find the other two where he left them. With a shudder, he pulled the last man in. The woman had a look of desperation in her eyes.

As he reached into his pocket, he noticed blood on his pants. He thought, at first, that it was from one of the intruders, but there was far too much to be from a busted nose or a cut lip. Looking down at his right side, he saw where the blood was coming from and began to feel woozy. The adrenaline had kept him going this long but was now wearing off. The wound in his side wasn't from a knife—it was a deep cut that let the blood flow easily from his body. With another cold shudder, he touched his side and winced as he looked at the woman, whose expression of desperation was now being replaced with a broadening grin.

Luis looked at the other two. One was starting to wake up. The other, who was lying at Luis's feet, looking up at him as if he'd just hit a home run. Luis saw him holding the weapon that did the damage; it was the old rusted screwdriver that he'd run over when he mowed his yard the other day. He gave another shudder as his arms and legs started to fall asleep.

*No!*

Panic set in as he realized that it was over. There was no one to help him. These three would simply watch him die. Closing his eyes, Luis grabbed his most prized possession, the Louisville slugger. He recalled his favorite memory—he and his younger brother playing baseball together.

In the background he heard noises—the one that cut him was freeing the other two. Finally, he slumped to the floor, resting his back against the wall. He pictured his brother running the bases after a long hit ball, Luis cheering him on to turn two. He could feel the warmth from that hot summer day, the roar of the crowd, the commentator calling the play, and his fellow teammates cheering his younger brother on as he watched in awe at how far he'd driven the ball into the outfield. He gave one last shudder and with that he smiled a little bigger. *I'm coming home, brother. I'm coming home.*

# CHAPTER 18

Riley walked into the kitchen from his first real night of sleep only to find Jonathan already working on breakfast and brewing coffee. His ongoing dream of the night his wife was taken from him hadn't occurred in some time. Perhaps finally learning to understand that it wasn't Jonathan's fault was the first step in letting go a little and learning to accept it.

A week had passed since the incident at the grocery store. There was no more blame when he looked at his friend, only remorse that it had taken him this long to find out that they were both in this situation until the end. They needed to depend on each other, and Riley needed to work with Jonathan, not against him. The training had intensified—Jonathan said they needed to push themselves further. They were running close to five miles a day, working on sparring in the garage, and as for target practice, they had moved from handguns to shotguns, which Riley didn't struggle with as much since he just had to point, aim, and fire at the wide pattern of a target.

His body ached, though, even if he was getting good sleep. It was as if constantly pushing his body to this breaking limit, day after day, was starting to get the better of him instead of helping him. His movements had increased considerably, as well as his striking. He didn't know whether this was due to training daily or if it was from being around Jonathan; perhaps his abilities were rubbing off on Riley.

"Good morning," Jonathan said without looking up from

scrambling eggs. "I felt we should load up on a healthy breakfast today. You're going to practice taking a shot at me."

Sitting at the table, and not registering what Jonathan had just said, Riley poured himself a glass of juice. "Good morning. You know, I've noticed the training is paying off. I'm getting a lot stronger and extremely quick. I mean, I wasn't in the best shape when we first met, but I was decent. Now I can feel a huge difference from when we first started."

"You ever notice that when a team has a really good defense that the offense usually starts to get really good as well, because they train with each other?"

Riley sipped his juice and then put his glass down. "So, you're not, like, rubbing off on me or spiking my drinks, or something? Because this change is pretty drastic."

Jonathan let out a soft chuckle and shook his head. "I will never do anything to intentionally hurt you. I'm here to protect you with my life, and as for me exchanging powers with you, no Earthly person could take just an ounce of what I could give them, without harming them to a point where it would take their life. You're simply getting stronger because of our routine. As for your speed and reflexes, we're going to test those out in a little bit when you try to actually hit me and shoot me."

Riley nearly coughed up orange juice all over the table. Jonathan grabbed a paper towel and handed it to Riley. He tried to catch his breath.

"What did you just say?"

Jonathan waited until Riley had control of himself. "I can feel you getting better every day. You're learning very quickly, and since time is always against us, I figured we should push our training further. Today, in sparring, I need you to go all out trying to hit me, and I will push the pace as well. I think we should get some paintball guns, too. They're the closest thing we can use to resemble real gunfire."

Riley thought back to the first, and last, time he had done paintball. He wasn't good at it and didn't enjoy it at all, but, at this point, why argue with his trainer? If Jonathan said they needed to do something, they did it, with no questions asked. Riley had learned to quit being objective since his life was in the balance now, and he had learned to accept it. "I don't really like paintball, but if you say so, then okay." He shifted his feet under the table like a nervous kid. "As for the sparring—when you say push the pace, does that mean you're going to try to take my head off?"

Jonathan smiled again. "I sure am. So, let's eat and then get started."

Riley, starting to feel a little anxiety growing inside him, shifted his feet again. Fighting someone was never his way of handling any situation, but he knew it had to be done. The idea of fighting not another person, but an actual angel who could rip him to shreds, wasn't sitting well with the orange juice, either.

Jonathan placed a plate of fresh sliced fruit in front of Riley, with two egg whites and some biscuits. He placed a hand on Riley's shoulder. "You're going to do fine. Remember, I'm not here to hurt you."

Riley felt that familiar sense of peace flow through him when Jonathan put his hand on his shoulder and smiled. "I appreciate the vote of confidence, but how am I supposed to actually hit you, unless you let me? I'm not too worried about hurting you, but if I do manage to land a good one, you're going to be okay, right?"

Jonathan walked back to the sink to wash his hands. "If I can take on several demons and walk away with just a few cuts and bruises, I think I can take a punch from you and keep moving. And besides, that's *if* you can hit me."

After finishing breakfast and putting everything away, the two headed out the front door and to the garage. The days were a little chillier now, with the temperature not getting above fifty-five and dropping at night to the forties, but once the sparring started, the cooler air felt great. As Jonathan walked a couple of paces in front of Riley, the nervous jitters started to come back again, making Riley feel as if he were walking to the executioner's guillotine, about to lose his head.

Opening the garage door with one quick pull, Jonathan walked into the three-car garage. Instead of housing cars, it only held boxing mitts, a heavy and speed bag combo stand, and various weights. Luis used the garage for storage and had left the items here for Riley to use in case he ever thought about taking out a little frustration. Jonathan started to shake his massive arms out and did some shoulder shrugs and neck rolls to start the warm up. Riley fell in line, mimicking the movements of the big man as they both jogged in place to get the blood pumping.

"You ready?" Jonathan asked.

Riley felt like the floor was falling out from beneath him, and his legs started to buckle. Jonathan, paying no attention, picked up a set of mitts and tossed them to Riley, who fumbled and dropped them. Jonathan put his on with ease, but couldn't Velcro them, since his wrists wouldn't allow it. Finally getting the last glove on, Riley looked up to see Jonathan standing there, watching him. *Come on, I promise it won't hurt . . . much.*

"Ready," Riley said, trying to sound confident.

Walking toward one another, Jonathan put out his mitt to start things off. Riley jabbed the proffered mitt, and it began. Immediately closing the distance with one quick step, Jonathan came in with a shot to the body that connected and then an overhand right that Riley barely saw coming but somehow managed to get out of the way, only to find the left that had caught him in the body now coming toward his head.

Riley staggered back, but Jonathan, once again, was already on top of him before he could recover. With his legs still underneath him, and not thinking of what to do next, he went down to one knee, as if asking for a ten count.

Jonathan stopped and looked down at Riley. "Not today, buddy, we're trying to push ourselves, remember? The demons will not give you any ten counts." With that, he threw a quick jab to Riley's head, but Riley scrambled out of the way. Back to an upright position and already breathing like a crazed animal, he just stared at Jonathan without quite knowing what to do next.

"Come on, Riley. You won't hurt me, I swear," said the angel. "Remember what I taught you thus far and use it."

Jonathan closed the distance again, and Riley threw a combination, but Jonathan was too quick for him. Still pushing the pace, Jonathan landed two more body punches before Riley could retaliate. Remembering to take a punch and keep moving, Riley countered with another combination, then sidestepped and threw a left cross that actually skimmed off the top of Jonathan's temple.

"Good job," Jonathan said. Then he threw another hook to Riley's body, once again taking the air from his lungs.

The sparring went on for a good hour or so. Jonathan only allowed Riley quick breaks for water before going again.

Over and over, the constant back and forth, Riley kept coming up short. As the session was winding down, Jonathan's pace stayed the same, but Riley felt like his lungs were breathing fire, and his arms were turning to jelly. He wondered if they were going to keep going until he actually passed out. His legs didn't seem to respond anymore to his brain telling them to move, and the punches he was throwing had absolutely nothing behind them. He dropped both arms to his sides, trying to stretch the muscles out for a moment. Again, Jonathan came at him. A right hook was thrown, and Riley had just enough in him to drop his head out of the way, but instead of countering, he lunged for Jonathan and wrapped him into an awkward bear hug, doing his best to tie him up.

"I can't go another minute," he said, gasping.

Jonathan backed out of Riley's grip. "It's about time. I didn't know you could go so long. Very good session, extremely good session. Your endurance has improved dramatically."

Riley bent over at the waist, resting his gloved hands on his knees and trying to make his breath come in at slow intervals. "You mean you were waiting for me to say no more?"

Jonathan slid his gloves off and then walked over to Riley, placing his hand on Riley's back. "Yes." Reaching down, he loosened the Velcro on Riley's gloves and pulled them off. Droplets of sweat formed at the bridge of Riley's nose and dripped onto the concrete, one after another. His shirt was completely covered, and the cool breeze from outside bit at his skin.

"I told you we needed to push the pace, and you did just that. I wasn't going to tell you that we had gone long enough since I don't get tired like you do. Now I think we should wait a bit until your energy comes back."

"Great idea," Riley replied. "I want food. Nothing healthy at all. I need the calories right now, because I am bushed." He stood up and put his hands over his shoulders, feeling his back muscles scream at him for what he just put them through. The burn felt good, though, and instead of backing off the stretch he bent more into it until his lower back relaxed. Shaking his arms out, he walked over to Jonathan and noticed that the big man wasn't sweating at all. He never did.

"That's the craziest thing I've ever seen in my life," Riley said. "We just sparred for over an hour and you didn't even break a sweat."

Jonathan looked at Riley's shirt, noticing how dark it was due to the sweat. "Well, you are aware that I'm not human," he said, smiling.

"Yes, but still, I mean, come on! I just went after you as hard as I possibly could. That's kind of a blow to my ego, you big freak!" he said with a cocked grin.

Jonathan began to laugh. "You did great. And besides, I don't produce sweat. As a matter of fact, I don't get tired. If you would like, you can add that to your list of rules."

They walked out of the garage and away from the shelter that the walls provided. The wind immediately wrapped itself around Riley's shirt and pressed the sticky clothing to his body. "I take it you don't get cold, either?"

Jonathan pulled the garage door down and turned to see Riley wrapping his arms around himself, trying to contain his body heat. "I don't. Nor do I get sick, but we'd better get you inside and warmed up so you don't get sick." With that, the two headed for the house.

Once inside, the warmth of the house started to take effect on his body. "I'm going to grab a shower, and then let's eat."

"What sounds good?" Jonathan yelled to Riley, as he watched him head across the living room toward the hallway.

"Anything fattening," he called over his shoulder as he disappeared down the hallway.

In the bathroom, Riley pulled his shirt over his head and caught a glimpse of his body in the mirror. He was looking for the bruises that should be all over his body from the shots he had just taken from Jonathan. Not one anywhere, and not so much as a scratch. He knew that he had been hit multiple times because he had felt them when they landed. Opening the bathroom door, he walked back down the hallway to the kitchen and found Jonathan peeling potatoes in the sink.

"I have an odd question, but would you look at me?"

Jonathan set the peeler down and turned to look at Riley and paused a moment. "Okay. I give up . . . what am I looking at?"

"That's just it," Riley said. "When we sparred, you landed several good punches to the point where I lost track. I felt them land, and each one took the breath right out of me. So, why isn't there one mark on me? I thought you said I couldn't take on your skills for self-healing, or whatever you want to call them."

"This will sound strange to you—not that any of this isn't strange, but when I hit you, even though you may feel it, it isn't real. I told you, I cannot hurt you in any way. Not in training, not in anything. I'm here to do whatever I can to protect you."

Riley was bewildered, as he was with all the conversations he had with Jonathan. He looked down at his body again. "Strange," he said. "Really strange."

Not sure what else to say, Jonathan stood there like a huge kid waiting for permission to go back to peeling the potatoes. "However, I have noticed that your muscle tone is coming out quite nicely," he said, trying to make a joke.

Riley looked back at Jonathan. "So, you don't sweat or feel pain, and I can't hurt you at all."

"That's not completely true. Feelings . . . I do have those. I can feel emotional pain, especially when it comes to you and Allison. As for everything else, yes, you're correct." He looked at Riley to see if it was okay to continue. Riley nodded. "When I lost Allison, I felt just as you did, like someone had taken something from me that I would never get back. Even though she went to Heaven, it wasn't the same. I was with her when she was birthed into this world, and I watched her grow up before my eyes. When she died in that accident, it was like a father losing a child. That's why, when I look at you, I'm happy to have a piece of her left in this world. So yes, I do have feelings, and I care for you very much and will do anything in my power to help you."

Riley stood there with tears in his eyes and nodded once more. He understood it all now. He no longer looked at Jonathan as something, or someone, that screwed up. There was only so much he could do.

"Thank you," Riley said softly. "I appreciate you being around. This is getting a little easier for me, understanding it all." He wiped his eyes with the back of his hand. Wanting to change the subject, he cleared his throat. "So, how about lunch? What did you decide on?"

"I was going to go with steak, mashed potatoes, and green beans, unless you have something else in mind."

"Sounds perfect. I'll grab a shower and be right back to help you."

"Take your time," Jonathan replied, as he turned back to peeling the potatoes.

Watching the big man in his kitchen, performing such a simple task like peeling potatoes, made Riley smile. Knowing that Jonathan could do so much more in this world, but instead wanted to stay and help him through these trials, a thought started to creep in: What if Jonathan got injured or killed by one of these demons because he wasn't ready enough? This entire time, Jonathan kept making the trainings harder and more intense—what if he was thinking the same thing? Riley headed back down the hallway to the bathroom. "I need to go harder," he said to himself. "I can't lose someone else who's like family to me."

# CHAPTER 19

"They go through the same routines, day in and day out. Training, training, and more training," Cassandra said to Thomas and Bill.

The three of them were sitting at Luis's kitchen table. They had to give him credit; he had put up a good fight, but with a little luck they had prevailed. After all, they were only as strong as the bodies of their hosts: two out-of-shape older men and a woman who didn't look a day out of college.

They had buried Luis in an unmarked grave out back in the woods. Although they weren't sure about what they were going to do next, they knew one thing for sure: they weren't going back to Hell without as much fight as possible.

"Well, at least we know their routine," Bill said. His nose had been smashed, and both of his eyes were completely black and blue. Although the break-in had taken place over a week ago, he had a hard time bouncing back. Cassandra's ribs had been broken. Thomas's nose still sat to one side, even though they'd tried to reset it, and he still had various cuts and bruises across his face. All in all, they were a sad-looking group. However, taking over this lake house couldn't have come at a better time.

"So, what's the plan here?" Thomas asked. "Sooner or later we're going to have to make a move."

Bill, thinking hard, got up from his chair to get another cup of coffee. "I say we hit them tomorrow," he said. He filled his cup and added creamer.

Cassandra and Thomas sat there in silence.

"What? No objections?" Bill asked.

"It's got to happen sooner or later," Cassandra replied. "Do you have a plan? You can't just wait until the last moment to spring it on us."

Bill sat back down at the table. The three had done nothing but watch Riley and Jonathan, in shifts, never taking their eyes off them, so that they could find a time to catch them when they were least prepared. "Originally, I thought the best thing would be to catch them at night, right?" Bill said.

The other two simply nodded.

"Well, I say that's a mistake. When I've watched them at night, I can tell you that the fallen never sleeps. Doesn't even so much as close his eyes. He checks the perimeters, looks in on Riley from time to time, and all the while he's constantly on alert, waiting for something to happen. He probably has backup plans on top of backup plans. He's probably expecting an attack at night."

A gloomy look fell upon the faces of Cassandra and Thomas. "So, what do we do?" Cassandra asked as she sipped her water.

"There is a small window of opportunity," said Bill, "but we have to make sure everything is done right in order for any of us to have a chance at surviving and coming out of this victorious."

"Their morning runs!" Thomas blurted out. "We can set up in the high pines and cut them down when they're completely off guard."

"Hmm . . ." Cassandra replied. "That may very well be our best chance."

"Nope," was all Bill said.

"Okay, then tell us, because I'm obviously not as smart as you," Thomas said sarcastically.

"Here is what I propose," Bill replied. He pulled out a sheet of paper with notes he had been taking while watching Riley and the fallen. "We know what time they get started in the morning, when Riley goes to bed, and what their training looks like each day." He turned the sheet of paper over and revealed a map from Riley's house to the only grocery store on the lake.

"This is our best shot," Bill said, pointing at the grocery store on the map. "They usually go together, but lately the fallen has been letting Riley go alone to pick up supplies. I have no clue why, because that makes him more vulnerable to an attack. Now, the store itself isn't very large. There's two ways in: the front door for customers, and the back door that only the storekeeper himself uses. Two of us can get in the back door, no problem, and hide while the other one walks in and shoots the store clerk. We should probably do this late in the day because the human always makes his trip to the store toward closing time. Not once has he tried to go during the day while I've watched him, since the two are usually busy training. They only go to the store for supplies, or to pick up something to eat. In and out in less than ten minutes. So, like I said, we have to pull this off as flawlessly as possible." Bill leaned back in his chair. "I know it's not clear and easy, but I'm open to suggestions."

Cassandra looked hard at the map, and then at Thomas, and then back to Bill. "I don't know if it will work. It's a good plan on paper, but let me throw a few scenarios at you," she said. Bill nodded for her to continue. "Okay, for one, we take the store. However, we don't know what day the human is going to come to the store. So, what do we do—open up every day and run the store ourselves until he finally does show up? And let's say that we do manage to get the store, and Riley does come the very next day. What if he brings the fallen?"

"Then we're screwed," Thomas chimed in.

Bill shook his head. "I know it's not perfect, but here we are.

We have to do this job. As for the fallen, we knew we were going to have to go up against him sooner or later. I understand if you two have doubts, but this is what we've got so far. Lucifer wants us to take the fallen out as well, so I believe it would be smarter to do one at a time."

Thomas stood up from his chair and walked to the window of the kitchen and looked out. Taking in the view of the lake and the pines surrounding it, he noticed that some of the trees' leaves had turned brown and were starting to fall. As for the evergreens, they stayed true to their name. Thomas reminisced about his past life, how imperfect it had been, and the predicament he was now in. He turned around to see Cassandra and Bill talking over the map. Cassandra was shaking her head and Bill was trying to persuade her that it was a solid plan.

"Your plan sucks," Thomas said. "This whole predicament we're in sucks." Bill and Cassandra turned to look at him. "But it's manageable. Look at it this way, Cassandra. Nothing that we can plan or say will go perfectly, but at least this gives us the element of surprise. Let's do it, and if anyone comes by asking questions, we'll deal with them."

Cassandra sucked in a breath of air and blew it out through pursed lips. "Well then, I guess we're all in, so let's see how we're going to carry this out."

Thomas came back to the table and they started working on the details of the plan.

"Okay," Bill said. "I'll take the store owner out while you two slip in the back. We'll use the dead guy's truck, and when we get there we'll park it in the back. There are only a few windows that look out onto the parking lot. I won't use the gun—we don't want to cause any attention. Since we're hitting the place right before closing time, there shouldn't be anyone around. If there is, then I'll act like I'm looking around until they're gone. Once

I have taken control of the store, I'll let the two of you in. Then we wait."

---

It was nearly ten o'clock, and as Paul watched the street and the occasional vehicle that would pass by, he thought of the upcoming days. His grandchildren would be down and, despite the stiffness in his knees, he couldn't wait to get on the floor with them and love on them as much as possible. How he wished that his belated wife Misty was here to cherish these memories with him. Losing her to cancer over two years ago had almost driven him back to the drink, but he was sober for over twenty years now and found his new addiction to be his grandchildren. Now he went home to an empty house full of memories with his dog Hershey. The reason he spent all his time at the store these days was due to the loneliness the house offered.

Hershey, his chocolate lab, whined at his feet. Looking down at the sweet old dog, Paul spoke back to him. "Yes, my sweet Hershey kiss, I think you're right. Let me close up, and then we'll go home and I'll get you something to eat."

His constant loyal companion had turned into his shadow, following him everywhere he went. During the day he had to leave Hershey in the stock room, which is where he should be now, Paul thought, but for some odd reason he had made it from his bed in the stock room out here to the grocery floor. "Just how did you manage to do that? Don't tell me you can open doors now!" Just then, something in Paul's core started to give way to fear. Something was off, and his old friend had come to alert him.

Walking back behind the register with Hershey hot on his heels, Paul picked up the telephone just as a man with bruises under his eyes walked in. He smashed the storekeeper over the head with a dull object. The storekeeper fell to the floor. Before losing consciousness, Paul heard Hershey growl once and then go silent.

Bill quickly shut off the lights to the store and parking lot. Moving as quickly as he could, he locked the door and drew all the blinds. In the dark, he heard the man start to moan. Bill hit him hard again. The dog was not going to be a problem. He could still see its brown eyes looking at him with fear right before he cracked it hard with the butt of the gun. He hurried through the stock room and pushed open the back door to find Cassandra and Thomas waiting.

"We have to move fast," Bill said. "The store owner and his dog are out by the register. The dog is dead but not the owner." They all made their way to the front of the store. Cassandra scooped up the dog and headed back to the stock room. Bill and Thomas followed, carrying Paul's body at both ends.

"We'd better hope that Riley and that idiot fallen come soon, or this place is going to start to stink," Cassandra said.

"Never mind that," Bill hissed at her. "Toss the dog into the dumpster out back and put something over it so that it's not noticed too soon. Thomas, grab some rope. I need to finish the old man off."

"Here, use my gun. It's easier," Thomas replied.

"Yes, you fool, I realize that, but do you remember what I said about drawing attention to ourselves? You think a loud gunshot coming from inside the store is the best way to go about that?"

Shrugging, Thomas turned and headed back into the grocery area. Bill heard the store owner start to come around again.

"Please . . ." he mumbled. "I need to see my grandchildren one more time."

It was more than Bill could handle. Straddling the man's chest and closing his hands around the storekeeper's throat, he stared hard at him. "Yes, well, I want to stay out of Hell. So, see them in the next life," he said, and he squeezed. The man didn't struggle. As the light in his eyes went out, Thomas finally reappeared.

"Great, you found the rope," Bill said, looking up at him. "Took you long enough. Now go grab some heavy-duty trash bags so we can wrap him up."

With the two bodies taken care of, Bill looked around and did his best to clean up any evidence of their presence. He then walked to the back of the store where Thomas and Cassandra were. "Well, now we wait. So, let's get comfortable."

# CHAPTER 20

**W**inding the afternoon down with the bench press in the garage and listening to Jonathan shouting words of encouragement—"one more big push"— Riley racked the bar and felt his body relax after getting the extra weight off his arms. This routine felt good; it took him back to the days in high school when he had started lifting so that he could impress one of the cheerleaders—Allison, the girl he knew would be his future wife. Since he didn't play sports, he figured maybe a nice physique would help him build up the courage to talk to her.

Smiling to himself, he grabbed his towel and wiped the sweat off his brow. "Hey, I have an oddball question for you."

Jonathan, taking the weights off the bar and putting them up, responded with a shrug, as if to say *I know what you're going to ask, but go right ahead.*

"When I was in high school, I took up weight lifting to impress Allison. Do you think that was why she started talking to me, or was that when she finally noticed me? I mean, we didn't run with the same crowd. I was her parents' lawn boy, but we didn't talk. Plus, I always knew that she was out of my league. Since I didn't have anything going for me athletic-wise, I thought maybe my being in the gym was what caught her eye."

Jonathan racked the last plate on the small stand next to the bench press and started to laugh. "Riley, seriously, it had nothing to do with your wanting a buff physique."

Riley was a little taken aback. "Well, then, what was it?"

Jonathan held up his hand for the towel, and Riley pitched it to him. Taking the towel and putting it over his shoulder, he started for the garage door with Riley following along behind like a kid following his father around. Once they were in the cold air and walking toward the front of the house, Jonathan looked at Riley, who was now walking along beside him. "It was your nervousness that first caught her eye; had absolutely nothing to do with your body."

"My what?"

"Your nervousness."

They walked up the front steps and Jonathan opened the door for Riley. Once they were inside the house, Riley pressed Jonathan. "Yeah, I heard that part, but when did she see me nervous? We weren't in the same social groups until after we got together, and we only had one class together all throughout high school."

"It was your sophomore year. The two of you had biology together, and you had to give a speech about—"

"The Earth's crust," Riley interrupted.

"Yes," Jonathan said. "Now, for Allison, being in front of people and doing speeches came as easy as breathing air, but you found it nerve-racking. When you got up to give your speech, you tripped on someone's bag on the way to the front of the room. All the prepping that you'd been doing went right out the window and your speech . . . well, let's just say didn't go as intended. You just stood there, holding your notecards, basically reading them word for word and pointing to your illustrations at the wrong time. I was there, and it was hard to watch, but Allison, well, she sat there and just watched you. She was completely intrigued."

Riley flashed a huge smile, thinking back to that day. "I was shaking the whole time. I had a heck of a time just reading the stupid cards, and all I could think was 'Oh my God, why do I write so small? I can barely read this!'" He started to laugh.

Jonathan chuckled and shook his head.

"Just as well," Riley continued. "It wasn't a good day for me, but I guess God works in mysterious ways if that was the reason Allison and I finally got together."

"And just think," Jonathan said. "It all started with a little clumsiness on your part." He chuckled again.

It felt good, and Riley could feel himself starting to like his friend more and more with each passing day. "I'm going to get something for dinner at the store. Want to come?"

"No, you go ahead," Jonathan said, getting control of himself. "Just grab me whatever you're having. I'm going to walk the perimeter and see if I can see anything out of sorts."

This used to leave Riley on edge, but now it just rolled off his back. He pulled his fleece jacket over his workout shirt and grabbed the keys off the key holder. "Grilled chicken sandwiches it is. Be back in a few."

In the truck with the heat on high and driving down the road toward the store, Riley let the events of the afternoon play out in his thoughts. A few minutes later, he arrived in front of Paul's Grocery. Getting out of the truck, he grabbed his wallet out of the console and saw the pistol lying next to it. Jonathan had told him to always keep it on him when the two were apart, but he decided to leave it where it was. He had known Paul for most of his life and, besides, he would be in and out in just a few minutes. Walking up to the store, he got an uneasy feeling but pushed it aside. He could practically taste the grilled chicken sandwich.

Pushing the glass door open, Riley expected to see Paul standing behind the register as usual, but there wasn't anyone there. *Must be in the back, working on inventorying the shelves.* "Hey Paul, it's me, Riley. I was just going to see if I could get two grilled chicken sandwiches, fully loaded, and two large fries," he yelled to the back of the store.

When no response came, Riley grabbed a basket and made his way down one of the aisles to get some other things they needed. Browsing through the magazines before heading to the other side of the store to grab shells, he noticed blood on the floor. He looked up to see a man standing at the end of the aisle, holding a shotgun pointed directly at him. Unable to think or say anything, Riley instinctively dove behind the end of an aisle, feeling the gust from the pellets as they passed by him and plowed into the wall right behind him. "Oh my God, what the hell!" He shouted before another shot smashed into the wall.

---

Jonathan watched Riley drive down the path leading to the small two-lane road. As soon as he couldn't see the truck anymore, he proceeded down to the dock where the boathouse was to check the boat yet again.

He usually started the small boat's engine every day, as well as made sure it had all the necessities: first-aid kit, oars (in case the engine gave out), the hidden compartment stocked with ammo, and underneath the ice chest a small handgun that could be accessed quickly. The whole time they had been there, Jonathan's security measures had remained the same. He knew exactly how many feet it was to get from the house to the tree line that surrounded the property and knew the easiest path to stay on so that once inside the tree line Riley could disappear on his own, if necessary. Riley knew all of the security measures in place and had walked them countless times with Jonathan, both during the day and at night, since neither knew when Hell would come for them. Jonathan had made sure Riley knew every security measure to the letter, along with all the what-if scenarios. He knew Riley found it taxing to hear Jonathan repeat himself, but Riley had learned this was what his life had become.

After looking over the boathouse, Jonathan headed up the path to walk the perimeter of the tree line, checking for anything that could be out of the ordinary, like foot tracks or even a scent of something in the air. Suddenly, Jonathan started to get a disturbing feeling in the pit of his stomach. Something wasn't right. Although Riley had only been gone maybe ten minutes, something seemed out of sorts.

Closing his eyes and focusing his senses on Riley, Jonathan detected gunfire in the distance. Focusing harder, he could sense his friend panicking for his life. Clearing his mind and taking in his surroundings, his keen sense of smell picked up the unmistakable scent of death in the air. The demons had found them—there were three of them now closing in on his friend. Jonathan's eyes opened at once to the sound of the lake lapping at the banks, the birds flying overhead, and the wind pushing up against the trees. It all played against what sounded like thunder in his head. With a feeling of helplessness coming over him, Jonathan mustered up one word.

"Riley!"

The firing had stopped. There had only been three blasts, and Riley knew there was at least one more in the shotgun. He had quickly figured out what was going on when the first shot was fired. They had been found. He had no idea how many he was up against or what to do next. Jonathan had told him to always carry the handgun on him. Now he cursed himself for not listening to the constant reminders of what he needed to do to ensure his own safety. The first hundred times were enough for anyone to have let it sink in, but lately it was like blah, blah, blah, do this, and remember to do that. He had let himself become placid, and now he would end up dying because of his stupidity.

*No! I will not go down this way. I will survive.* Unfortunately, all he had was the small basket he was clutching to his chest. Trying to make a run for the front door to get to his vehicle for protection was not an option. He peeked around the corner of the shelves. There was a woman standing at the front by the door. There was no way to get around her. He needed a diversion.

Suddenly, another shot hit the wall and then there were more voices, men's voices.

"You have him pinned down; he's not going anywhere."

"Do you know if he's carrying?"

"Better not assume anything. Let's take this slow—us three against him—we should be able to do this without a hitch."

"Just like you planned."

Riley's mind raced, matching his heart racing inside his chest. He had just one thought—what the hell should he do next? There were three of them. Even if it was just hand-to-hand combat, he didn't think he would come out of this alive. The only thing he could do was outsmart them. His only advantage was that they weren't sure whether he had a gun.

"Listen," Riley called out, "I don't know what you want, but if you so much as peek your heads around the corner, I'll have no problem blowing them off."

"Oh, yeah? If you're packing, then why haven't you opened fire?"

"I've got six shots and I will make them count! You don't believe me, just keep on coming down the aisle. I'll make you a believer!" Another shot hit the edge of the shelving that Riley's back was pressed up against. He almost pissed himself. He quickly looked around. Just four feet away from where he was crouched, there was a collection of do-it-yourself books and magazines for house repairs. Next to that were hammers, glue guns, staple guns, and a few axe handles, but no blades. Nothing he could use as a weapon. *What am I going to do, staple their eyes shut? Hot glue their hands together and then beat them with an axe handle?*

He had to think fast to stay alive. He knew Jonathan could read his mind when they were together. Did he know Riley was in trouble? Could he have picked up on the gunfire? He hadn't been gone long. How long would it take before Jonathan would be worried about Riley not coming back? He knew he didn't have time to wait for Jonathan to rescue him. He reached for one of the axe handles and pulled it to him as fast as he could. Another shot hit close to where he was.

"Would you quit firing that thing!" one of the men growled. "I'm trying to see if I can get a better view, but every freaking time it goes off I think I've just been shot. So, cut it the hell out!"

"Well, then, move your ass!" the woman snarled back. "Who knows how much time we have until someone shows up!"

"Quiet, the both of you!" the other male said. "He's not deaf."

Riley cautiously peeked around the corner and saw a man not ten steps from him, crouched down and coming toward him. He jerked his head back, hoping he hadn't been seen. He felt the shelving he was pressed up against shift against his body weight. They were made of wood and weren't the sturdiest; each was approximately twenty-five feet long. Each section was about five feet wide and almost six feet tall. Paul likely made them himself when he first opened the store years ago. Riley considered trying to heave one over on the guy coming down the aisle, and then try to maneuver behind another one before being picked off, but it was risky. But risky or not, it could give him a little more time until Jonathan could get there—that is, if he was even coming.

Thinking no more of the argument playing out in his head, Riley pushed as hard as he could. To his relief, both the shelf and its contents started to lean, and then fell all at once.

Riley made a rush to his right to get behind the next shelf. A shotgun blast and two pistols went off, almost simultaneously. One shot went right over the top of Riley's head. The shotgun blast sprayed the wall, yet again. The guy in the aisle managed a shot just as the shelf fell over on him.

The bullet caught Riley right in his side.

Tucked behind the next shelving unit, Riley cried out in pain when he reached down and touched the fresh wound. The blood was almost black and was spilling out of him and onto his shorts. He felt himself slide to the floor. Everything around him grew dark. He wanted to close his eyes. He could feel his legs sprawling out in front of him. Fear coursed through him as he realized he was becoming an easy target. More shots were going off all around him. He heard the splintering of wood, the breaking of glass, voices in the background yelling out—then nothing. Pure blackness crept in. It grew quiet. There was no smell of gun powder. There was no pain. Nothing seemed to exist anymore.

# CHAPTER 21

The darkness of the room seemed to amplify the somber mood as Jonathan sat looking over his friend while the doctor worked on him. Riley was practically on death's doorstep. The bullet had hit him in the abdomen; the loss of blood was the most dangerous part. The bullet had missed his kidney by a hair. Had it hit the kidney, he would have bled internally and died within an hour.

The man was the local doctor in the nearby town and the only one who still did house calls. His name was Josh Hardin. He appeared to be in his late fifties and knew quite a bit about the town and all its inhabitants. He'd had no problem finding Riley's lake house. He had thinning gray hair and slightly shaky hands which would make one question his ability to operate. He didn't treat gunshot wounds very often. However, as soon as he started working on Riley, his hands were steady and true as he asked Jonathan question after question, staying calm despite the intensity of what was happening. Dr. Hardin worked swiftly, cleaning the wound with warm water. Then he stuck Riley with a needle in different areas around the wound. Jonathan did his best to answer the doctor's onslaught of questions while keeping his eyes on every movement the doctor made.

Dr. Hardin was in the middle of putting the stitches in when he finally looked up at Jonathan. "I'll have to report this, you know. I imagine it has something to do with what went down in the grocery store earlier tonight. Why didn't you take him to a hospital to get treated? There's one not far from here that would be better equipped to treat him."

"I know, but I need you to understand that this situation requires special circumstances," Jonathan answered quickly.

"I've known Riley since he was born," the doctor said, ignoring Jonathan's comment. "I actually assisted in his birth. I treated every scrape and every sniffle when he was growing up, so to be working on him when he's in this kind of shape gives me pause about you, big fella."

Jonathan hadn't considered that, being in a small town, everyone probably knew everyone—and their business. He sat there, not sure how to answer.

"Tell you what," the doctor said, not taking his eyes off Jonathan. "While you think of a story, why don't you put the coffee on. This is going to be a long night, so leave for now. If you tell me the truth, then I'm sure I can make this all go away; but if you don't, then I will report it." He then returned his attention to Riley.

Still sitting there looking at Riley, Jonathan wasn't sure he should leave his side. "Well, I, ah . . ."

"I take my coffee black," the doc interrupted. "I will meet you in the kitchen as soon as I finish up."

Jonathan, still not moving, stared at Riley. His face was pale from the loss of blood and had an absolutely helpless expression written on it. He started to wish he could do more for his friend.

"I said to leave," Dr. Hardin said, interrupting his thoughts. His voice grew harsher. "It's not a request!"

Taken aback, Jonathan stared hard at the doctor, but Dr. Hardin just stared right back, not giving an inch. Jonathan got to his feet and, saying no more, walked to the bedroom door and left the room. Once the door was closed behind him, he paused. He could hear the doctor's voice. "Riley, this is no worse than the time you broke your wrist on that bike and I set it back in place. You're going to be down for a little bit, but you'll bounce back from this stronger than before."

Jonathan moved away from the door and headed to the kitchen. He opened the cabinets, pulled out the coffee, and started the coffee maker. He placed two coffee cups next to the coffee maker. Yet again, a feeling of helplessness came over him. His friend, his most precious thing in this world, was lying in the next room getting patched up from a gunshot wound, and he was standing here making coffee.

Jonathan sat down at the kitchen table and went over the events that had happened merely an hour before. He had been in the yard checking the perimeters when the feeling that something was wrong had hit him hard. He'd turned his senses way up and focused only on Riley. The sound of gunfire had broken his senses. The first shot had put his feet in motion and, what seemed like just moments later, he had reached the grocery store and discovered that demons had overtaken three human bodies. The first had been a woman reloading a shotgun, the second a man pinned under an overturned shelf. The third, an older guy, had not been ten feet away from him and had had a gun pointed at Riley, who had been hunkered down at the end of an aisle.

In a flash, all of Jonathan's abilities had sprung into action. He'd grabbed the guy with the gun, who'd had his back turned to Jonathan. With a quick jerk of his hands, Jonathan had snapped the man's neck. Before the body had hit the floor, he'd been upon the younger woman, slamming her hard into the wall. He'd grabbed her shotgun and had snapped it like a twig. He'd ended her with a quick snap of her neck. Jonathan had gone over to where the other guy was crawling out from under the overturned shelf. With one hard punch, he'd delivered a blow to the man's face that had crushed the skull upon impact. The body had fallen dead to the floor.

Jonathan did not take comfort in committing violent acts but had known it must be done in order to send the demons who'd overtaken these human bodies back where they came from. The demons inside each of the overtaken bodies had let out horrific screams as they began to emerge, only to be sucked into a black hole that appeared in the floor. The hole then had sealed itself up, leaving no trace behind. He would have to deal with the overtaken bodies later.

Jonathan had gone to Riley's side as he'd lain limp against a shelf. Jonathan had picked him up and gotten him back to the lake house. He'd gently placed Riley on the bed and then had gone through the contact list in Riley's phone to see if it listed a doctor, but had found nothing. Then he'd remembered the notepad on the wall in the kitchen. He'd seen various notes and phone numbers scribbled on it. He'd raced to the kitchen and pulled the notepad off the wall, flipping through the pages. He had been relieved to find the name Josh Hardin M.D. with a phone number. He'd said a prayer of thanks, then had punched the number into Riley's phone and placed the call. Not twenty minutes later, Dr. Hardin had been standing over Riley, taking care of him.

Jonathan now rested his face in his hands. "God, please give him strength, and help me know what to do."

"I hope you have a better answer for me than that."

Jonathan looked up and saw the doctor standing in the doorway of the kitchen with a hard look on his face. The man was five foot ten inches tall and heavyset. The wrinkles on his face made him look more like an outdoorsman than a doctor who spent his hours in hospitals saving lives. He wore blue jeans and a polo shirt, tucked in, with a pair of tennis shoes. Dropping his medical bag, he stared at Jonathan without saying anything. He looked at him as if he knew they were partners in some crime. In truth, Jonathan was to blame for all that had happened.

"Let me get you some coffee," Jonathan said, standing up. "I do have an explanation for all of this." With that, Jonathan turned and walked to the counter to pour the coffee. When he turned back around, he found Dr. Hardin right behind him.

The doctor didn't back away even an inch. "That boy in there means the world to me. I knew his family very well, and I also knew his Allison. I don't know who the hell you are, but you need to leave."

Jonathan opened his mouth to speak, but the older man poked his finger right in his chest several times. "*I said leave!*"

Jonathan blurted back, "*No!*"

The two men locked eyes, waiting for the other to make a move. "I can explain all of this if you will just listen," Jonathan said, calming his voice. "I will tell you everything, and I won't lie to you because . . . I can't lie to you."

Dr. Hardin stared intensely at the big man.

Jonathan offered him a cup, and after holding it out for a long moment, realized he was not interested in it. He started to put the cup back on the counter, but the doctor jerked it out of his hand, spilling most of it on the floor. He then moved to the table and sat down. "I'm waiting," he said.

Jonathan sat down across from him. "I will tell you the absolute truth. However, if I were in your shoes, I would be just as skeptical about what I'm about to tell you. I just ask for you not to interrupt until I'm finished."

The older man took a napkin out of the holder on the table and wiped his hands of the coffee he'd spilled.

"To start things off," Jonathan said, "I'm an angel."

Dr. Hardin reached inside his pants pocket, pulled out his

phone, and started to dial. Knowing where this was heading, Jonathan snatched the phone so quickly the doctor didn't even realize it was gone until he went to press the call button. In a flash, Jonathan wiped up the spilled coffee and filled the doctor's coffee cup as the older man looked down to see if he had dropped it. He then looked back to Jonathan who was holding the phone in his hand.

"Like I said, please give me time to finish what I'm telling you," Jonathan continued. "I know that you will have questions, but calling the police is not going to help either of us. I cannot lie to you because it's forbidden by God."

Dr. Hardin just sat there, flabbergasted. Jonathan returned the cell phone to his hand. Astonished, he dropped it on the table and looked at Jonathan, his face growing white. "What the . . . "

"Please don't swear," Jonathan said gently. "It, well, it doesn't sit right with me."

The older man just stared wide-eyed at Jonathan.

"I will not harm you. I'm in your debt for helping Riley, but please, let me continue now."

Dr. Hardin didn't say a word, just simply reached down for his coffee cup and saw that it was full. He looked disbelievingly at Jonathan who placed his hand on the doctor's, sending out peace to calm him. The heart that was once racing now began to calm, and he understood that what Jonathan was about to tell him would, indeed, be true.

As Jonathan took his hand off the older man's, he looked up at Jonathan. "How . . . I mean, what are you?"

Jonathan started at the beginning, telling Dr. Hardin about his assignment to watch over Allison from the first moment she entered the world and explained everything that had happened up until this point. The doctor listened intently, taking it all in, with question after question beginning to overflow inside him.

Two pots of coffee later, Dr. Hardin leaned back in his chair, amazed by all that he'd been told. He blew out a long breath then waited, trying to gather his thoughts. "Good thing I didn't try to take a swing at you, huh?"

Jonathan smiled. "I don't know, you look like you could've taken me apart piece by piece."

Dr. Hardin began to chuckle. "I can't say I understand everything you've just told me, and I do have lots of questions, but I guess maybe what I'd like to know first is—do you know my guardian?"

Jonathan had sensed he would be curious. He looked at Dr. Hardin for a moment before responding. "Yes."

The doctor smiled. "So, how come you don't all come out of the woodwork and help us out more?"

"It's God's will for us to stay behind the scenes," Jonathan replied. "We do it each day—not as dramatic as coming to Earth and working side by side with our humans, but by doing simple things like calming nerves when rough times come or providing a sense of assurance when life seems to be too much. I know your next question is probably going to be, 'Wouldn't it be easier if we were always around?' And my answer to that is that life is not supposed to be easy, it's supposed to be beautiful, but with trials. It can be triumphant based on the decisions one makes. It's called free will, and it's one of the greatest gifts that God gave humans."

The doctor smiled at Jonathan, amazed at everything he'd just been told.

Jonathan wanted to know about Riley and was just about to ask when Dr. Hardin interrupted. "Last one, I promise, big fella, and then I'm done."

"Please, go ahead," Jonathan said, knowing the man had lots of questions building inside of him.

"It's simple, I promise, and I won't follow up with anything else."

Jonathan nodded.

"My guardian . . . I would like to know his, or her, name so that I can thank God in my prayers for what he, or she, has done for me. I've lived a wild life and have had a lot of close calls. I'm often shocked that I'm still alive."

This time Jonathan couldn't help but smile. Of all the questions that he could have asked, he wanted to know the name of his guardian. Hearing his thoughts throughout the whole conversation, there was no way to know which one he would ask, since he jumped from one to the other. Reaching across the table and taking the doctor's hand in his, Jonathan sent peace to him yet again. "Your guardian's name is Leeann, and she loves you very much."

Dr. Hardin closed his eyes, said a quiet thank you, and a small tear started down his cheek. With that, Jonathan released his hand and gathered up the two cups on the table. After placing them in the sink and rinsing them both out, he turned to see the doctor watching him. Jonathan didn't want to ruin the moment, but he needed to know how Riley was doing. However, this time it was the doctor who could read minds.

"Riley is fine. Do you think I would have let you tell me a story if he was in any kind of immediate danger?"

Chuckling, Jonathan shook his head. "I suppose not."

"The bullet went in and out without causing too much damage. I don't see a lot of gunshot wounds, but if there is a place to be shot, then that's it. Any further in the middle and he would have died in the store."

Jonathan whispered another thank you to God.

"Figured one of your gifts would be to heal someone."

Jonathan smiled. "You would think so, but unfortunately that is one thing I can't or, I should say, won't do, because of what could happen." He could hear the next questions coming into Dr. Hardin's mind. "If I heal someone, a piece of me goes into that person, and they could end up living hundreds of years—or more. Or some of my attributes might transfer to them. Not knowing how to properly use them, they could end up hurting themselves or someone else."

"Big fella, I'm afraid if I hear any more, my head might explode. This is far too much to take on in one night."

"I completely understand," Jonathan replied.

"I have some antibiotics that I'm going to leave you. They will help with the recovery. As for pain medicine, give him ibuprofen, but if it gets to be too much pain, then give me a call and I'll write him another prescription. I'll check on him in a week. Oh, and as for the police, don't worry. I'm not going to report it," he said with a smile.

With that, Jonathan walked over to the man and offered him his hand, but Dr. Hardin gave him a hug. "You call me if you need anything. I'll do everything I can to help you." He then picked up his bag and walked out the front door and into the cold night.

After the door was shut, Jonathan was taken aback by the man's kindness and warmth toward him. He realized that no matter how big he was, or how powerful he may seem, he had just learned his place when dealing with Dr. Josh Hardin. A smile spread across his face.

# CHAPTER 22

T he room had arched ceilings, stained hardwood floors, a fireplace at one end, and a long throw rug with a strange star on it, and beautiful leather furniture. Thousands of portraits displaying gruesome scenes lined the walls. Cassandra, Bill, and Thomas found themselves dumped here, pulled back into Hell once their mortal bodies had been fatally wounded. Lucifer and Legionaries were in the room with them. They had been expecting them.

"Six of them were let out," Lucifer said as he looked at the three standing before him. "Or am I missing something here, Legionaries? One failed to overtake a body and immediately resumed its place in the pits. I banished another for acting like a little shit. Now I see just three before me. Where is the fourth?"

"Master, the fourth—Jason—he . . ." Cassandra interrupted.

Lucifer backhanded her and grabbed her by the throat, pulling her toward him as a predator pulling its prey. He snarled. "Don't ever interrupt me, do you understand that? Not ever." He pushed her to the floor, and blood began to spill from her smashed nose. She grasped her nose and fought back her pain, daring not to make a sound as she tried to struggle to her feet.

Thomas and Bill stood there, doing nothing. They knew their place and feared being subjected to the same discipline. Legionaries stood by looking at Lucifer, not knowing what he should do. Lucifer took a seat in one of the leather chairs and leaned back to ponder what he should do next. He began to chuckle, and then it turned into a full-blown hysterical, maniacal laugh. Legionaries had first seen his Master do this as the hounds ripped his mortal body apart.

Finally, Lucifer controlled himself and directed Cassandra, Bill, and Thomas to take a seat. They positioned themselves on the couch across from him. Legionaries took a seat to the right of Lucifer, as if to position himself as far away as he could from the three that had failed in their task.

"Well done to each of you," Lucifer said as the three looked nervously at one another. "I could not have asked more from you. I didn't think any of you would have a chance at pulling it off, but for the most part you have made your Master very, very pleased. The bar was set high. I, for one, will be the first to admit this, but each of you should be happy—I would say even more than happy, with your efforts."

Legionaries started to relax, feeling he was owed some credit. However, he sat there with a stern face making sure he didn't overstep. Cassandra, Bill, and Thomas sat dumbfounded. Could this really be happening? Did they really go above and beyond even though they didn't manage to bring the fallen, and the mortal, down?

"Cassandra, or I should say Tricia, as you were known in your past life, you should know better than to ever interrupt me. After all, you have been in Hell for over seventy years. But what you have proven to me on this task is that you are reliable and persistent, whereas in your past life you were an addict and prostitute who would steal and hurt anyone to get what you wanted.

"Now, Bill and Thomas, or shall I say, Jake and Greg, as you were known in your previous lives. Jake, you were the brains of the outfit and did a fine job getting your two companions to work as a team. I really didn't see that one coming since you used to be a rapist with only one thought—where you would get your next prey. Now, as for you, Greg, I really thought you would have jumped ship right off the bat. After all, you did kill your family and then yourself when life got too rough for you. However, the three of you complied with my wishes as a single unit. Each of you helped play a vital part in wounding the mortal."

The three felt completely exposed now that they had just had their past brought back to life. Each had the same question on the tip of their tongue: *What would happen to them now?* However, they dared not ask. They were promised, if they succeeded, that they could stay in the house with Master; but they didn't exactly succeed.

"Now, I know each of you wants to ask me the same question," Lucifer said. "I can hear everything going on in your heads." He placed his hands in his lap and then crossed one leg over the other. "You are the only three to survive long enough to go on the expedition to find the mortal and his fallen. You methodically and carefully laid out a plan. But when it came to completing the deed, you fell short."

Legionaries already knew where this was heading and had a hard time looking at the three. Just moments earlier they were under the illusion that, by some miracle, they would actually be free from the eternal tortures of Hell and would be able to come and go as they pleased in the household of their Master.

He looked at the rug that was stretched out before them. What a strange-looking rug. He'd never quite noticed it before. It was deep blue, the color of the night sky just after the sun falls below the horizon and the stars begin to emerge. As he looked closer, he could see one star in the center of the rug. It began to sparkle and then it slowly began to move from its position. Legionaries's focus was so strong that he no longer heard what Master was saying. Everything fell silent. He needed to touch the star, to feel it, to let the beams shoot out all around him.

The room disappeared. Master disappeared. The three souls disappeared. All that was left was one beam of light, filling up everything around Legionaries. A voice from within the star started to speak to him.

"Legionaries, you are more than what you appear."

"What do you mean?" asked Legionaries. "What do you mean?" he said louder, as he leaned toward the beam of light. He could feel the pressure of a hand gripping his shoulder. The star made a crackling sound. It was the most breathtaking thing he had ever experienced.

"Magnificent!" he said to himself. He reached out for it, but it was just beyond his fingertips. He continued to reach until, suddenly, something stabbed him in his side. It stabbed him again and again, but he would not allow it to distract him.

The star pulled away from Legionaries. He tried to run toward it but couldn't move. Something was holding him back. He felt himself burning with pain, but he accepted it. He would use it. He could feel himself losing control. It had been so long since he had felt a release. He continued to stare at the star as it pulled further away from him. Suddenly, everything went black as a mighty roar overtook him.

"You just placed your hands on the wrong God, you piece of filth!"

Legionaries saw his Master standing in front of him, blood spilling from his mouth. At once he felt his knees buckle. Looking down at his hands, he saw the blood on his knuckles. He closed his eyes. The hand he'd felt was Lucifer's, trying to pull him up off the rug. Legionaries had looked like a damn fool, lying there facedown on the carpet. He had thrown the hand off, knocking Master back into his chair. He called for the hounds, who jumped on Legionaries and bit and tore at him, his sides, his face, legs, even his groin.

This time Legionaries had fought back, snapping the necks of two of the hounds, ripping another in half, and tearing the spine from another. Lucifer then ordered the three damned souls to attack. Reluctant as they were, they did so, but one by one, Legionaries fought back, smashing their faces in with blow after blow.

Now he was left to face off with Master himself. With one violent blow he struck and knocked Lucifer against the wall. He stood face to face with Lucifer, who was staring at him through black eyes. The three damned lay at his feet, their faces starting to slowly morph back into shape. The hounds were also coming back to life, their forms coming together.

"I'm going to put you in the depths of Hell and enjoy listening to your screams," Lucifer hissed at Legionaries. At once, Master pounced upon him, holding his throat with one hand, strangling the life out of him, as the other came down on him like a hammer, releasing one blow after another.

"The star, the star made me do it!" Legionaries gasped. "It pulled me in!"

Lucifer continued to deliver blow after blow. Then, suddenly, he climbed off Legionaries. "Come with me!" he ordered, then grabbed Legionaries and dragged him out of the room and down the hall to the front door that led to the entrance of Hell. Once there, Lucifer pulled open the door and began dragging Legionaries down the narrow staircase to the pits. The walls on either side of the staircase immediately came to life, throbbing and pulsing under the force of untold numbers of faces of the damned, all begging and screaming to be let out. Lucifer ignored them as he cursed at Legionaries for daring to strike him.

They journeyed farther and farther down the staircase. They were reaching the point Legionaries had never gone before. The damned continued screaming to be released. Blood ran down his ears, and Legionaries was too terrified to imagine what was coming next. Lucifer stopped and reared his head—the head of a giant beast—at Legionaries. "You are in the depths of Hell," Lucifer snarled, "right where I want you, and where you will remain for the rest of eternity!" His was the voice of pure madness.

"Please, Master, I would never do anything to hurt you. I only wanted to help and protect you," Legionaries begged. He watched in horror as Lucifer's body continued to morph into a beast, his hands and feet becoming hooves.

Legionaries tried to turn away. Lucifer pushed him, sending him into the wall, a place he hadn't been for a thousand years. At once he was attacked by the damned on the other side of the wall. Teeth clutched at and then sank deep into his neck. The beast pulled back, holding a hunk of Legionaries' neck in its mouth. Countless of the damned tore at Legionaries as he screamed out in terror. Suddenly, his body burst into flames as his flesh was torn apart. Legionaries knew he was now truly trapped. There would be no more second chances.

The beast, Lucifer, stood grinning at Legionaries, watching, then laughing. Legionaries reached out to him, begging for forgiveness. Lucifer, now satisfied, turned and walked back up the stairs, touching the walls and caressing the faces of the damned.

---

After returning to his lavish surroundings, Lucifer assumed his human form once more. He stood before a full-length mirror on the wall, seeing his complexion for the first time since the whole ordeal. The red smudge where blood had dried below his lip caught him completely off guard. He leaned toward the mirror to get a better look and realized that Legionaries had actually caused him to bleed. This had never happened before.

He had felt the blow, yes, but to actually have been cut, and in front of these three lackeys whom he had sent out on a mission that he knew they would certainly fail! This could very well cause a problem. If the three started to whisper to others that their Master himself could be caused to bleed . . . maybe he should go and get Legionaries out of the pits of Hell so that he, too, wouldn't begin to whisper.

Then another feeling started to overcome him. If Legionaries could be controlled, maybe he could bring down the fallen and the mortal. After all, he had caused Lucifer to bleed, which he'd always thought impossible.

"Where do I go from here?" Lucifer asked his reflection in the mirror before being interrupted by a sound in the hall. Wiping his lip with the back of his hand, he gave himself one more quick look in the mirror and then walked out to the hall to see Tricia standing there with an odd look on her face.

"Master, um . . . are you okay?"

In an instant Lucifer knew he was right—she knew, which meant the others knew. Word was out that Legionaries had gotten the better of him. There was only one thing left to do. Smiling at her, he walked over to Tricia and put both hands on her shoulders. "Everything is fine now. Legionaries simply lost his mind, and I have dealt with him accordingly. Let's resume our talk with the other two back in the living room, shall we?" He wrapped his arm around her waist and guided her back to where Jake and Greg were already waiting.

"Not to worry," Lucifer said. "Everything has been taken care of. I would like to pick up where we left off." After everyone was seated again, Lucifer continued as if nothing had happened. "As I was saying . . . although you weren't able to complete the job, I was impressed with how well each of you had

done. Let me tell you what I am going to give you." He paused
a moment, enjoying watching the three of them shift about
nervously. "None of you will ever go back to Hell."

The three wanted to cry out with joy from the news that they
would never have to be unwilling participants of Hell. Almost as
if they had accomplished the task that they never quite fulfilled
and would still receive the benefits as if they had.

"I thought that might please each of you," Lucifer said, a
smile also crossing his face. "Excuse me for just a moment. I will
be right back." He stood up and exited the room through the
door that he and Tricia had just come through.

Once he was gone and his footsteps could no longer be heard,
the three exchanged glances, and each of them started to cry out
with joy. Who cared at this point if they could be heard? They
were finally going to be granted the closest thing to freedom that
any of them could ever have. When they heard their Master's
footsteps coming down the hall again, they quickly regained their
composure. As Lucifer walked back into the room, they saw that
he was carrying three large sterling silver boxes. He placed them
one by one in front of Tricia, Jake, and Greg on the coffee table.
Then he took his seat again and smiled.

"Inside each of these boxes is your freedom—freedom to walk
among these halls with me as equals. You may even spend a little
time on Earth as well, without having to take a soul or fear being
pulled back to Hell. I am so grateful for what each of you have
done. So, please, open your boxes, and afterward I will embrace
each of you as equals."

The three sat there, completely stunned at what they had just
been told. They sat wide-eyed, staring at Master, not knowing
what to say or what to do, except to open their boxes. Could this
really be true? They could come and go as they pleased, roam

around the house, or even walk right into the world that they once knew and view things as they once did?

Lucifer watched the three and leaned back in his chair. He then called one of his hounds to his side and stroked the massive animal's head, rubbing his hand over the muscular body. The hound never took its eyes off Lucifer, giving him a dead, icy glare, as if it would rather be chewing on him. This once annoyed Lucifer but he'd come to accept it, given the hounds would do nothing but protect him and help to strike fear into any who would try to challenge him.

Jake reached for his box first while the other two watched. He closed his eyes for a moment then proceeded to open the box. Taking the lid in one hand, he looked into the box to find a necklace with a small square charm. It was absolutely beautiful in its simplicity. He thought it must represent freedom. It had been such a bizarre journey that had led him here. Although he had failed in his mission, here he was, being rewarded for his efforts. He wasn't going to question it; he did the job to the best of the capabilities that he had been given, and he deserved this. Tricia and Greg opened their boxes as well and were each holding their necklaces. Then they held their necklaces inches from their faces, admiring what they had been given.

"Look at the inscription inside the amulet," Lucifer said, breaking the silence in the room.

The three placed their boxes on the floor, on top of the blue rug, and opened their amulets, looking hard to find the inscription.

Tricia, finding it first, said, "Oh, I see something." She squinted harder. Inside her square amulet she saw not just an inscription, but something was moving. It appeared inside the amulet, a view of what her life could have been if she'd never gotten hooked on drugs. She could see that instead of falling in love with the man who eventually would get her to try heroin, only to leave her strung out and fending for herself, if they would each have gone down different paths. Her life would have been a blessing, with a man who loved her and children she adored. She would have lived a long, happy life instead of overdosing at such an early age. Tricia wanted that ever so badly, and she looked harder and harder into the little square, tears rolling down her face as she saw what could have been.

Greg's amulet also revealed what his life could have been like. Instead of being overworked and pressured by everything that life threw at him—to the point where he took the lives of his wife and two children and then turned the gun on himself—he now saw flashes of what his life could have been: watching his two sons grow up, making him a granddad, and how much he and his wife loved one another and their life together.

Jake's amulet showed him that, instead of being bounced around from foster home to foster home, where he was molested by the people who were supposed to take care of him and growing up to become a rapist—he could have been raised by an elderly couple that had met too late in their lives to have children of their own. They would have loved Jake wholeheartedly and given him a wonderful life.

The three damned souls, who had been sitting next to one another across from the one they were forced to call Master, now found themselves looking out at the room as Lucifer sat admiring his work. Each of them were frozen in time, trapped inside a frame on the wall. The lives they'd seen in their amulets were merely illusions. They would never have those lives.

Finally, he spoke to them. "Absolutely magnificent, isn't it?"

Tricia looked down at herself, inside the frame that was now her new world, and saw a needle stuck in her arm. Jerking it out, she cried out in pain as yet another one was inserted into her arm. She pulled it out, and immediately another one was pushed into her arm, and the process continued, over and over. She began frantically screaming and begging for it to end.

Greg found himself looking out at Lucifer as well. He could hear voices behind him, calling to him, but it was impossible for him to move. The voices grew louder. He recognized them— they were the voices of his family. He looked down and saw his two young sons peering up at him. "Hello, Father," they said in unison, sounding like something from a horror movie. Greg felt a shiver run up his spine. His mouth opened, but nothing came out; he was just pinned there in the frame, looking down at his two boys.

Meanwhile, Jake was trapped in a frame on the wall across the room, watching everything taking place, knowing he was next. He looked down and saw his ten-year-old body. He heard someone coming up the stairs—it was his first foster parent. Jake closed his eyes as he heard the door open. Then he felt a hand on his shoulder. "You should be in bed. What are you still doing up?" And with that, the man picked him up and placed him in bed. The strong smell of liquor on his foster dad's breath lay heavily in the air. "I'll just lie here with you for a little bit until you fall asleep."

Tears welled up in Jake's eyes, for he knew what happened next would lay the path for the rest of his life, where he sought out innocent women and forced them to do things they didn't want to do.

"Perfect," Lucifer said to himself. "Three more for my walls, and they are absolutely breathtaking. Couldn't have picked a better spot for them." Running his hand down the hound one more time, he stood to his feet. "It's time I dealt with the fourth one who is out there undermining me. I must say, this last one does intrigue me a little."

Lucifer walked out to the hallway leading to the back door of the house. Several of the hounds emerged from different rooms and followed him. He stopped and turned to find six hounds standing there, as if waiting for instructions. He smiled at them.

"Let's not rush to judgment, shall we? I will let you pick his bones dry, but first I want to speak with him and find out exactly what he is doing. Of course, he will fail once he feels my wrath. When he does, I want each of you to see to it that you take your time when you rip him limb from limb. And remember: don't go for the throat at once. I'd rather hear them scream for mercy!"

With that, Lucifer rubbed the head of each hound, then turned and opened the door. He walked through it and found himself standing in front of a hotel bar in the middle of the night. "Just as I expected—the little maggot is drinking on my dime, trying to lure a female into his bed. Or was he into males? Legionaries should be here. I don't enjoy trying to keep up with all of this."

He thought of Legionaries and the last he saw of him: screaming and crying and begging. Lucifer had enjoyed watching him going mad and then lashing out at others. Smiling again, he strolled toward the bar with a new gleam in his eye.

# CHAPTER 23

"C oming," Jonathan said in response to a knock at the door. He had just gotten off the phone with Dr. Hardin to give him a progress report on Riley. The doctor assured him that everything was okay. Thankfully, Riley's wound to the abdomen was healing well. He wondered who could be at the door. He didn't sense a threat but was prepared for the worst. Throughout these past five weeks at the cabin, he had only met Luis and Dr. Hardin. It was nice and peaceful, and people seemed to keep to themselves.

Luis was supposed to have stopped by, but he never did, which gave Jonathan pause. But Riley had reminded him that Luis was planning to be gone for a month or so and probably just got tied up preparing for his trip. Reaching the door, he peered through the peep hole. Jonathan stopped dead in his tracks. Two men from the sheriff's department were standing outside the door. Jonathan scolded himself—he had become too relaxed; his senses had gone soft. If he hadn't dropped his guard, he would have heard them as soon as they started down the driveway and could have prepared himself.

Had they found something at the grocery store that led them back to the lake house? Jonathan had gone back to clean up the blood from where Riley had lain after he was shot. He had been so thorough it would have been impossible for them to find any evidence that Riley had been wounded there. Besides, the whole ordeal had happened two weeks ago. If they knew Riley had been there, the sheriff would have come out a lot sooner than this. According to the newspapers, authorities suspected it was someone just passing through who had gone into the store to rob the place as Paul was closing up, and then fled. It had put a damp mood on the inhabitants of the small community because of the brutality of the murder. This kind of thing just didn't happen out here.

Paul was simply an innocent victim who had been sucked into this horrible situation. When Jonathan had gone back to make sure there was no evidence of Riley ever being at the grocery store, he'd found Paul's body in the back room and knew he hadn't had a chance against the three demons. Jonathan just hoped that he hadn't suffered. The best thing he could do was unwrap Paul's body from the plastic bag, kiss him on the forehead, and offer a prayer to see the man again one day. Jonathan had smelled a dog the first time he entered the store. He'd found it in the trash out back. He'd cleaned it and had placed it next to Paul with its head resting atop Paul's leg.

Unfortunately, horrible things like this were to be expected. Jonathan knew anyone near Riley was at risk. It was the reason Jonathan wanted to leave the city as quickly as possible.

But evil found them faster than he'd anticipated.

The other three bodies would never be found. The doomed souls had been immediately sucked back into Hell, and the overtaken bodies had been buried far away—Jonathan had seen to that. He'd given them a decent burial. He tried not to think about the families they may have left behind.

Returning to the current situation at hand, Jonathan un-locked the door and opened it, putting a smile on his face. "Good morning, officers." As with everyone else who came into contact with Jonathan, the two men exchanged a quick glance at the giant in the doorway.

"Damn," the younger of the two of them said, as he looked Jonathan up and down. "You've got to be the biggest man I've ever seen in my life!"

Jonathan smiled. He was getting used to the shocked expressions people made when first meeting him.

"Excuse my partner's rudeness," the second officer said, "but we were wondering if we could ask you a few questions."

"Absolutely," Jonathan replied. "Why don't you come in out of the cold?" The two men stepped inside, and Jonathan closed the door behind them. "My name is Jonathan. I'm a friend of Riley's." He extended his hand to the older of the two.

"I'm Sheriff Baker and this is Deputy Miles."

"Pleased to meet you both," Jonathan said. "What can I do for you officers?"

"Well, first off," the sheriff began, "is Riley around? We would like to speak with him."

"He is. He's asleep right now. Came down with a stomach ailment the other night." Jonathan knew the rules. He could not lie. And this wasn't exactly a lie. Riley was sick in the other room and it was because of a stomach problem—just not the kind you get from eating bad food, or a bug that you catch at work; those were minor details that Jonathan didn't feel compelled to tell the officers.

"Oh," the sheriff replied. "Sorry to hear that. Well, then, we'll just talk to you for now. I definitely don't need to catch anything, especially with the forecast saying we have colder weather coming in."

"I understand that," Jonathan said, thanking God under his breath for small miracles. "Why don't you come in? I've got coffee in the kitchen." He turned, motioning for the two officers to follow him.

"We are investigating a missing person that recently happened in the area," the sheriff said. "Do you know of a man by the name of Luis Perez?"

"Why, yes I do. He looks after the place for Riley. I met him when we first got up here a few weeks ago. Said he was going to be taking off for a month or so. We haven't heard anything more from him. Is something wrong?"

He took down three mugs from the cupboard and poured a cup of coffee for each of them. Handing the officers their cups, he blew the steam off the top of his own mug while motioning for the officers to take a seat at the kitchen table. "Would either of you like something in your coffee, or do you take it black?"

"I'm good here," the sheriff said.

"You wouldn't happen to have some hazelnut creamer, would you?" the deputy asked.

The sheriff looked at him sideways for a moment as if to say, *We're here to conduct an investigation.*

"Sure do." Jonathan said. He got up and went to the refrigerator, took out the creamer, and then handed it to the deputy with a spoon. "So, is something wrong? Did something happen to Luis?"

"So, you just met him the one time?" the Sheriff asked.

"Yes, sir, that's correct. From what I understand, he and Riley are good friends. I believe he even leaves some of his boxing equipment here in the garage."

"Do you box?" the deputy blurted out, not wanting to be left out of the conversation. This earned another sidelong glance from the sheriff. The younger man gave him a sheepish look, knowing he should let the sheriff lead the conversation.

Jonathan smiled. "As a matter of fact, I do box a little bit, but it's more to stay in shape rather than to actually get into the ring with someone. The men and women who do that for a profession are far tougher than I will ever be."

"Oh, man, I don't know why you wouldn't try to compete," the deputy said. "With your size alone, you would intimidate your opponents. Besides, you look solid as a tree trunk; I don't think you could get in any better shape or—"

"Deputy Miles, do you mind?" the sheriff said sharply.

"Oh. Sorry, Sheriff," he said, and went back to staring at his coffee. "So, you have met Luis?" he asked again.

"Yes, just that one time," Jonathan replied.

The sheriff took out a notepad and pen from his left front pocket, placed it on the table, and began to scribble something on the pad, being careful not to let Jonathan see what he was writing down. Jonathan knew that the sheriff didn't believe that he, or Riley, had anything to do with Luis's disappearance, but at this point everyone was a suspect, and rightfully so.

Jonathan just sat there, watching the sheriff as he made his notes and tuned into the thoughts that were running through their minds. The deputy's were simple. You didn't need to be an angel to know what was going on inside his head. *If we have to arrest this big guy, I have no clue if the cuffs will even fit him. He seems like a nice enough guy, I mean, inviting us in and giving us coffee. This is some good coffee. I wonder what brand they use. Maybe they grind it themselves.*

The sheriff's thoughts were marred. Although his face and disposition said one thing, his thoughts said another. They were guarded, due to years of being on the force. He never knew what he was up against until everyone revealed their hand, but he believed Jonathan had nothing to do with whatever had happened to Luis. However, he needed to get the whole story. Jonathan sat there, waiting patiently. Then suddenly, Jonathan felt the sheriff's thoughts turn to Riley. *Maybe while we're here I can take a look at Riley and see if his story fits with this big fella's.*

A moment later, Riley walked into the kitchen, breaking Jonathan's train of thought. He looked disoriented for a moment. The sheriff stood up from his chair. "Hey, Riley. How are you doing? Your friend here tells us you came down with something, and by appearances, you look horrible. Must really be a bad bug."

Jonathan looked at Riley and nodded at him, ever so slightly, to let him know to play along. Riley saw the look and smiled a little. "Yes, sir, whatever I had really has taken me down. I can't remember the last time I've felt this terrible. So, what brings you out here?"

Before the sheriff could respond, Jonathan walked over to Riley to help him take a seat at the table. "It appears that Luis Perez has gone missing, and with the recent activities at the store, it seems to be tied into what's been taking place around the lake here lately."

Jonathan could tell that Riley wanted to reply, but was thankful when his friend began to cough, unable to ask his question.

Imagining how this must appear to the Sheriff, Jonathan again jumped in.

"Let me get you something to drink, Riley. With all the fluids you've been heaving up, I imagine you're extremely dehydrated."

Walking to the fridge, Jonathan called over his shoulder, "Would either of you like a refill?"

"We're good here, but thank you," the sheriff responded, answering for the deputy.

Coming back to the table, Jonathan placed a bottle of Gatorade in front of Riley, and then took his seat.

"I really would rather have water, if you don't mind," Riley said.

"Your electrolytes are way down; you should drink this instead," Jonathan insisted.

Riley was barely able to twist the top off, then took several long pulls from the bottle before finally coming up for air. As always, Jonathan was right. The liquid did seem to quench his water-deprived muscles.

Looking at the Deputy and then over at the Sheriff, Riley asked in a dry voice, "You said Luis has gone missing?"

"That's correct," the deputy answered, looking over at the sheriff for approval.

"He has gone missing," the sheriff said matter-of-factly. "And we're here to investigate. Just asking the neighboring lake owners that are still here, when they last saw him. Do you recall the last time you saw him?"

Riley, never breaking eye contact with the sheriff, or looking to Jonathan for answers, said, "Luis is my groundskeeper when I'm not around. We got here about a month ago, and he was here doing some finishing touches on the grounds when we arrived. We had made plans that day for him to come over and grill with us, but with his busy schedule . . . I know his plans change from day to day. How long has he been missing?"

Sheriff Baker was jotting down what Riley had said and didn't respond right away. "Probably a couple of weeks at most. Some of the students from his gym told us that much," Deputy Miles answered.

Sheriff Baker made a sound with his throat that let Deputy Miles know that he had overstepped.

"Since he's just missing, are there suspects? Or is there anyone new in the area, besides Jonathan and myself, who have raised any suspicions?" Riley asked.

Jonathan knew Riley must be wondering if there were any more demons, other than the ones they had already encountered, who could be in the area.

"No one new in the area that we have come across," Sheriff Baker said. And with that, he stood and tucked the notepad and pen back in his breast pocket.

"Thank you for the coffee, Jonathan. I appreciate both of your cooperation."

Deputy Miles stood as well and shook hands with both Riley and Jonathan. "Get to feeling better," he said to Riley, and then followed Sheriff Baker to the door as Jonathan showed the two out.

# CHAPTER 24

**R**iley sat at the table, numb to the news he had just heard. He let the word "missing" play over and over in his head. Then it hit his weak, tired mind: Luis wasn't missing; he was dead, probably because he was living so close to Riley on the lake. Even though he knew that his friend must be dead, he couldn't accept it.

Jonathan reappeared in the kitchen and took a chair across from Riley after refilling his cup. He didn't look at Riley. He just sat there as if waiting to be reprimanded for his shortcomings. It was almost as if he could feel Riley's eyes boring into him, and the question he was about to ask weighed heavy in the air. Jonathan could taste the sarcasm coming from it.

"What went wrong?" Riley asked.

Jonathan said nothing, letting the silence in the room become almost deafening. He imagined that the soft tick, tick, tick of the grandfather clock might soon be followed by a boom.

"All I can say is . . . I'm sorry, Riley. I'm sorry for my short-comings. I take Luis's death upon myself. I will try to right this wrong."

The world had just come crashing down on Riley's shoulders. "How do you know he's dead?" Riley asked. It was as if asking the question would generate a different answer, but deep down, Riley knew it too. His friend was gone.

The mood in the room shifted immediately when Jonathan didn't answer; Riley let the tension come out through his voice. "I thought the whole reason for moving away from the city, and being more isolated, was so I wouldn't have a body count start to add up all around me. Paul has been murdered, I've been shot and left on death's doorstep, and now Luis is gone as well. I have to tell you, so far, your plan of protecting me hasn't gone so well."

Riley knew he couldn't blame the deaths of the two men on Jonathan, nor the fact that he was wounded—that was because of his own failure to carry a firearm. But he wanted to blame someone. It might help relieve some of the pressure that now weighed so heavily upon his shoulders.

Jonathan looked at Riley as if asking whether he really did blame him for all that had happened. Riley caught Jonathan's cool blue eyes looking at him. They seemed to have such hurt behind them. He decided to remain quiet and refrain from saying anything further.

"Coming out here has helped our chances of not only keeping the demons away from loved ones, or any innocent bystanders, but it has also improved our chances of keeping you alive," Jonathan said. "I know it doesn't feel that way right now, and it shouldn't, because I take this as my fault. I didn't know they would come after your friend."

"Didn't know?" Riley asked, almost mockingly, but then he decided to tone it down. "How could you not have known? I thought you could sense when they were close."

Jonathan looked down at the floor as if to acknowledge that Riley was correct for being upset with him. "I was a watcher, now I'm just a guardian. I still have many of the same powers, but I let my guard down, Riley. I got comfortable with our regimen day in and day out. This was an unfortunate wakeup call. I don't, and never will, have all the answers, but I will work twice as hard for you."

Sitting quietly for a moment, Riley let everything that Jonathan said sink in. They had become so engrossed in their day-to-day rituals that even Riley had started to believe this was a new normal and that all the training they were doing was going to protect them.

"I'm sorry," Riley said weakly. "This is not your fault. My being shot, the loss of Luis and Paul; none of it is on you. The things I said were out of anger, that's all. Lately, just when I feel like I have control of it, like I'm in the clear, it creeps back in."

Jonathan placed his large hand on Riley's shoulder, sending a flood of peace into him. Riley did not jerk away from Jonathan's hand, but instead allowed it to rest upon him.

"So, what do we do now?"

"Now, we change your bandage and get you back to bed. As for me, I'm going to check the perimeter again," Jonathan said.

"My bandage?" Riley looked down at his side only to see a small red spot starting to form on his white shirt. "I didn't even notice until now. Good thing I have an angel around to help coddle me."

Jonathan grinned. "I'm just grateful that those officers didn't notice it. I guess it's helpful when their attention is on the elephant in the room."

This made Riley laugh, but he stopped when the pain from his sutures pulled against his skin, causing him to half laugh and wince at the same time. "I can see how this little red blot could have caused quite a bit of damage."

"Not at all," Jonathan said. He headed down the hall and returned with the first-aid kit. "I would have just had to wipe their memories and put them back in their car so that they would think they had just pulled up to the house!"

This made Riley pause long and hard, but before he could ask, Jonathan answered, "Yes, I can really do that." He bent down so that he was in front of Riley. He held the gauze in his hand and a Q-tip between his teeth. "Okay, let's take a look."

Riley lifted his shirt up. The once-white gauze had now become red. "How do you wipe someone's memory?"

Jonathan started to work on the tape that was holding the gauze in place, even though half of it had started to come undone from the sweat that Riley had been producing while his body was recovering from its wound. He peeled it off slowly, so as not to cause any more harm to his friend.

"Simple, really. I send out a large amount of peace, to the point that it causes the person or persons that are around me to almost fall asleep. When they come to, they aren't aware of what happened." He removed the gauze and applied ointment with the Q-tip before applying a fresh gauze. "Really, it's as easy as changing a bandage." With that, he gathered up the old bandages and discarded them.

Riley wanted to know more. This was definitely the most fascinating skill one could possess. "So, will it work on anyone?"

"Well, there are limits, of course, just as there are with all my abilities."

"Give me an example," Riley said, as he pulled his shirt back down, never once taking his eyes off of Jonathan. He was simply too fascinated.

"Okay, well, it won't work on demons, I can assure you of that, nor on you," Jonathan said. "I can't wipe your memory. I can only distort it, the way I did on that dreadful day. I belong to you now, Riley. I've pledged myself to you. As for demons, they know no peace; they are set out to do one thing only, and it involves hate."

This presented Riley with yet another question. "You what?"

he asked. "No, Jonathan, you do not belong to me. We're friends and we help each other. If anything, you are my aide; you try to help keep me alive, and I'll do the same for you."

Jonathan took his chair once more across from Riley. "You're thinking that 'belong' pertains to how one would own another, but it's really not that way. It's difficult to explain, really. You have the authority to tell me to leave, and I have to do it, if you mean it. And from then on, I would have to go and make my own way in the world."

Riley leaned over and touched his friend's hand. "Look," Riley began, "I know that when I get upset, I take it out on you because of how our situation started. I've learned that it wasn't your fault; not everything I go through is going to be your fault. If we fail, then we fail trying, but we fail together. This whole belonging-to-me thing. If we survive, I don't want you to feel obligated to stick around because of some loyalty rule. I want you to live and enjoy everything that you possibly can. I appreciate everything you do for me and everything you have done for me."

Jonathan smiled at these words. "And there is the man that my Allison fell in love with—calm under pressure and wisdom beyond his years. You should let him out more often, you know."

Despite hearing the mention of his late wife's name, Riley knew what his friend was driving at and offered a pained smile.

"I'll try to do that." He started to stand, but grimaced from the stitches in his side. Jonathan reached out to help his friend. At once, Riley felt the peace flood into his body; he enjoyed that feeling. They walked down the hallway together, and Jonathan kept his hands on Riley to steady him. Riley felt like a little kid being taken to bed. "I have no idea how I'm going to sleep," Riley said. "My mind is racing, but my body is telling me to rest."

When they reached Riley's room, Jonathan helped him into bed. "I can tell that sleep is going to be difficult for you. Just lie back and try to think of nothing; it should help your body to relax."

"Or," Riley chimed in, "do you think you could sit with me and send out peace, to put me into a deep sleep?"

"I can do that, but I have to have your permission to do so," Jonathan replied.

Riley smiled. "By all means, feel free to knock me out."

Returning Riley's smile, Jonathan placed his hand on Riley's arm, and the peace began to set in once again. It was almost a high; one could get addicted way too easily.

"How long until I fall . . ." and with that, Riley was out and snoring.

Releasing his hold on Riley's arm, Jonathan stood up to leave. As he reached the bedroom door, he turned and looked back at his sleeping friend. "I will never fail you again, Riley . . . never."

# CHAPTER 25

T he bar was the typical scene one would expect. Young adolescents buying the latest illegal drug—anything for the cheap thrill of appearing cool to their peers. Once someone had a few drinks in them, the real person that stayed locked inside Monday through Friday came out and was allowed to express themselves however they wanted. A couple of shots could make the mellowest guy someone of interest and the nerdy girl appear as somewhat of a catch. People broke established rules and set their own, all because of what was held inside of a glass.

The bar was not big but was packed due to its location. The bar stretched the length of the room on the left side, with several bartenders behind the counter exposing as much flesh as possible; anything for tips. The dance floor was to the right, and though not very big, it fit just right in the place, as it seemed that personal boundaries no longer existed.

Smoke filled the air, making it difficult to see, but all in all— outside of everyone exposing themselves, being one step closer to death, and deaf from the loud conversations and the blaring music—everyone seemed to be having a good time. There were no empty booths, and even though the bar had some stools lined up against it, no one was using them. The men just pressed themselves against the bar, peering at the neatly placed bottles on the shelves. The women behind the bar were flirting back at the patrons as if the poor schmucks had a chance.

The Devil himself was already getting eyed by several of the females in the place; and why not? He was absolutely gorgeous. His jet-black hair hung around his face. His dark mysterious eyes were inviting, and his physique was slim and fit. His dark, faded jeans and designer button-down shirt made him fit right in.

He walked up to the bar. Instead of pulling out a stool, he leaned over, copying the other male patrons. A bouncy redheaded bartender came over to him, ignoring the requests by other patrons, and offered a polite smile. She was young, maybe early twenties. By her looks alone she could have anyone in the place. She had a perfect figure—large chested, tight body, and wearing a shirt way too small that was cut to reveal as much as possible.

*Vanity, thank you for the seven deadlies,* the Devil thought to himself. He flashed a perfect white-toothed smile at the bartender. She blushed a little, as if she had met her match. *Oh, if she only knew.*

"What can I get you, handsome?" she asked, leaning over the bar to reveal more cleavage. A couple of the men standing next to the Devil leaned in a bit more, hoping to catch a glimpse of more skin.

However, the Devil's attention was focused elsewhere. He stared directly into her green eyes, never once breaking eye contact. "Jennifer," he said, "I'm a very thirsty man."

She smiled, looking down at the name tag positioned over her right breast. She was accustomed to men hitting on her. She knew how to hold her ground. "Thirsty, huh? Well, you've come to the right place."

"I don't think so," the Devil replied. "You see, what I'm thirsty for is not on the menu."

Lucifer knew that when someone spoke to her in this manner,

that she was turned off and quickly shut the person down. However, he had spent thousands of years whispering thoughts to fools, knowing exactly what someone wanted to hear.

Not sure how to respond, she took a napkin and pen, wrote something down on it, and slid it over to him. Before she could lift her hand off the napkin, the Devil placed his hand on top of hers and, immediately, pure ecstasy shot into her, causing a soft moan to escape from her lips. Pulling the napkin toward him, without looking at it, he folded it and tucked it into his back pocket.

"For now, how about you get me a nice, tall glass of water?"

Blushing and pulling her hand down from her mouth, she blinked as if she was just coming out of a lost moment. She placed a glass of water in front of him, gave him another grin, and then headed down the bar, looking back at him as she took more orders and crude requests from the patrons.

"Damn," one of the men standing next to the Devil said. "You are one lucky guy. I've been coming here for two weeks now, and all I get is 'what can I get you' and the occasional 'yes, they're real; quit staring or you will go blind' response."

"Well, it takes practice," the Devil replied. "Besides, when you've been doing this for as long as I have, it comes pretty easy."

"I've been way out of practice and for way too long."

"Well, let me see if I can help you out. How about I buy you a drink, and I'll give you a crash course on how to manipulate the opposite sex."

The man started to laugh and slapped the Devil on the back. "Sounds like a hell of a good idea to me. I'm drinking—"

"Jameson's and Coke," the Devil replied smoothly. "I heard you order just before I walked up." With that, he turned and motioned at Jennifer to come over. She almost dropped the drink she was pouring and bounced over to him.

"Do you know what you want now?" she asked.

"I don't think I have ever seen anything sexier than watching you work, and you do it with such ease. Do you think you could pour my friend here a nice stiff Jameson's and Coke?"

Smiling back at him, Jennifer grabbed the soda nozzle and the Jameson's bottle and poured both at the same time into a glass, then slid it across the bar. "Anything else I could get you?" she asked.

"Oh, I could think of a few things, but for now I believe we're good." And with that, the Devil pulled out a one-hundred-dollar bill and offered it to her.

"Uh-uh, not like that," she said suggestively, then leaned over the counter, pushing her large chest toward him. The Devil smiled and tucked the money into her top, running his pointed finger along her breast. Again, she moaned and then stifled a small shudder, closing her eyes. She smiled and then looked at him. "Just call me whenever you need anything else."

"Will do, beautiful," the Devil replied. He slid the drink over to his new friend, with a sly grin on his face.

The man looked at the Devil, once again in awe of his way with women. "I have definitely been out of practice, to say the least," he said. He finished off his drink, set the empty glass down, picked up the new one, and took a long pull from it.

The Devil smiled at how easy the immature could be manipulated. "My name is Cross. What's yours?"

"I'm Jason, but if you can help me get lucky, then you can call me whatever you want," he said with a sheepish grin. He took another long pull from his glass, finishing it.

"You seem to be very fond of that drink, to say the least," the Devil said. "How about another?"

"Absolutely. But this time, let me buy you one. What are you drinking?"

"For now, just water. I haven't made up my mind about what I feel like having."

"To each his own," Jason replied. And with that, he looked at Jennifer, who was at the end of the bar taking orders. He waved at her but she gave him a disinterested look that said *hang on* and turned back to what she was doing.

"I don't think she likes you much," the Devil said. "How about you try someone else?"

"Yeah, I think you're right. If that bitch only knew who I am and what I could do, and that I outwitted the greatest fool in the world, she'd be falling all over me."

The Devil slammed his glass down, spilling the water on his hands and the bar. He could feel his anger starting to grow. This lackey, this impertinent louse, one of whom he had set free, now calling him a fool?

Jason jumped back a bit, not sure what was going on.

"Sorry about that," the Devil said, trying to regain his composure. "Glass almost slipped right out of my hand." He looked up, and Jennifer hurried over and offered him a towel. "Thank you, sweetie. Didn't mean to disturb you. I feel like watching you from this distance has made me clumsy."

"Please," Jennifer replied. "You have nothing to apologize for. Besides, I was hoping you were enjoying the view."

The Devil smiled at her. "I'm more than enjoying the view. However, my friend and I think we are going to have our drinks in that booth," he said, pointing to one in the corner which was already occupied. "Would you mind bringing them over?"

"Not at all," she said. "Just let me finish up with these jerks at the end of the bar and I'll be right over."

"Thank you." The Devil pulled out another hundred-dollar bill and tried to hand it to her, except this time she pushed his money back.

"This round's on me." She gave him another beautiful smile, paying no attention to Jason, and turned and walked to the other end of the bar.

"So, I guess we're going to the booth," Jason said.

"Why not? I'm tired of being surrounded by all these people. And besides, maybe we can convince Jennifer to come and sit with us." The Devil made his way through the crowd as Jason followed. Several women noticed the Devil and made sure he noticed them. One woman tried to put an arm around his waist, trying to pull him in. The Devil took her hand, kissed it, and whispered something in her ear that made her, too, sigh and moan a little. He continued to make his way to the booth where two couples were already sitting.

"Excuse me," he said. The group seemed to be in deep conversation. The Devil leaned in and tapped the man closest to him on the shoulder.

"No thank you, we're fine right now," he said, not bothering to look up. He continued talking to the others in the booth.

The Devil then leaned in and whispered in his ear, "Did you know, your sister, the one you took advantage of at an early age, was never the same? What strikes me is that after she took her life, you swore you were going to turn yours around; but yet, here I find you in a dingy bar occupying my booth. It's okay, I save a special place for people like you in Hell. I like to hang them on my walls . . . purely for my own amusement."

Startled, the man turned and came face-to-face with the Devil who, instead of looking disturbingly evil, appeared downright beautiful. Fear traced the man's brow, and his complexion suddenly faded in the dimly lit bar. The Devil leaned in closer.

"Get your friends out of my booth," he hissed, "or I'll have your sister visit you tonight. Except this time, she will be the one doing bad things to you. Now, don't cause a scene. Here, have a drink on me." He handed the man a hundred-dollar bill. "Now, get out of my booth."

At once the man stood up and grabbed his girlfriend's hand, almost pulling her out of the booth. "Come on, this guy has offered to buy us a drink." His date started to complain. She wanted to stay right where she was. The Devil flashed a menacing smile at her. She quickly stood up and got out of the booth. The other couple did the same. The Devil slid into the booth and Jason followed.

"There you go again," Jason said. "You must have a hell of a knack for persuasion."

The Devil smiled as Jason leaned his head back against the booth, as if letting whatever weight that he seemed to be carrying around slide right off his shoulders in one long breath. Sitting back up again, his eyes were becoming heavy from all the alcohol he'd been consuming. He peered at the Devil. "Well, Cross, tell me, what kind of work are you in?"

The Devil leaned his elbows on the table. "I'm a negotiator. I can pretty much negotiate whatever I want, but I'm sure you don't want to hear about that. Besides, here come our drinks."

Jennifer walked up to the booth and placed the drinks on the table. Climbing into the booth next to the Devil, she placed her hand on his leg. "I think I preferred you better at the bar, that way I can keep a better eye on you."

The Devil let a small chuckle escape his lips. "Well, I prefer you better over here in my booth." And with that, he leaned in and kissed her mouth.

She let the kiss last, and the passion that seemed to come from it made her almost lose herself. She threw one leg over him and straddled him right there in the booth. The Devil pulled back, however, ending the kiss abruptly, leaving her wanting more. Jennifer's steady green eyes now appeared nearly black as her pupils dilated. "Oh my God," she said. "Here I am throwing myself at you, which doesn't happen, ever."

"Yeah, sure," Jason interrupted. "Doesn't ever happen, my ass. Or does 'ever' mean it hasn't happened since the last guy tipped you good?"

Jennifer turned and gave Jason a dirty look and was about to tell him off.

"Jason, now that's downright cruel," the Devil cautioned. "This sweet girl just bought you a drink, and this is how you repay her?"

"You're right, I'm sorry; must be the booze talking."

"Yeah, it's pretty much an-every-night-thing," Jennifer said, her voice edged in sarcasm, "when some jerk comes in here who can't hold his liquor and then starts spewing the nastiest crap. One minute, it's I love you, and then next it's where's—"

The Devil interrupted her by placing his finger under her chin and pulling her toward him for another passionate kiss. This time he lingered a little more before Jennifer pulled back.

"Well, I've gotta get back, but please don't leave without saying goodbye."

"Wouldn't think of it," the Devil replied.

Standing up, she gave him another smile and then looked at Jason and mouthed *Go to hell*, and walked off.

Jason jumped in as soon as Jennifer was gone. "So, you say you're in the negotiating business? Are you some kind of big attorney?"

"Yes and no. Why, are you looking for a job?"

"Hell, no," Jason replied. "I'm just here for the party, nothing serious. And, I don't know how long I'm going to be around, anyway."

"I see," the Devil said.

"No, you definitely don't see," Jason replied. "I don't think anyone could see, or even understand, my predicament."

"No, I do see, Jason. I do understand your predicament." The Devil stared directly into Jason's eyes, a little grin spreading across his face.

Jason sobered up at once as reality set in. Now he knew who the stranger was. It was the beast himself, Lucifer. Jason knew he was done for. Wanting to run, but knowing that he wouldn't make it very far, he just sat there, frozen, looking back at the Devil.

"Jason gets it," the Devil said, letting his black eyes turn a little darker. The Devil leaned in. "So, what shall I do with you now?"

"I . . . I'll cause a scene," Jason stammered. I will not be taken back so easily, even if that means I have to bust this damn glass over your head and run out of here.

"Go ahead. Jennifer knows you've been slamming drinks back all night, and everyone will just think that it's another lightweight who can't hold his liquor. And besides, do you really think you have a chance if you tried to do anything physical to me? I would tear your arms off before you could even think of raising them to your God. No, the real question is, do I just drag you back to Hell right now and let my hounds rip you apart, or do I give you an encouraging speech and send you back out to do the job I sent you here for in the first place?"

Jason couldn't look at him any longer. He focused his gaze on the drink in front of him.

"Look at me, Jason," the Devil seethed under his breath. "Or I'll rip you apart myself, right here."

Jason looked up at the Devil. "Please don't hurt me anymore."

The Devil was silent. Jason could feel his eyes piercing right through him. The silence seemed to last forever. He began to panic.

"I'm in a generous mood," the Devil said. "I'm actually going to give you another chance. You see, you simple-minded fool, I want that fallen, and I want him bad. The other three fools failed miserably, so, rather than try to replace them, I will allow you to assist my sons in bringing this thing down. Listen carefully. This is what you're going to do: You are going to finish the job that I assigned you. If you fail, at least you can be thankful for the few extra days you've had. Now, don't say another word, just get up and follow your nose to the fallen angel and kill it, or the human—for now, either will do."

Jason slid out of the booth and turned away from the Devil. He ignored the urge to look over his shoulder to see if he was still sitting there. Instead, he headed for the door, wanting to get out of the bar as quickly as possible.

Once Jason was no longer in sight, Lucifer slid out of the booth. He stood, made eye contact with Jennifer, and gave her a wave. She returned the wave and gestured for him to call her. He smiled back at her, taking in her beauty, eager for the day when she joined him in Hell. He would punish her in his own personal way, over and over again, till she literally went mad. With that thought dancing around in his head, he exited the bar and then stepped from this world back into his own.

# CHAPTER 26

As Bryce and Abel took the winding road up to the lake, they couldn't help but notice the landscape; the rolling hills, the beauty of the pines stretching toward the sky, the gray cloud cover—and a stench that made them both breathe through their mouths. They knew it was coming from the thing they were in search of—the fallen. They could tell he was almost within their grasp. This would be where their stories would either come to an end, or they would receive praise from their father for a job well done.

The road was narrow, leaving no room to pass other vehicles, so they were forced to stay behind an old, beat-up truck, barely going the speed limit. Meanwhile, the stench was pushing them to their wits' end. They knew they were closing in on the fallen and his human. They had stolen a truck out of a garage parking lot as soon as they stepped into this world. At least they didn't have to overtake a human body and be limited to whatever attributes it may have. This would give them a huge advantage once they met up with the fallen.

Moreover, they didn't have to use inferior weapons like guns and knives to beat their prey. They were each carrying a cat-o'-nine-tails whip, similar to what was used on Jesus, but crafted to their own liking. Abel's whip had a sharp, almost tooth-like structure running the length of each tail. Once it was slapped upon its prey, the teeth would come to life and begin chewing and ripping deep into whatever it was set upon. Bryce's whip was much simpler, but just as potent. There was a toxin inside the tails that drained the life out of its prey almost instantly. On the end of each whip was an engraved star, and in the middle of the star was a knife-like structure that would penetrate and break off into whatever it came in contact with, sending out another toxin that would cause immediate paralysis. The whips were contained in wooden handles that, when activated, would shoot the tails out, ready to inflict damage. It was almost as if they took on a life of their own.

"Honk at him," said Bryce. "Get him out of our way. I can't stand the stench of him."

Abel furrowed his brow, knowing that giving into Bryce and causing a disturbance would only draw more attention to them. Instead, he turned the heater on high to help clear out some of the stench that assaulted their nostrils.

"That only forces more of it in my face," said Bryce. "Damn you."

Abel tightened his grip on the steering wheel, remaining quiet.

Bryce reached over and turned the heater off. "There," he continued. "Now I don't have to have that stink stuck on me. It smells like rotting meat left out in the sun . . . or Legionaries after Father has ripped him a new one."

This last comment made Abel loosen his grip on the steering wheel, and a small grin started to form on his face.

Bryce, picking up on his brother's reaction, continued. "How many times do you think Father has taken pride in disciplining a buffoon like Legionaries? What satisfaction can be had with beating someone day in and out and declaring yourself a fearless leader when the fool can't even defend himself! If you ask me, that must be the smallest victory in a pitiful existence."

This made Abel take his eyes off the truck in front of them and look directly at Bryce. "I'm sure he does find some kind of enjoyment in hurting people, but seriously, you can't say things like that. You know as well as I do that Father knows of every thought we have. Nothing is private and never will be, no matter how far we are from him. We are pawns in his game of life, and there is nothing that we can ever do to change that outcome. So, knock it off, and let's stay focused on what we're supposed to do."

Bryce let the thoughts of Hell and being trapped there float around in his mind for a moment, and then leaned back in his seat.

Abel again looked over at his brother, expecting something sarcastic to come from him, but Bryce just sat there looking out the window. Abel looked back to the road and the truck in front of him. After a while, the truck finally turned off onto a dirt road, and Bryce flipped the driver the bird. Now that the truck was out of the brothers' way, they increased their speed and let the stench pull them closer and closer to their target.

They both had their senses on full alert, anticipating everything and anything. Both could hear Lucifer's words about the fallen and the powers that surpassed their own. They would have to stick together to pull off a victory. If not, they would be forced back into Hell where they would have to answer to Father and whatever torments he laid on them. He would have no mercy on them. They would become just like the multitudes of others, banished to the pits of Hell and unending torment. They would no longer be called Lucifer's sons. They would no longer have regions to oversee. Hell's flames and worms would lick and eat at them each and every day.

"Pull over," Bryce said, suddenly.

Abel pulled to the side of the road, knowing they were thinking the same thing. Bryce stepped out of the vehicle and began to puke. Abel got out as well and went to the passenger side where his brother knelt, heaving. He was about to place a hand on his shoulder and lie to him by telling him everything was going to be okay, but before he could, Bryce held up his hand, waving him away. After a few more dry heaves, Bryce's posture returned. He turned to look at his brother, yet said nothing and showed no expression.

"We have a chance here—it's two to one. We can do this. It'll be difficult, but I know we will come out victorious in the end," Abel said.

Bryce looked at his brother for a moment. "What the hell is wrong with you? I don't need a pep talk. I'm not worried about failing. It's that damn stench in the air. It's gotten so heavy that I can taste it in the back of my throat. Can't you?"

Abel nodded. "Get in the truck. The smell is only going to get worse. It just means we're really close." He walked back to the driver's side and got in behind the wheel as Bryce climbed in on the passenger side.

They continued down the road, completely silent. Bryce looked at Abel with a sarcastic grin on his face. If you're too afraid, perhaps you should leave me to complete this task alone."

"I'm not the one who was just on the side of the road puking my ass up," Abel replied.

"As I said before, it's the stench."

"Of course," Abel said, as he continued driving.

When they came to the top of a hill, they saw a massive lake below. They knew they were in the right place. Another ten minutes more, and they would be face-to-face with what they were sent here to do. The anticipation had been growing, and now they were finally here. Their plan was simple: Instead of sitting around and studying the fallen and the human, they were going to drive right up to the house and pick a fight. They had been going over this. They knew that sooner or later the fight had to happen, so why draw it out? They knew the fallen could smell them coming, so there would be no element of surprise.

Abel had no memory of what his life had been like before he was paired up with Bryce. It was as if one day he had just appeared in the role. Just like the leaders of the regions, they didn't have memory of what their lives used to be like. He did ask Bryce once, of course, since they were basically stuck together. Bryce brushed him off, saying maybe it wasn't worth remembering, but Abel was a thinker, someone who always wondered, and was intrigued by what else might be out there. Perhaps one day Father would reveal the answers to his questions.

"Are you listening to me?" Bryce yelled.

"What?" Abel said sharply.

"Have I been conversing with myself for the past five minutes?"

"It's what you do best," Abel replied.

"I suppose you're wondering why we're out here doing this when Father could just snap his fingers and finish the job himself."

"Actually, now that you bring it up, I was thinking that of all the people I had to get paired up with in this ordeal, why did it have to be you?"

"I actually have an answer to your question on this matter," Bryce replied. "It's simple, really—you're the quiet, conservative one, and I'm the one who brings excitement into your life."

Abel ignored him as he turned off onto another small two-lane road. A sign with an arrow read: *To lake properties, bait shop, and downtown.* "We need to stop and get gas," he said.

"Good," Bryce said. "You know how much I enjoy mixing with the locals."

Abel looked over at him with his eyebrows raised.

"Don't worry. I promise not to make a scene."

The last time they'd been sent out, it was to pull back a demon that had gone rogue. They never caught him, but they did manage to bring mayhem to a small city. Many were injured, to say the least, and all Bryce and Abel had to show for their efforts were damaged egos and beaten bodies, to the extent that Lucifer had to put them out of commission for a while. Abel still wanted another chance to try and get the demon back, but that would have to wait since Father had sent them to track down the fallen.

Driving into the small downtown area, they saw just a handful of buildings, including a combination bait shop and gas station, an outdoor sporting goods store, and a small grocery store at the end of the street.

"Good thing it's small," Abel said to Bryce. "I don't think even you could get in trouble here."

"Don't underestimate me," Bryce replied with a wry grin.

Pulling into the bait shop, next to the gas pumps, Abel started to get out but first looked over at Bryce. "Either stay in the car or be on your best behavior. We will have our fight soon enough with the fallen. We don't need to draw any more attention to ourselves."

"You're the boss."

Abel climbed out of the truck, slammed the door a little harder than necessary to make his point, then proceeded to pump the gas. Another vehicle pulled up to the pump next to them, and an older man got out and proceeded to fill up his tank. The man looked at Abel but didn't say anything, just gave him a long, hard look. Abel continued on about his business until the gas pump clicked off. As he put the nozzle up and the cap back on, he once more caught the eye of the man who was now glaring even harder than before. Ignoring him, he walked into the building and paid the cashier, then came back out. The other man was still filling up his tank. Rounding the driver's side and about to climb in, he saw the man still glaring at him.

"What's your problem?" Abel asked the man, doing his best in his voice and mannerisms to blend in as just another human.

The man made a snort. "I don't have a problem, but your friend in the car seems to have one. He's been giving me the bird this whole time."

"Should have known," Abel mumbled, shaking his head. "I apologize about that. He's got an illness. I like to get him out of the house every now and then, but sometimes even that can be too much for him, which is why I make him sit in the car." The old man didn't seem satisfied by that answer and snorted again before turning to head inside the gas station. Abel climbed into the truck and looked over at Bryce. "As I said before, we don't want to draw attention to ourselves."

"That'll teach you to make me stay in the truck like a dumb animal," Bryce said.

Abel started the engine and then made his way back onto the two-lane road. "The sooner we finish this, the better."

# CHAPTER 27

R iley looked out the window to see the snow clouds hanging low, ready to pop at any moment and cover the ground in a soft white blanket. He had forgotten how much he enjoyed the lake house, especially in the winter. His abdomen was still feeling tight from the gunshot wound. The injury had taken a lot out of him, and he was sleeping most of the day. Today, he seemed to feel better. A lot better.

He left his room and headed for the kitchen to see if Jonathan had already started breakfast, only to find it empty; even the coffee pot hadn't been turned on. That was unusual. Jonathan was always up early. Riley couldn't remember the last time he had actually been the one to start the coffee. He walked over to the counter and opened the coffee maker and found fresh grounds ready to start. Jonathan was ridiculous when it came to being precise with everything, especially here lately. He seemed to check everything twice, even when looking over the rifles and their ammunition supply, just to make sure everything was tidy and ready to go.

Riley pressed the start button on the coffee maker and looked out the kitchen window, taking in the scenery: the calmness of the lake, the pine trees with their leaves a constant green, and the leaves of the oaks and cedars all brown and scattered on the ground. Normally, this was a peaceful setting. However, one eerie thought was on his mind lately. Something was coming for him and threatened everything he had here. How could he even try to enjoy this place knowing that death could be around the corner at any moment? The thought made him shiver. He needed to find Jonathan. He walked to the front entry and retrieved his jacket off the coat hanger. When he opened the front door, the cold wind slapped him in the face and the air bit at his exposed skin. It must be somewhere in the forties today, but the wind chill made it feel a lot colder.

Riley headed down to the boat dock, since Jonathan usually spent his mornings down there checking to make sure everything still met with his approval. He walked into the boat room to find it empty. Starting to feel nervous, since Jonathan was always around, Riley headed back up the small incline to the house, and headed for the garage. Looking around nervously, he saw only the trees that surrounded the house.

"Jonathan!" he called out. He heard the tinge of desperation in his own voice.

At once Jonathan appeared, barely five feet in front of him, causing Riley to stumble and almost fall. Jonathan reached out and steadied him.

"Something the matter?" Jonathan asked.

A little out of breath and filled with relief, Riley smiled. "No, I was just being silly, I guess. My mind started playing tricks on me."

"No worries. Come with me; I want to show you something."

Following Jonathan up to the house and toward the garage, Riley found the doors were already open. The grueling workout sessions played out in his mind, and he couldn't help but think how long it would take for him to get back into shape. He didn't want to dwell on it since he knew that with each passing day, as he got stronger, Jonathan would be like an army sergeant pushing him beyond exhaustion.

"Don't worry, Riley. You've got a few weeks before we can start my crazy workouts again."

Riley chuckled to himself. "Can't a guy get some privacy around here?"

Jonathan looked over his shoulder at him. "Yes, you can have some privacy, but aren't you the one who was yelling my name like a little girl a minute ago?"

Riley enjoyed the way they went back and forth at each other, joking around. Not long ago, he hated Jonathan and all his powers. Now, he loved and accepted him as a close friend and would do anything for him. His powers were a bonus, especially if Riley was having trouble sleeping. He could just ask Jonathan to lay a hand on him and flood him with peace, and he was out like a light.

"So, where are you dragging me to when we could be inside drinking coffee and eating breakfast? Besides, it's freezing out here."

"This won't take long," Jonathan said, "then we can go inside. Here, this will help." Jonathan reached back and laid his hand on Riley's shoulder, sending a sense of complete warmth through his body.

"Why didn't you do that a long time ago?" Riley asked. "It would have saved me from buying another jacket."

Jonathan looked at his friend. "If I would have tried anything like that a while back, you would have bitten my head off, or even worse, banished me from your—"

"Okay, I get it," Riley interrupted. "I was only teasing."

Walking into the garage, Riley saw at once that there was a door laying on the ground. Glancing at it again, he could see it was actually attached to the ground like a trap door.

"What have you done to my garage?"

Jonathan laughed. He reached down and opened the door. Riley peered down into a stairwell with steps leading a good twelve feet down. "Here, let me show you. I'll go in first," Jonathan said.

"Are you sure you'll fit?" Riley asked.

"Yes, Riley, I will fit. After all, I am the one who made this."

Disappearing down into the hole, Jonathan called out to Riley to grab a flashlight and come on down.

Looking around, Riley found the flashlight on the workout bench. He turned it on to make sure the batteries worked, and then proceeded down the steps. At the bottom, he saw that Jonathan had carved out a small room and stocked it with bottled water, a couple of rifles, ammo, and blankets. A tunnel broke off from the room and went farther than the beam of the flashlight could reach.

"What's down there?" Riley asked.

"A passageway that goes beyond your property line; it comes out about thirty yards into the woods."

"That's almost a hundred and fifty yards from the house!" Riley exclaimed.

"Yeah, I've been working on it since you fell asleep last night. I'm almost finished. I need to wire it up; that way, you'll have power down here and you'll be able to see all the way down the tunnel."

Riley only now noticed how dirty Jonathan's clothes were. "I would be a horrible detective," Riley said.

"Because you didn't notice how filthy I was?" Jonathan asked. "Yes, I agree, you would be a horrible detective," he fired back with a grin.

"So, what is this for, anyway? Is this our fallback position, or something?"

"No, this is your escape if things go terribly wrong for us," Jonathan said.

Riley wanted to interrupt but knew Jonathan had a reason for everything he did, so he kept his mouth closed for once and listened.

"The demons who are coming can move extremely fast. They aren't like the others. And they're close. There's a dead smell in the air that has become so strong that I know they're practically upon us."

Riley started to feel like the walls were closing in on him. The air was becoming hard to breathe. He began to panic a little more with every word that Jonathan said.

"What I want you to do when this all starts," Jonathan continued, "is to come down here and wait for me. If I don't show up within a certain amount of time, I want you to run through the tunnel and out into the woods. Then you get yourself into town to Dr. Hardin. He'll assist you in getting out of here. I've told him all he needs to know, and he understands. He'll do whatever he can to help you."

The small room began to feel more like a dirt coffin. Riley was having a hard time getting the air to fill his lungs. Looking around fiercely, he started to go into panic mode for the second time this morning. He felt dazed. He leaned against a wall and felt his legs getting wobbly. Then he felt Jonathan's hand on him, and the peace that he needed was given to him. Calming his breathing, he looked up at Jonathan. "What happened?"

"I believe you almost passed out. Come on, let's go inside the house and I'll tell you more over breakfast."

Riley let Jonathan help him to his feet and up the stairs until, finally, they were back in the garage. Closing the door to the garage, the two walked toward the house. Once again, Riley looked at the scenery that once was so clean and pretty. Now it appeared dim with gray clouds hanging so low it was as if they held something evil. Inside the house, Riley hung up his coat and walked over to the coffee maker and poured two cups. He placed one cup in front of Jonathan and sat at the table, taking the seat opposite him. He looked at his friend in earnest.

"The smell that these two have on them is death," Jonathan said. "It was only a couple of days ago that I first caught their scent, but now it's so strong it seems to cover everything. I wouldn't be surprised if they are already in town and searching us out. It will happen either today or tomorrow at the latest."

Riley felt a chill run down his spine and wanted to immediately run into his room and start packing his things so they could flee.

"Wouldn't help," Jonathan said.

Riley looked up from his cup of coffee and looked right in his friend's big, blue eyes. "I know, but I feel so helpless just sitting around here waiting for something to happen," he said, frustration and fear in his voice. "Oh, and as for me not fighting? That part is not acceptable. We did all that training so that I could help, not just sit around and watch you take a beating."

"Riley, we did that training so that if I fail, you'll be able to keep yourself alive. You'll only be in my way. I'm sorry, but I can't protect you if I'm trying to keep a watchful eye on you."

Riley didn't know what to say. He leaned back in his chair and blew out a hard breath. "This sucks, you know that?"

Jonathan smiled at his friend and replied, "Yeah, I know."

Riley was ready to change the subject, and stood up. "Well, what do you want for breakfast?"

Jonathan stood to his feet. "No, you take it easy. I'll make breakfast."

"No, seriously, I'm making breakfast," Riley said. "Besides, you need to get cleaned up. Run the wire in the basement another time. If today is our last day together, let's sit around talking rather than working."

Seeing Jonathan give him a forced smile, Riley knew they didn't have that kind of time. "Bacon, eggs, and pancakes then?"

"Sounds good," Jonathan answered, then turned and headed down the hallway to the bathroom.

Riley turned and went to the refrigerator for the bacon and eggs. Reaching into the pantry, he grabbed the mix for the pancakes and got started on breakfast. Ten minutes later, breakfast was ready. He couldn't help but start to nibble at his plate until he realized he was halfway done. Getting up to serve himself another helping, he saw Jonathan appear in the kitchen. His posture had changed significantly to the point that it made Riley's skin crawl.

Jonathan's eyes had turned a fierce blue; they were almost purple. It hurt to look at them. Every muscle on Jonathan's body was tensed, making his frame appear even larger. His face, usually soft with an easy-going smile, was now hardened with anger. His mouth opened, and the two words that came out broke the quiet in the room. Riley felt the blood drain from his face.

"*They're here!*"

# CHAPTER 28

J ason pulled into the parking lot of the outdoor sporting goods store of the tiny town. Although time was of the essence, he didn't want to hurry into what awaited him. He was outclassed on every level when it came to fighting, and knew a bad outcome would take him straight back to Hell. He had to avoid that for as long as possible. The only advantage he had was the element of surprise, but even that went out the window when he really thought about it. The fallen's one job was to protect and defend his human. Nothing else. Jason knew he'd be waiting for him.

Putting the stolen car in park, Jason climbed out and stretched his legs and back. The drive had been a long one, and so far the only thing he had going for him was his sense of smell. He had followed it from the city all the way out to this lake, and he had picked up on two things: He knew the fallen was here; he could smell him. And the other smell he detected was that of death. The air reeked of it. But where was it coming from and who was it here for?

The store was an old wooden building with a glass front. The entryway was comprised of two full-size glass doors with wooden handles to complete the outdoorsy feel. Pulling open the door and stepping inside, Jason saw that the place was empty except for an old man behind the counter and an elderly woman sweeping the floors.

"Howdy," the older man said to Jason.

Immediately, Jason felt like he was in some Old West show. The scene itself was just too unreal; the only thing missing—well, a few things missing—a piano man, some beer maids offering him a brew, and a bunch of cowboys playing poker.

"Hello," Jason replied, as he walked over to the counter where the older man was stocking shelves of ammo. Not knowing what he was looking for, he stared at all the rifles lined up on the walls and the handguns in the glass display case.

"So, what can I do for you?" the older man asked.

Not knowing anything about guns or ammo, Jason immediately felt hopeless with the task that now seemed like a sure ticket straight back to Hell. "I'm looking for a gun," Jason casually replied.

"Well then, you've come to the right place," the old man chuckled. "We're the only store for about seventy miles that carries guns. What are you looking for? Big game rifles? Handguns? We even carry bows and arrows."

"I think big game should do it, but I really don't know a thing about them," Jason said, feeling like a complete idiot.

"Don't worry, stranger; I'll help you out. Besides, everyone has to start somewhere. So, is this your first hunting trip?"

"Yes," Jason said quickly. "I mean, I've hunted small animals before, but mostly with a pellet gun." It was all a lie, but he thought he should try to make some kind of conversation.

"Well, these rifles kick a lot harder than any pellet gun," the old man said, chuckling just a bit. "Tell you what, how about I give you a crash course on deer rifles, because bows and arrows are for experts." And just like that, the man had made Jason feel better. "The most commonly used deer rifle is what is called a 30-

06. Now, you are in luck, because I have several in stock that fit the 30-06 shell, but one which I think will fit you perfectly. Plus, this rifle can bring down just about any kind of animal you're hunting."

Reaching behind him, the old man grabbed the rifle off the shelf and placed it on the counter for Jason to examine. "This is a Remington 700 BDL bolt action rifle, with a gloss walnut stock. Now, it's a little pricy, but this rifle—if you clean it and take care of it—will last you forever. It holds four shells, and the bolt action works like this: When you fire one shell, you eject it by pulling the bolt. In return, it will kick out the fired shell and inject a new shell."

Jason admired the man's sales pitch; he certainly seemed to know what he was talking about. "May I hold it?" Jason asked, sheepishly.

"Of course you can," the man answered.

He picked up the rifle and offered it to Jason. Taking the gun in his hands, Jason felt the weight of the gun and suddenly felt empowered. Maybe he had a chance at this after all.

The old man showed him how to position the butt of the gun against the crook of his shoulder and look down the barrel. Jason focused on the end of the barrel and followed the sight out of the glass doors to the gas station across the street.

The older man came from behind the counter and said, "Well, you almost have the hang of it, but you're holding it wrong."

Jason lowered the gun and looked at the man, feeling his face starting to turn red.

Noticing how he had just made the young guy feel, the older man started with a story. "You're doing better than I did when I first held a rifle. I shook like a leaf in the wind. The weight alone made me feel insecure and then trying to balance the long barrel was just too much. Took me almost a week before I could actually hold my first rifle and feel secure about it. Let me give you a few pointers." He picked up the rifle to demonstrate. "Okay, first off, the shell, when you eject it, comes out the right side. To avoid getting burned by the hot shell, you want to put the butt of the rifle to your right shoulder."

He assisted Jason in repositioning the rifle and then took Jason's left hand and placed it a little farther down the end of the barrel. "This hand is for balancing the gun while your right hand will be placed on the trigger, ready to take the shot. There, try that," the older man said, letting go of Jason. At once, Jason felt the difference in holding the rifle and again peered down the barrel out the doors, focusing on the gas station.

After holding his aim for a little longer, Jason put the gun back down to his side. He saw that the man was smiling at him. Jason returned the smile. "Don't worry, you have a sale, and I appreciate you helping me out here. By the way, my name is Jason," he said, shifting the rifle to his left hand so he could extend his right hand toward the old man.

"Mine's Steven," the man said, as they exchanged a handshake. He walked behind the counter. "So, let's get you finished up here. How many boxes of shells do you need?"

"Not sure," Jason replied.

"Well, how about you start with two boxes? And you're going to need a cleaning kit, which is $15. I will also have to run a background check on you, which is mandatory, and it costs $25."

Jason reached into his wallet, pulled out his new credit card, and said, "I've been saving up for this, so I plan on splurging."

"While you have your wallet out, go ahead and hand me your license as well, so I can start the background check. Plus, I have some paperwork for you to fill out."

"Seems that buying a gun is like going to the doctor's office, having to fill out paperwork. Do you need a blood sample, too?" Jason said, giving the old man a grin.

"Yeah, I hear you," Steven replied, smiling back. "But the law is the law. Unfortunately, there are a lot of people out there that aren't as trustworthy as you and me."

Jason couldn't help his grin turning into an almost wicked smile. *If you only knew,* he thought to himself. He handed over the driver's license and placed the gun back down on the counter. Then he thought of another thing that may come in handy. "Do you sell knives here as well?"

"Sure do," Steven replied. "After all, we wouldn't be much of an outdoors shop if we didn't. We have all types of knives; they're over here." The old man walked down a few display cases, and Jason followed. "The first two shelves are the pocket knives, and then the bottom two are an assortment of filet and field knives."

Jason immediately saw the one he wanted. It was the biggest one in the case, with a good six-inch blade, with little divots on the top of the blade. "Let me look at that one," he said, pointing to the knife inside the case.

"Absolutely," Steven said, reaching inside the case and handing it over to him. The knife had a black handle and a black blade. The weight was heavy in Jason's hands.

"That one comes with a protective sheath and a belt clasp, so you can just hook it right onto your belt."

"I'll take it too," Jason said.

"All right, let's get you started on the paperwork, and then if you would like, I have a shooting range right behind the shop. We can go out there, and I can give you some pointers."

"Thank you so much," Jason said. "I could definitely use some more pointers."

Jason walked over to where Steven had placed the paperwork on the counter. He took the pen and started filling it out when Steven told him the bad news.

"Now, the knife, ammo, and cleaning kit you can take today, but the rifle you'll have to wait on a few days."

Looking up from the paperwork, Jason replied, "Seriously?"

Steven stopped ringing the items up on the register. "Well, yeah, like I said, there's a lot of untrustworthy people out there. Just can't sell guns to anyone who wants to buy one."

"Dammit!" Jason all but spat at the old man. "I mean, sorry, but damn, I was hoping to have it today. Is there any way you can push this through for me, like charge me extra or something? I wanted to go hunting as soon as possible."

"Sorry, sir, I can't. I do apologize. Guess I should have told you about that first."

Jason resisted telling the man something hateful. "It's not your fault. I'm the newbie around guns and such. So, how long do you think?"

"Shouldn't be more than a couple of days. Do you still want me to ring this stuff up?"

"Yes," Jason said, disappointed by the thought that he wouldn't be able to go on his way today.

"Think of it this way: you purchase the gun today, and then if you're staying around here, you can come by and I can teach you how to break it down, clean it, load it, set the sights in, and fire it. How does that sound?"

"I don't guess I can say no to that," Jason replied, going back to filling out his paperwork. "However, I don't know the area. Do you know of a hotel or a place I can stay?"

"Hmm, nope. The closest one is seventy miles away. Tell you what, if your background comes back clean, you can stay here with me and my wife. We have an extra room that used to be our son's before he moved out years ago."

"I can't thank you enough for helping me out," Jason said again. "Really, I appreciate it."

"Think nothing of it. We can always use the extra company. Your license says you're from Miles City. You've come a pretty long way to buy a rifle, not that I'm questioning you, or anything."

Jason looked up from the paperwork once more. "Yeah, well, this is kind of a last-minute hunting trip before the season ends."

"Oh, I see," Steven said. "Well, I am envious of you. I hope you tag a big one.

Jason smiled to himself. "Yeah, I hope I bring down a really big one too."

# CHAPTER 29

L ucifer walked into his media room—the one place where no framed "art" was hung on the walls—to enjoy tonight's show. There were several large screens at one end of the room, with a large, ornate chair in the center, several projectors at the other end, and speakers positioned all around. The walls were covered in heavy drapes. This was where he came to relax and watch whatever he pleased.

He hoped tonight's show would feature the capture of the fallen and the death of the human. After all, a dead fallen was worthless to him. No, he would strip him of his powers and then string him up on a wall to look at day in and day out. Having the fallen in his possession, he would drain him little by little. He was eager to once again experience the intensity that a false God blew into the angels. Lucifer took his seat and leaned far back into it. "Screen one, show me Jason. Screen two, show me my boys. And screen three, show me the town."

At once the screens came to life. Lucifer saw Jason at a shooting range with some old man. They were carrying on a conversation about how to take aim on an animal. He watched with interest as Jason took in a breath, let it out a little, and then pulled easy on the trigger. He hit the target at the other end of the range. "Good boy," Lucifer mused.

"You're getting the hang of this," the old man said. "That was a perfect shot—it kills the animal instantly, and you hit it in the right place so as not to ruin any of the meat. Plus, if it's a big buck and you want to get it stuffed, it'll be an easier job for the taxidermist."

"What a fool!" Lucifer shouted at the screen. He motioned for one of his hounds to come to him. The hound obeyed and stood next to the chair. Lucifer rubbed the hound's ears. "I should have gone into that bar, grabbed that little weasel, and dragged him back to Hell kicking and screaming. Or better yet, brought him back here and let you boys rip him limb from limb, just for causing me so much grief. What do you think about that?" He continued rubbing the hound as he stared into its cold, blank face.

Looking at the other screen, Lucifer saw the twins riding in an old truck. Bryce was talking nonstop and Abel was behind the wheel, his eyes fixed on the road ahead of him. "I tell you, hound, that boy Bryce can talk, can't he?" Then something caught his ear and he sat bolt upright. "Leave me now," he ordered the hound. "Rewind screen two," he called out. The images flashed backward. "Play!"

"How many times do you think Father has prided himself in disciplining a buffoon like Legionaries?" Bryce was saying. What satisfaction can be had with beating someone day in and out and declaring yourself as a fearless leader when the fool can't even defend himself? If you ask me, that must be the smallest victory in a pitiful existence."

Lucifer sat there and began to fume. Closing his eyes, he wished Legionaries was there in the room with him just so he would have something to beat.

"Rewind again, screen two." Again, the images on the screen flashed backward. "*Play!*" Lucifer screamed into the empty room, and he watched the scene again. "My own worthless sons . . . making a mockery of me, thinking that all of this is just a silly little game!"

Lucifer rose to his feet and stormed out of the room. The hound was standing just outside the door. With one quick movement, Lucifer ripped its head off, pulled out its tongue, and slung the head down the hallway. The other dogs cowered, unsure what their Master would do next. Charging at them, Lucifer morphed into a devilish hound himself and lunged at two of them. He bit and tore at them, tearing their throats out. The hounds fell lifeless to the cold tile floor, blood pooling around them. Lucifer quickly reassumed his body and stood smirking at the remains of the two dogs. Their blood trickled down his chin, and he licked his lips. The salty flavor washed over him. He dipped each finger into his mouth, sucking the salty blood off each digit. Once he finished, he looked down at the floor and saw that the dogs' necks were beginning to heal. They would be as good as new in no time.

"I think it's time for a bath." Lucifer walked into one of his many bathrooms, picked up a small bell, and rang it four times. Four women appeared and shuddered when they saw Lucifer. He put his finger to his lips, directing them not to utter a sound. "This day has been particularly taxing on me. And I would like for you to draw me a bath . . . and join me."

Two of the women moved toward the tub and began murmuring to themselves. Lucifer turned swiftly and glared at them, causing them to vanish under his icy stare. The third woman began to violently shake and shudder and soiled herself. One glance from Lucifer and she evaporated into nothingness.

"Why is it that the damned cannot seem to follow very simple instructions?" Lucifer growled, staring at the fourth woman. She dropped her head and looked at the floor, not knowing what to do. "Well . . . are you going to draw me a bath, or do you want to go join your friends?"

Not knowing how to answer, the woman continued to look down at the floor, hesitating. Then she raised her hand like a school girl asking for permission to speak.

"Oh, I like you already," Lucifer said, moving toward her, taking her in. She was a little on the chubby side with short brown hair and a dark brown complexion. She stood completely naked before him. Lucifer smiled to himself. "Please, go ahead and speak, little one," he said, his voice softening, coaxing her now. "I promise, I won't send you back. I like a woman with manners, which is so hard to find these days."

The woman hesitated, choosing her words carefully. "How would you like your bath drawn, Master?" she finally asked in a meek voice.

This little lady was going to serve him just fine. "I like it hot. And throw some of those bath rocks in with it. I just love the sizzling sound they make. It relaxes me."

"Yes, Master." As she turned back toward the tub, Lucifer grabbed her by the shoulder, slowly turning her to face him.

"I don't think you could have made this day any better," he said. "Your coming here has been worth all the unpleasantness I've endured thus far."

The woman stood looking at Lucifer's chest, not daring to make eye contact with him. Releasing his hold on her, he took a step back.

"I never do this, but tell me your name."

"My name is Esperanza," she replied, still not able to make eye contact. She then slowly turned, walked over to the bath, and began filling it.

Lucifer stared at her backside and found himself drawn to her. He hadn't felt desire in a very long time. Others may look at her and not find her attractive, but Lucifer saw pure beauty radiating from her. She was born to serve, and even better, she was born to serve him. Lucifer typically had slaves undress him, but he didn't dare ruin this mood. Instead, he leaned against the bathroom counter and waited patiently for the bath to fill. Esperanza did as she was told to perfection. She picked up a glass container holding blue rocks and sprinkled them in. When she started to put the lid back on, Lucifer stopped her.

"Go ahead and put more in. I love nothing more than a nice bath."

"Yes, Master."

She took more out and dropped them into the hot water. Once she completed her task, she put the lid back on the container and placed it back on the shelf. Then she turned to one of the many drawers and pulled out a robe and hung it on a hook on the wall. She pulled a towel from another drawer, placed it on a corner of the bathtub, and then turned off the faucet. She turned to face Lucifer. "Shall I undress you, Master?"

"Actually, I think I shall do it myself." He began unbuttoning his black silk shirt. "There's something that caught me as odd. Why did you take out a robe for me?"

A look of worry came over the woman's face. "I, ah, well, I thought ..."

"No harm done," he stopped her. "I was just curious, that's all."

Esperanza looked down at the floor. "I thought that after your bath you might wish to put on a comfortable robe instead of having to fuss with clothes. Then you could relax. I didn't mean to offend in any way."

Lucifer felt himself actually being drawn to this woman, as if she had cast some kind of spell on him. He walked over to Esperanza, gently took her hair in his hand and smelled it. She

reeked of ash. Something would have to be done about that. He
was thinking of making her his own personal servant, but this
smell would not do.

"I have come to a conclusion," Lucifer said. "You will stay
here, in this house, with me. Not as my companion, but as my
own personal servant. We will not share a bed, nor a room; you
will have your own living quarters. You will simply serve me in
whatever way I wish. Once you have done everything that I ask
and are precise in doing these tasks, I might take you on as my
personal assistant since I had to cast out the last one for trying to
turn against me. What do you think?" He looked at her intently.
Never before had he given someone the option of becoming a
servant. This woman was different.

"Yes, I would like that very much," Esperanza replied, still
looking at the floor. "Thank you, Master. I will do everything I
can to please you."

"Splendid," Lucifer said. "First things first. We must get
you cleaned up. Use this bath to clean yourself. When you've
finished, you may put on the robe, and I will show you around my
luxurious home. Then we shall have something to eat," he said.
He saw Esperanza hesitating. "I will not hurt you, unless you do
something that I am not pleased with. Get into the bath, and I
shall wash your hair."

With that, Esperanza stepped into the tub. After she had
relaxed, Lucifer poured from a crystal vase some scented oil into
her hair, then began rubbing her scalp, all the while humming to
himself.

# CHAPTER 30

"I will not argue with you about this," Jonathan said to Riley. "I need you to go now!" He was at once standing right next to Riley, so close that he was literally in Riley's face. "You will do more harm than good trying to help me fight the demons. I can't afford to take that risk; it would put me at a disadvantage. I need you to listen to me and let me do what I committed myself to—protecting you at all costs. If you want to stay alive, you go to the garage and go down into the space I created for you. Stay there until I come get you."

"Jonathan, I . . ."

"Go, Riley. *Now!*" Jonathan yelled.

Never had his friend spoken to him in this manner, never even raised his voice. Riley's knees felt weak at the thought of whatever might be out there coming for them. There was so much more he still wanted to do, so much to say to his friend, but now he wouldn't have the chance.

Jonathan's posture relaxed for a moment. His piercing blue eyes softened a bit, and he placed a hand on Riley's shoulder. "I know you want more time. I know you have questions. However, we knew this day would come, and now it's here. God willing, we will overcome this, and then maybe you can enjoy the rest of your life. Perhaps we can be friends, but if that isn't in God's plans, I want you to know that I do love you—as much as I loved your beloved Allison and always will."

Riley felt his eyes starting to glisten. He didn't know what to say, so he threw his arms around his friend and squeezed him hard, hoping that, if he held on tightly enough, nothing bad would happen to Jonathan. He closed his eyes, not wanting to let go. When he finally pulled back, suddenly his arms were empty. Jonathan was gone. And Riley was no longer in the kitchen. Startled, he quickly looked around. He was sitting on top of the blankets in the space below the garage. There was a rifle and a handgun on either side of him, loaded and ready to fire. The flashlight had already been turned on and was sitting to the right of Riley. It offered what little light it could to the room's dark.

Putting his face in the palms of his hands, Riley understood that Jonathan had swept him down here with one quick movement, all to preserve and protect him. His friend was now out there, somewhere, doing what Riley couldn't. Suddenly, he had the urge to pray. Not just for himself and the trials that he was being put through, but for the one thing left in this world that he cared so much about.

He dropped to his knees on the dirt floor and clasped his hands together, doing something he never imagined he'd ever do again. "Father God in Heaven, I come to you now, not for myself. I know I'm a sinful man and have gone away from you. I believed you had forsaken me, which I know is wrong, but I ask at this time, that you watch over my friend, Jonathan. You know him as one of your many angels, but I call him friend because we have grown close in this short time. I didn't want him, but now I don't know how I can go on without him. He's more than my friend: he's family, and I beg and ask that you watch over him and protect him in his hour of need. This is all I ask, Father, in Jesus's name, Amen."

Pulling into the long, narrow driveway, Abel looked over at Bryce who, for the first time, was quiet. While his brother was completely still, Abel was ready for action and ready to rip anything and everything apart that stood in his way. However, he was also nervous to the point that he was starting to shake, but he somehow kept Bryce from seeing it. For the past couple of miles, his grip on the steering wheel had been so tight that his forearm muscles begged for relief from the strain. He didn't have to tell Bryce that they were there. They could both smell it—it was so thick in the air now. In a matter of minutes, they would be fighting the fallen for all their worth.

Arriving at the end of the driveway, past the pine trees that enclosed it on each side, they came to a clearing where the driveway became a circle in front of the house. The place was beautifully set near the lake and the landscaping was well manicured. There was a three-car garage to the left of the house and what appeared to be a deck with an upper section attached to it down on the lake. When they pulled into the long driveway, they stopped before going all the way up to the house. Abel put the car in park and shut off the engine.

Bryce started to get out but stopped for a moment and looked at Abel. "Well, brother, here we are."

Abel looked back at his brother and, neither smiling nor responding, just sat there in the driver's seat.

Bryce, usually so upbeat and always having something witty to say, reached over and slapped his brother on the shoulder. "I don't know what to say, other than let's rip this fallen apart and go back with one hell of a story to tell!"

Abel grinned, and with that, they both stepped out of the vehicle.

The air was completely still, and the coolness of the day was in the thirties, for sure. The sun was hidden behind gray clouds that loomed overhead, and the woods around the house prevented anyone driving past from seeing what was about to take place. Not that it mattered. One thing was for sure—both sides were about to spill their fair share of blood. Abel, Bryce, even the fallen knew it. No one would come out of this unscathed. As for the poor little human, he would be the first to die, unless the fallen had already stashed him some place; they'd just have to hunt for him.

Their ability to simply transport themselves, as they did when they were collecting the dead for Father, had been removed upon setting foot on Earth. The only abilities they possessed now were what resided within their whips. They could still move faster, and were stronger than any human, but they were limited as to what they could do.

And then, just like that, it happened: The fallen walked out of the house, stopped for a moment as if to survey the scene, and then stood looking directly at Abel and Bryce.

"What a pity," Bryce said, placing his hand on his whip and moving around the front of the truck as Abel did the same. "I was thinking there surely must be more than just one of you, given that rank stench that's in the air. But I guess that just makes you one rancid fallen!"

Bryce was now just fifteen feet away from Jonathan. He pulled his whip out, activating it in one simple move. The tails immediately shot out and came to life, slapping at the ground, ready to suck the life out of its victim. Abel walked a little farther away from his brother, making it harder to be easy targets. He, too, activated his whip, releasing the tails.

Jonathan watched the two demons, knowing they were afraid of him, fearful that he might be able to use his powers to defeat them and send them back to Hell. He looked up at the sky, closed his eyes, and breathed deeply. He thought about the path that had brought him to this moment, from watching as the most beautiful being had been brought into this world, watching her grow up, meeting the love of her life, to her horrible, senseless ending. He still blamed himself. He thought of Riley and the love that he had for his new friend, how close they had become and how he wanted one more day with him.

He whispered, "With your will, it shall be done."

Then he opened his eyes and glared at the two demons. "I am Jonathan. The meaning of my name is 'Gift from God'. I will send you both back to the hole you crawled out from."

Moving quicker than lightning, he smashed his fist into Bryce's face. The demon made a shrieking sound as black bile shot from his mouth. Just as Jonathan grabbed his head and began squeezing it, Abel lashed his whip around Jonathan's arm, tearing at it. Jonathan released his hold and gave Bryce a hard knee to the chest, making him double over. He then looked down at his arm and saw the blood beginning to drip from it. He turned into the whip that wrapped around his arm.

With a quick snap of the wrist, Abel released the tails. As Jonathan charged the demon, he snapped his wrist again, wrapping the tails around Jonathan's head, tearing at his face and eyes, and the smell of blood immediately soured the air. Abel pulled the tails taut, as blood started to run down the sides of Jonathan's face. "*Send me back to hell, will you?*" Abel screamed. A sharp pain struck Jonathan in the back over and over again, causing him to cry out and fall to his knees.

Bryce leapt upon him now and stabbed him with something that, with each blow, seemed to be sucking the very life out of him. Jonathan reached up and grabbed the whip that was wrapped around his head and jerked hard, ripping the whip out of the demon's hand. The tails immediately fell away from his face, and he saw the demon fall facedown. Jonathan threw the whip out of the demon's reach and turned to the other, who was several feet away from him, slapping the tails of his whip against Jonathan's back. Blood had soaked his shirt, which now was no more than strips of cloth clinging to his sticky red body.

Rising to his feet, Jonathan charged the smaller demon, taking slap after slap to his body and feeling each blow. Tackling the beast to the ground, Jonathan began smashing the demon as hard as he could, but his energy was quickly draining from his body. He delivered blow after blow to the demon's face. The smaller demon was laughing at him; or was Jonathan losing it and starting to go crazy?

Then Jonathan understood. The whip was sucking the very life out of him. Despite his growing weakness, Jonathan was able to land several solid punches, causing the demon to spit his broken teeth out. Somehow, the smaller demon overpowered Jonathan, got on top of him, and hit him with a barrage of punches so violently that it drove Jonathan's head into the ground, and he could do nothing but lie there and take hit after hit.

The demon, still mounted on top of Jonathan, took his whip, turned it around, and activated a blade that came out the end of the whip, about nine inches in length. Smiling through its cracked and broken teeth, it jammed the blade all the way into Jonathan's leg, causing Jonathan to cry out in pain. The demon broke it off, activating the poison in the blade, causing Jonathan's leg to go limp and lifeless.

Feeling the life going out of him, Jonathan looked up at the sky, staring at the gray clouds over him. He imagined them as a soft blanket about to cover him up. He had failed his beloved Allison and his friend, Riley. He feared his fall to Earth had been for nothing. These two demons were nothing like he had ever faced. He was able to inflict damage on one of them, but they managed to quickly overpower him. They were the first type of demon that Jonathan had told Riley about. Able to walk Earth without having to take a mortal nonbeliever's body as well as keep the powers that the Devil had allowed them to.

"Move!" Jonathan heard someone say. Then he felt the cracking of the whip once more, its teeth digging into his beaten body. It felt as if they were inside him now, chewing at him. "Let's find that damn human and kill them both together. Should be a nice farewell party for them," Abel said.

"Damn it all," Bryce said through a broken mouth. "Let's just end this now, and then go look for the human."

"If the human saw any of this, he's surely gone by now, but we'll catch up with him so we can end this," Abel replied. "Besides, this fallen isn't going anywhere. Now, let's go get the human."

# CHAPTER 31

"Holy hell!" Jason all but yelled out from his view deep in the tree line where he saw everything unfold. He had perched himself up in a tree, so that he could try to pull off a miracle shot if he got a chance. He knew that if he missed, running away wasn't an option since there was no way to outrun the fallen.

The speed in which everything had just taken place was eerie. He couldn't keep up with half of it, but he saw how it ended—with the fallen slowing down, nearly stopping, and letting the smaller demon get the better of him. The whips had saved both Bryce and Abel from being defeated, and they had left their marks all over the fallen, who now looked mortally wounded. The fallen just lay there, not moving at all, while one of the two whips were wrapped around its body and appeared to be writhing back and forth.

*What the hell do I do now?* Jason wondered. These two had overpowered a fallen. Now all they had to do was find and kill the human. *My journey is now over. Lucifer will come looking for me, to pull me back to Hell.* What were his options? Staring at the trees around him, and wishing he had more time, Jason shook his head and cursed himself for not staying with the others that he was originally released with. Now he was alone, and there was nothing else for him to do except wait for Lucifer to come along and punish him to his own liking.

After Lucifer finished cleaning up Esperanza, he showed her around the place and then left her alone to do some of her own exploring. If that's what the sweet thing wanted to do, then by all means, he couldn't be happier. She had lifted his spirits. Humming to himself, he returned to the media room, plopped himself down in his chair, and leaned way back to watch the rest of his sons' exploits unfold as well as those of the treasonous Jason.

Seeing them all in position, he watched his boys standing in front of the house, getting ready to take on that damned fallen. He could feel his anger starting to grow again when he remembered Bryce's vile disrespect of him. He would deal with him later. Looking at one of the other screens, he saw Jason in the distance perched in a tree, like the half-brained idiot he was, with his rifle cocked and raised, ready to shoot. "What in hell's name, Jason," Lucifer said to himself. "More and more, I believe I should just pull you back this very instant."

The fight began, and Lucifer found himself on the edge of his seat, watching it all take place. Blow after blow, Abel and Bryce worked together, just as he told them they needed to. In fact, they were following his instructions to the letter. It wasn't long before the fight was over and the fallen was on the ground, defeated. Lucifer leapt to his feet, feeling victorious. Not even the disappointment of that worthless Jason, perched in the tree, could bring him down at this moment. He would have a fallen in his house this night! *My boys came through for me in the biggest way.* Finding himself much more relaxed than usual, Lucifer stopped and stared at the screen, looking at the fallen, beaten and defeated.

"Somehow," Lucifer said to himself. "I feel that was a bit too easy." He started to question himself now. If it was this easy to beat one of them, then why, in the past, had he always failed? *Maybe I was sending the wrong ones to do my bidding. Sure, in the past the others had gotten the human, but never the fallen.* Lucifer turned his back to the screens, pondering what might be going on. Suddenly, something flashed through his mind. He spun around to face the screens again. He scanned the images. Bryce with a beaten-in face. Abel no worse for wear. The fallen a bloody mess. But wait—the fallen just moved.

"Turn around, you fools!" Lucifer yelled at the screen. "Turn around!" Then he looked at another screen. "Well, do something Jason, you stupid, insignificant little man. You were sent to help, so help! Blast that fallen all the way to Hell! Do it! Do it now!"

---

As Jonathan lay wounded on the ground, he could hear the two demons planning the demise of his human. But then he heard Riley—praying. He knew one's prayer went straight to God. The fallen—or even angels, for that matter—were never allowed to listen in. So, how was he hearing Riley? God must be allowing him to hear Riley's prayer this time. Jonathan was pleased and found that his heart was overwhelmed with joy. He had worried that Riley had turned his back on God. However, Riley's prayer was serving to strengthen Jonathan's powers so that he could continue to fight the demons in order to protect Riley. Jonathan knew that the power of prayer could bring about miracles. He opened his eyes and looked at the gray sky overhead. Using one arm, he struggled to free himself from the whip, ripping some of the tails in half until the whip was lying at his feet. As he looked around, he saw the demons heading up the steps of the house. "I told you I would be sending you both back to Hell!" he yelled at them. "Now, let's finish this!" He spit out a wad of blood and then gave the demons a defiant grin, ignoring the pain he was in.

Bryce and Abel turned to see the fallen standing with Abel's whip ripped apart and lying at his feet. "What the hell?" Bryce mumbled. "You just won't stay down, will you?" Coming off the porch first, Bryce walked toward the fallen. "I'm not going to stop this time. Like I said, we should have done it before!" Now just five feet away from the fallen, Bryce took his whip out and pitched it to the side. "I will crush you into pieces, you big—"

Before he could finish, Jonathan grabbed Bryce's head and smashed it like a cantaloupe. Holding up Bryce's lifeless body, Jonathan looked hard at Abel, paused for a moment, and then released his hold of what was left of Bryce's head, letting his body fall to the ground.

Abel jumped down off the porch steps, ran to retrieve Bryce's whip, and activated it. "I'll kill you!" He began lashing out at Jonathan as hard and as fast as he could. Each crack of the whip hit its mark, repeatedly hitting the fallen all over his already bloodied body. The whip landed over and over. He could barely stand. Finally, the blows weakened him, and he fell completely to the ground. Abel let up for just a moment to adjust his grip, but a moment was all Jonathan needed to gain enough strength so the next time the whip came down, he would do his best to catch it. Seeing the demon looking down at him, Jonathan smiled a bloody smile, just enough to provoke it. It worked.

"Take this, you pitiful, wretched thing!" Abel yelled as the whip came down faster than the last. Jonathan held up his arm and allowed the tails to wrap around it, causing his body to sprawl out in front of the demon. Abel stood there, trying to wrench the whip from Jonathan, but it didn't budge. The demon was standing over Jonathan now.

Jonathan reached out and pulled the demon off balance and

onto its back, releasing his grip on the whip. Jonathan had just enough energy to grab the demon. He then jumped on top of it, put it in a head choke, and pressed down with all his weight to squeeze the life out of it. Jonathan started to feel as if he wouldn't have enough energy to finish the job.

Jonathan felt a burning sensation slam through his body. The demon stopped moving for a second, but then kicked out frantically, trying to escape Jonathan's grasp. Then, just as quickly as it had arrived, the demon was gone, out from underneath him, now just a gray mist that quickly faded.

Lying there on the ground, Jonathan knew it was over. He had been pushed beyond his limits. He needed more time, a chance to look upon his friend's face once more and let him know that he loved him. He pushed himself up with his arms, although they trembled and cried out in resistance from the movement. He could feel the pains brought against him directly from Hell. Bringing himself up to one knee, he looked toward the garage and saw Riley running toward him. Tears ran down his face as he held a rifle over one shoulder.

Jonathan tried to speak, but nothing came out. He couldn't find the strength to make it all the way to his feet. All he could do was let his friend come to him. It was all worth it, just to see Riley. Then the world turned sideways as he saw a look of shock and terror cross Riley's face. Jonathan's body was shutting down. His eyes were open, and he was registering everything, but he couldn't move. *Not like this,* Jonathan tried to scream out. *Just let me hold my friend once more, please, God, not like this.* His body became motionless on the ground. He stared at Riley, who was now firing round after round at something behind Jonathan. This set off a new alarm. Were there more demons? Jonathan couldn't do anything but lie there helplessly and watch his friend try to defend himself.

Riley threw down his rifle, yelled "Christ, no!" and rushed to Jonathan's side. Doing his best to lift the angel's massive body, finding that he could do no more than to cradle Jonathan's head in his lap.

"It's over," Riley said. "It's okay, it's all over now. Just stay with me, you hear me? I don't want to lose you, not now. We've gone through too much, please, keep looking at me, stay with me."

Riley pulled his cell phone out of his pocket, punched in a number, and started speaking frantically into it. Jonathan wanted to reach up and touch his friend, but instead he just lay there and felt himself start to drift away. Riley slapped him hard. He was yelling at him, but Jonathan couldn't hear him. Everything began to dim. "Don't you dare!" Riley yelled, inches away from Jonathan's face. He looked up into Riley's eyes and saw hope. And faith. He saw faith in Riley's eyes.

# CHAPTER 32

R iley and Dr. Hardin lay Jonathan's broken and beaten body on top of the kitchen table. "My God!" the doctor said. "What happened out here today?"

Riley, too distraught to explain anything, just looked at him. "What do you need me to help you with? What can I do?"

Jonathan's eyes were closed, and he was barely breathing. He had dried blood all over his body. He had been shot in the back, and the bullet had exited his chest. The gash on his leg remained open, exposing ripped flesh all the way down to the bone.

Dr. Hardin, not knowing where to start or what to say, just looked at Riley with questioning eyes. *How do you heal one of God's angels?*

Riley stared back at him, realizing that the man had no solutions. He had to help. He had to think of something. He ran down the hallway and returned with his first-aid kit. He jerked it open, sending supplies everywhere. Grabbing the alcohol and gauze, Dr. Hardin began working on the chest wound first. The bullet had passed clean through. He poured rubbing alcohol over the wound and then applied large amounts of gauze to try and stop the bleeding. He then cleaned the leg wound, stitched it up, and wrapped it in gauze.

Riley felt helpless. "There's got to be more we can do for him."

Dr. Hardin just stood there, looking over Jonathan's beaten, bloody body. "Riley, I don't know how to help him. This is out of my—or for that matter—anyone's expertise."

Riley knew he was right, but he just needed a small sliver of hope that it was going to be okay. This couldn't be the end. Riley was doing his best not to break down. He pulled out a chair and fell into it. Jonathan had gone above and beyond to protect him, and had actually fulfilled his duty. Those two demons were not what put his friend down. Although they had nearly killed Jonathan, they had lost. No, there had been another rogue demon—just like the night that took his wife's life—that actually took Jonathan down with one shot, straight through his back and out his chest.

After seeing his friend take the bullet, Riley had returned fire, and had dumped three shots into the rogue demon. The first one was a kill shot; the other two were for revenge. All the practice had paid off, but now, here they were. Jonathan was lying on the kitchen table, so close to death. All Riley could ask for was a miracle.

Dr. Hardin took a seat on the other side of the table and looked solemnly at Riley. "I just have no words that can express my sympathy for your loss, Riley."

"I would like to pray for him," Riley whispered softly, "but I don't have the words to say what needs to be said, nor the strength."

Dr. Hardin stood up and placed his hands on Jonathan. Riley did the same. Then Dr. Hardin began to pray. "Precious Father, we come to you, thanking you and praising you for allowing us to have this angel in our presence. He was just as you are, a blessing. And he was the definition of what is good in this world."

The room began to shake. Both men opened their eyes, expecting Jonathan to be looking at them. However, the room was eerily dark. It was as if the sun had suddenly been extinguished; now there was only darkness.

"That one is now mine," a voice said, causing both Dr. Hardin and Riley to quickly scan the darkened room. Then, feeling the presence of something evil, they turned to see the Devil himself, standing at the end of the table. His eyes were black as coal. He was dressed in white. He was surrounded by an eerie illumination.

"What the . . ." Dr. Hardin started to say.

"I will not be bothering you anymore, Riley. As you can see, my sons and my 'rogue demon,' as you call him, succeeded in bringing down the fallen. "I'm here to claim him—and take him with me."

"This is one of God's guardian angels," Dr. Hardin said, his tone becoming hard. "You have no power here, and nothing you want can be claimed."

"This doesn't involve you, old man," the Devil sneered. "Let me remind you that at one time you were unclaimed. You used to cheat on your wife. You may now serve a false God out of guilt, but tell me, Doctor—does your past not still keep you awake at night?"

"Yes, I have sinned in the past. I'm still a sinner, but I can tell you, serpent, that my sin is not bigger than me, which is why God carries those sins for me," Dr. Hardin said, not backing down. "As for you, there is nothing that will ever satisfy you, and one day soon you will be the one begging for mercy amongst the multitudes that are trapped with you."

"This debate bores me," the Devil replied. And with that, he reached for Jonathan. But Dr. Hardin grabbed the Devil's bony fingers and wrenched them backward. The Devil shrieked. The older man didn't back down. Instead, he leaned right into the Devil's face.

"I will enjoy what I'm about to tell you."

"What's that?" the devil sneered. All the anticipation was so much fun.

"I am washed in the blood of the Lamb, and in the name of Christ I demand you to leave this place."

Riley had used those same words that night when the Devil appeared at his house trying to cut a deal with him to betray Jonathan. The words still held their power.

The Devil shook loose of Dr. Hardin's grip and let out another shriek. The floor opened up and sucked the Devil back into a deep, dark hole. As the hole sealed itself back up he managed to scream, "I will be back for what is mine, Riley!"

The house shook violently, causing several dishes to fall out of the cabinets. The grandfather clock danced across the floor and then fell against a wall, breaking the glass of the clock face. The kitchen table shook, jostling Jonathan about, but Riley and Dr. Hardin were able to keep him from falling off. Then, as suddenly as it started, the shaking stopped.

Dr. Hardin cried out in pain as he grabbed his wrist. The hand he had used to grab the Devil's fingers was badly burned. The once smooth palm now looked ragged and bloody. "I never in my life thought I would ever experience anything like that," he said, trying to compose himself. "Are you okay, Riley?"

"Y-yes, I'm okay," Riley said, stunned by the surreal nature of what had just happened. He was shocked by the way he had taken on the Devil, stood up to him, risking his own life to stand between the Devil and Jonathan. And himself, for that matter. He didn't want to think about how things might have gone. "You saved us. I don't know what would have happened if you hadn't been here." He looked at Dr. Hardin's badly burned hand. "You're injured. What can I do?"

"Well, let's talk about all that later. We need to figure out what to do next." Even in this kind of pain, Dr. Hardin treated Riley with patience and kindness. "Can you get me a damp cloth?" Dr. Hardin asked.

"Yes, of course." Riley rushed to the sink, grabbed a clean towel, ran it under cool water, and then hurried over to Dr. Hardin.

"Thank you, Riley," he said, placing it on his wounded hand. "I'll clean it first and apply some cream to it. Do you think you could get me some gauze and antibiotic ointment?" Riley rummaged through the first-aid kit and located the ointment. "Okay, open one of the packets and spread the gel out slowly, onto my palm."

"Am I hurting you?" Riley asked.

"No, you're doing just fine. Thank you."

As the doctor wrapped his hand, Riley turned and looked at Jonathan, his body so still and lifeless. "I had no clue I would get so attached to him," he said. "And now here he is . . . so broken. I don't know what to do for him."

Dr. Hardin finished wrapping his hand with the gauze. "Actually, Riley, I think I have an idea," he said and then paused. "Now, it's a peculiar one, but given everything we've gone through here, it may be our only option—but first, we'll have to move Jonathan to your truck. I'll explain the rest once we're on the road."

# CHAPTER 33

Riley didn't know which was harder—getting Jonathan off the table or trying to squeeze him into the backseat of the four-door truck. It took strength and determination that neither Riley nor Dr. Hardin knew they had. After thirty minutes of working together to negotiate Jonathan's size, they finally managed to get him in the truck.

Both men were drenched in their own sweat, despite the cold temperature eating at their skin, and neither complained about setting himself up for a likely hernia. One thing that stayed on Riley's mind, though, that made him fear his friend might really be gone was when he touched Jonathan and didn't feel the immediate sense of peace wash over him. He told himself maybe it only worked when Jonathan was the one initiating the touch. Otherwise, if he gave into his fears, he would surely lose control of what he had to do next.

Dr. Hardin and Riley both climbed into the truck. Riley stuck the key in the ignition, turned it, and the engine came to life. He looked at Jonathan and then at Dr. Hardin. "So, where are we heading?"

The doctor pulled his cell phone out of his pocket with his good hand, scrolled through the contacts, and then hit send. "Head to the church." A moment later, he began talking to someone on the other end of the call. "Micah, it's me, Josh. Oh, I'm doing okay.

Say, I was wondering if I could come by the chapel and pray for a friend. Would that be okay?"

Riley was amazed at how calm he sounded. Unable to hear the other end of the conversation, he put the truck in drive and headed down the driveway. Any evidence of what had just taken place in the yard was now gone. No dead demons. No whips. No blood. However, the yard did look as if someone had driven all over it with heavy equipment.

Dr. Hardin finished his call and put the phone back in his pocket. He looked over at Riley with a strained face. He was obviously in pain. "Micah said we could stop by. He's going to unlock the church so that we can let ourselves in; just told us to lock up when we leave. He also told me we won't be disturbed. No one has the chapel booked for any church activities this week since Vacation Bible School was last week."

"That's good to hear," Riley replied. "I don't know how I would begin to explain why we're bringing a bloodied man into the church instead of taking him to the hospital."

Dr. Hardin gave him a small smile and nodded.

Riley knew Micah Hargrave and his wife, Ryan. He was the only minister in town, and when he wasn't delivering powerful sermons to his small flock of maybe forty on a good Sunday, he was out back of the church where he ran a local firing range and was one of the best skeet shooters in the area. Ryan ran a law firm in the closest town, some seventy miles away. She was quite successful at what she did and loved it with a passion.

"I'm guessing Micah is skeet shooting today?" Riley asked.

"What else would he be doing?" the doctor replied. Riley realized that he knew his friend too well and would have laughed if it hadn't been for the seriousness of the situation.

The rest of the trip to the church was quiet as both men were caught up in their own thoughts, hanging onto a small, thin thread of hope that this might actually work. Riley wasn't exactly sure what Dr. Hardin had in mind, but he trusted him.

Ten minutes later, Riley screeched to a stop next to the side of the chapel, so they wouldn't be seen by anyone driving down the road.

Dr. Hardin hopped out first. "I'll go through the front and unlock the side door for you."

Riley got out and opened the driver's side back door, where Jonathan lay bunched up in the back of the cab, which was actually quite large. Grabbing hold of his friend and trying to be as gentle as possible with him, Riley pulled as hard as he could, but only moved Jonathan a couple inches. "This is going to be just as taxing as getting him into the truck," Riley grunted.

The side door of the church opened, and Dr. Hardin came out pulling a dolly. He hurried to Riley's side. "I know it's not the best-case scenario, but I don't think we could carry him any farther," he said, almost sheepishly. He knew both of them had taxed their muscles to their limits.

It was a two-way dolly: you could use it standing upright, or flip a lever to lay it flat with handles that popped up. Putting the dolly into the flat position, Dr. Hardin got on the other side of Riley, and together both men pulled Jonathan's body out, not able to avoid having it land with a thud on the dolly.

"Careful!" Riley snapped, not realizing that he had just scolded the one person who was trying to help him. "I mean," he said, backpedaling now, something Riley seemed to do so well nowadays.

"Think nothing of it. I'll try to be a little more careful," the doctor assured him. He then closed the doors to the truck and hurried to the side door of the church, opening it for Riley to push the dolly, with Jonathan's body sprawled on it, inside the church. Dr. Hardin locked the door behind them and then led the way down a long hallway straight to the sanctuary. Riley was thankful there weren't any turns. Once inside the sanctuary, Dr. Hardin went to the front of the church and locked the front doors to ensure that no one would be coming in.

"Let's lay him on one of the front pews," Dr. Hardin suggested. Riley nodded. They then went through the process, yet again, of lifting Jonathan and laying him down as gently as they could. After several minutes of struggling, they managed to get Jonathan halfway onto the pew. He looked like an oversized child trying to, somewhat uncomfortably, take a nap on a pew.

Dr. Hardin's beeper went off. He took it out of his jeans pocket, looked at it, and shook his head. "I don't know what to do next—pray for him, or simply wait and hope that God will grant him healing. I'm so sorry, Riley, but I need to go. One of my patients is going into labor and is on her way to the hospital the next town over. I need to be there."

"Are you going to be able to do anything with that hand of yours?"

Dr. Hardin looked at his hand for a moment. "Guess I will have to do the best I can. Besides, I have helped thousands of babies come into this world, and there is always a nurse there to assist me."

Realizing that they came in Riley's vehicle, Riley dug in his pockets, handed over the keys, and quickly gave Dr. Hardin a hug. "Thank you so much for everything you've done. I can't imagine what I would have done without you."

Dr. Hardin looked right into Riley's eyes and held them for a moment. "Thank you for allowing me to help you in your time of need." The man truly was the closest thing that Riley had, in a human at least, to a role model and a dear friend. He cherished the man for his giving nature, kind heart, and the protection that he had over not just himself but now Jonathan as well.

"I'll be back soon as possible, shouldn't be longer than early tomorrow morning at the latest. You have my numbers, so text or call me if there is any change at all." And with that, the doctor squeezed Riley's shoulder with his good hand and headed out, calling over his shoulder that he would lock the door on his way out.

Riley took in his surroundings. The vaulted ceiling had the exposed anchors running through them. Micah's voice echoed off them on Sunday mornings. The carpet was old. It was once a deep blue, matching the cushions on the pews. Now it was faded in spots from heavy walking traffic. The cushions themselves had worn thin; their padding compacted after years of use. The pulpit, however, was still in good condition, and the cross on the front of it looked as new as the day it was installed. Behind the pulpit was the baptismal font which had been used to baptize dozens of children of God over the years.

After standing near the front of the church for a bit, Riley's eyes then fell back to Jonathan, who still laid motionless in the pew. Riley felt his heart drop, as if the day couldn't get any sourer. All he wanted was to have his friend to talk with again. Taking a place in the pew next to Jonathan, he lifted his friend's head up and positioned it in his lap. The pew was, in fact, as uncomfortable as Riley presumed. Checking the watch on his wrist, it was nearly five o'clock. The day was halfway over. However, Riley would stay the whole night in the church and wait for a miracle to happen.

Looking at the pulpit, yet again, Riley found his thoughts starting to drift. He went back to a scene in his own church, back in Taupe City, when he was a teenager. He was in the youth group, and while many of the kids sat near the back of the church, Riley's parents insisted that he sit in the front of the church, or with them, so that they could keep an eye on him. It never bothered him, though, because he liked to be down front, since that's where the music and praise team were located. Plus, he had the added bonus that this, too, was where Allison and her friends sat. It was the only time during the week that the two actually spoke, since the school they went to was fairly large, and it wasn't often that they passed each other in the hallways. Even so, when he did see her, she never looked his way. She was usually caught up in her own conversations with friends. So, Sunday mornings, and any other time the church was open, were his only chance for her to really see, or for that matter, recognize him, and he always cherished any glance she stole his way.

The cross and the pulpit in this chapel were similar to the ones at his old church. The cross was a different kind of wood than the pulpit, making it stand out a little more, creating a three-dimensional quality. Below the cross was an inscription of John 3:16. Riley knew the scripture by heart. It was one of his favorites. To him it meant not just everlasting life after death, but hope that there was a bigger plan than he could anticipate or fathom.

Looking harder at the pulpit now, Riley couldn't be certain, but it seemed like it could actually be the one from his old church— he just had the strangest feeling about it. Only one way to be 100 percent sure—check for something that he and Allison had once left underneath the pulpit itself. He laid Jonathan's head back on the worn pew cushion and walked up to the pulpit. What were the chances it was the same pulpit? But if it were, there would be a note taped to the bottom.

When Allison and Riley had been together for a little over a year, they had spent a day that summer helping to restore the furniture in their church with the other members of the youth group. They had been assigned to the pulpit, and when they were finishing up, Riley had made a joke about how well the piece turned out, and like artists leaving their mark on something, they should do the same. Allison had laughed at his response, since all they had done was slap some new paint on it, but in the end they had pulled out a piece of paper that was stuck to the bottom of the pulpit, in a plastic sleeve that had the details of the furniture—what kind of wood it was, the model number, and manufacturer. Allison wrote in her beautiful handwriting, *This piece was restored by Allison and her boyfriend, Riley, who she cares for very deeply.* And then she added the date.

Riley leaned down and lifted one corner of the pulpit, ever so carefully, making sure he didn't knock it over on its side. He saw the plastic gray sleeve and some pieces of paper stuck inside. After tussling with the sleeve for a bit, Riley finally slid the papers out, slowly, to make sure not to tear any. He walked back to the pew and sat down next to Jonathan and once again placed his head in his lap. He then began to shuffle through the pieces of paper. There was the manufacturer slip and the receipt from the manufacturer, and then he saw it, the scrap of paper Allison had used to write her note. It was faded, and felt as if it would fall apart in Riley's hands if he tried to open it too quickly.

This was all so surreal. However, he knew that Micah had once been a member of the Taupe City Church before moving out to the lake, where he had always wanted to live. So, the connections to his past church were, of course, there. Riley carefully unfolded the piece of paper, already knowing what he would find. He gazed at his Allison's beautiful, faded handwriting, and read over the two lines. It brought tears to his eyes. He didn't fight them, but instead allowed them to build, like water collecting in a rain gutter before it flows to the ground. He closed his eyes and leaned back against the pew.

"I miss you so much, sweetie."

He put the note down next to him and continued sitting there, his eyes closed, letting his thoughts carry him to better times, or so he thought. Suddenly he felt himself being sucked into a deep darkness, an emptiness where nothing seemed to exist. There was no church and no pew. Not even Jonathan. Riley found himself utterly alone, with no one to turn to. He couldn't speak. He now found himself where not even dreams exist. He wanted to shake himself and open his eyes to find the church still around him and his friend with him, but something held him back. He shuddered hard and was doing his best to awaken, but the fight seemed hopeless.

"Help me!" Riley tried to scream out. "Someone, please, help me!" No words could escape his lips. He continued to struggle. Then, finally, the darkness gave way to light. He opened his eyes. Things were dim at first, but then the light grew so bright that Riley couldn't look at it any longer. An outline of a man was coming toward him. He strained to see it. Then, a rush of peace poured into his very being. He experienced a feeling of pure warmth, and in the warmth, he felt as if it was telling him that there was no reason to be afraid. He wanted to answer, but found yet again that his voice seemed to have escaped him. The light started to dim again, and he was finally able to make out the figure in front of him. To kneel would not be enough. Riley sprawled out on the floor and moved as close to the figure as he could until he felt a hand upon him.

*My beloved, please rise and see me.*

Riley slowly got to his feet, but was unsure what to do. All he could manage was to stare at the ground before him. Then God's voice spoke—it was soft and filled with assurance.

*I know the trials you have endured have pushed you beyond doubting me, but you have found your way back to me. This is not the end of your trials, Riley, but I will be with you through them all, my beloved. Never stop putting your faith in me. I will always be a light upon your feet.*

Riley couldn't find the words to express what he was feeling. Everything then fell silent. He opened his eyes and found himself back in the pew of the chapel, staring once again at the vaulted ceiling. Tears were still wet upon his face. He wiped at them with the back of his hand. He sat up. His eyes saw the note from Allison, and he smiled. The fear of the unknown was quieted within him.

"Riley, was meeting God everything you thought it would be?"

Almost jumping out of the pew, Riley looked down to see Jonathan looking up at him. His eyes were a dim, bluish gray. Jonathan was smiling up at him. His broken body was still covered in dried blood and he appeared so weak.

"Oh, Jonathan, oh my God!" Riley blurted out, scooting off the pew and kneeling on the floor in front of Jonathan. "Thank you, God! Thank you so much for giving him back to me." Riley grabbed Jonathan's hand and squeezed it in his. "Everything is going to be okay."

Jonathan looked at Riley, his eyes barely able to remain open. "I doubt it," he said, giving Riley a weak smile. "Otherwise, God wouldn't have sent me back. Seems that our trials together have only just begun. There will be more, my friend, there will be more."

# EPILOGUE

Mary sat aimlessly looking at the charts on her laptop and trying to appear in tune with the conversation concerning the new company structure following the takeover of Mass Communications. Her thoughts drowned out the tedious arguments going on in the room. She couldn't shake what had happened that night, the night when her life changed, all because of a man named Jonathan. He had literally saved her life, that hulking big man that came out of nowhere to beat those two thugs who attacked her in the alley. At first she had been afraid of him, but he was so gentle and caring with her. He was like a great big walking teddy bear. Jonathan had arrived just in time to save her, but then just as quickly, disappeared. It felt like finding a long-lost family member only to have them go away again.

That was seven months ago. She had been searching since then to find him again, but there was nothing. She convinced the chief of police to allow her access to the security camera footage in the area, hoping to spot him again. She had written out a large check to local law enforcement as a thank you. When she wasn't dealing with the many day-to-day tasks of running her company, she spent all her time combing through the footage. The security cameras outside the hospital had, indeed, shown them walking up to the entrance, but after she told Jonathan goodbye, he seemed to have just vanished. It was as if she had been escorted by her own personal guardian angel.

"Do you agree, Ms. Gregory?"

She snapped out of her thoughts and saw all eyes on her, eagerly awaiting her approval. She quickly glanced over at her friend, Stuart Branch, who was her second in command at Gregory Portal Provider. He realized that she wasn't aware of what was taking place and stepped in to save her from embarrassment.

"I think we both agree with everything that we have talked about so far. Let's take a lunch break, so Ms. Gregory can take another look at the numbers and we'll have an answer when we come back together at two o'clock."

Mary could see the disappointment on all the faces in the room as they got up to leave. After everyone else left the room, she looked over at Stuart. "Thanks for the save."

"Well, that's what I'm here for," he responded in his strong Louisiana accent, "to cover your ass when you drift off to wherever it is you've been going these past months."

She knew he was joking, but it was true. Nothing about the business she and her parents had built interested her in the slightest anymore. She had been thinking about it for a while, but now she was sure. She knew it was for the best. "Which is why, as my Chief Operating Officer, I am turning all decisions over to you. Whatever you think is best, you have my full support, and I won't interfere."

Stuart looked at her and then laughed. "Oh sure, you're going to turn over a $1B family business to a black man whose only education came from two years at a junior college—which I never completed, I might add. I think it's time we had you checked by a shrink."

"I'm serious."

"Oh, I can tell, and I'm serious about finding you a psychiatrist."

"Come on, Stuart. You have the respect of everyone here, including me. Who cares about your education? You have a knack for business just as well as someone who graduated from a top business school. It's the whole reason I hired you in the first place when we first got this up and running. Do you think it was a dumb decision?"

Stuart looked at her for a long moment, then wrinkled his forehead. "You are serious, aren't you?"

"Stu, you have been one of my oldest friends. I trust you like a brother. You have stood by my side even when others told me that we would never be able to compete in the market by providing cheaper internet and cable. So, I'm asking: please, would you oversee my company?"

Stuart was still looking at her as if she had lost her mind.

"I promise that whatever decisions you make, I will support you. Just don't bankrupt me, please."

He looked at her with his dark brown eyes, and she could see the fear and confusion in them. "Okay, Mags." It was a nickname that he and a few others called her when they were behind closed doors. "I will agree to run the day-to-day under one condition."

"Let's hear it."

"Whatever it is that you have lost, been confused about, or are searching for, promise me that you won't let it eat you up. I have no desire to lose a friend or, for that matter, a sister to something foolish. Understand me?"

She loved him for how good he was to her. He was big-hearted, kind, and so slow to anger that at times she could swear he was not a normal person. She smiled and placed her hand on top of his. "Deal."

"I'm serious, Mags." He turned his hand over and held hers with a strong grip. "Don't get lost in wherever you are heading."

Squeezing his hand, she nodded at him and then gathered her belongings and left the conference room. "Time to find Jonathan," she whispered to herself.

# ABOUT THE AUTHOR

**Kelly Hollingshead** is an avid reader who prefers books over music. He found entertainment in books as a child due to growing up in a large family where money was tight. However, the library was free and entertainment was endless, simply waiting between book covers.

Kelly has been married for ten years to his wife Melissa and they have a one-year-old daughter whose nickname is Ms. Brynn.

From an early age, Kelly has approached writing as an enjoyable pastime until his wife convinced him to try to publish at least one story.

When not working on the *Riley* series, Kelly enjoys extreme workouts, cookouts on the grill with his friends and family, and late nights of watching UFC fight pass.